Praise for Alexis Morgan's Steamy Paladin Series
"Intriguing and unique . . . compelling characters."
—Romantic Times (Top Pick!)

"Great sexual tension and action—
I love these hunky, heroic guys!"
—New York Times bestselling author Katherine Stone

Jarvis's voice came from right behind her, his breath sending a chill dancing down her spine.

"Am I making you nervous, Gwen?"

She could feel his body heat all along her back. She lied. "No, what makes you think that?"

"Because I'd hate to think I'm the only one in the room wondering if we're ever going to kiss again."

She ought to step away, out of his reach. But when she started to move, it was only to turn to face him. He fingered the edge of the fabric at her shoulder.

"Ever since that first morning when you were sleeping in the chair, I've been dying to see firsthand where all you have freckles."

He leaned in close and whispered, "I have to tell you, Gwen, that I'd give anything to get the chance to count them all."

This title is also available as an eBook.

ALSO BY ALEXIS MORGAN

The Paladin Series

Redeemed in Darkness
In Darkness Reborn
Dark Defender
Dark Protector

The Talion Series

Dark Warrior Unleashed

ALEXIS MORGAN

Pocket Star Books

New York   London   Toronto   Sydney

Pocket Star Books
A Division of Simon & Schuster, Inc.
1230 Avenue of the Americas
New York, NY 10020

First Pocket Star Books paperback edition February 2009

POCKET STAR BOOKS and colophon are registered trademarks of Simon & Schuster, Inc.

For information about special discounts for bulk purchases, please contact Simon & Schuster Special Sales at 1-800-456-6798 or business@simonandschuster.com

Cover design by Lisa Litwack.
Cover Illustration by Craig White.

Manufactured in the United States of America

10   9   8   7   6   5   4   3   2   1

ISBN-13: 978-1-4767-8693-3
ISBN-10:   1-4767-8693-3

This book is dedicated to one of my favorite people in the world—my son. Evan, you make me laugh and you make me proud. You've turned out great—Mom.

Chapter 1

*D*ust and the humidity made the air too heavy to breathe. Jarvis Donahue leaned against a tree and rested his weary body for a few seconds. Sweat stung his eyes, making it impossible to see clearly. When he used the hem of his T-shirt to wipe off his face, it came away stained with dirt, sweat, and old blood. Some of it was his, some of it not.

There was one more Other to track down and kill before he could think about some serious sack time. He was in no condition to fight, but there hadn't been anyone else left to send.

He reached out with his senses on full alert, listening for the presence of his enemy. Pushing away from the tree, he picked up his sword. At least he was still upright and functioning. That was more than he could say about Jake and several more of his fellow Paladins. The Handlers were scrambling to patch wounded Paladins back together, shoving the walking wounded back out the door as fast as they could. Only the dead were given a chance to rest, but they'd be sent right back into the fight as soon as they had a regular pulse.

For the past two weeks the barrier had been down more than it was up, and anyone strong enough to hold a sword was ordered to hold the line against invasion. If those bastard Regents didn't bring in some replacements pretty damn quick, the whole state would be overrun with murderous Others on a killing spree.

Jarvis started down the slope toward the narrow river that ran along the valley floor. Some cool water would bolster his energy, and the going would be easier down where the ground was flatter. Slipping and sliding, he hauled his weary ass down the hill, not caring if the noise he made carried to his enemy's ears.

He wanted the bastard to know that death was on his trail. As long as the Other was busy avoiding the sharp end of Jarvis's sword, he'd be too busy to look for innocent victims along the way. Right now Jarvis still had the advantage, because the bright daylight would leave the Other all but blind. But once the sun dropped behind the hills to the west, all bets were off. He and his mortal enemy would be stalking each other in the darkness.

There was no sign of anyone along the river. His

sword at the ready, Jarvis knelt down and scooped up handfuls of water, splashing almost as much on his clothing as he got into his mouth. The cool, clear water tasted sweet, washing away the coppery taste of blood from his tongue. When he'd had his fill, he dunked his head underwater and then raised up quickly, shaking off the excess water and sending a spray of droplets sparkling through the air.

It was better than a jolt of caffeine for clearing the head. But now, it was time to get back to business. Once darkness fell, the Other would be in his element. Keeping to the edge of the water, Jarvis watched the top of the ridge.

There. Just ahead, someone crested the hill, heading away from the river. Jarvis charged up the hillside, the familiar sizzle of adrenaline surging through his veins. Out here in the countryside, he didn't have to worry so much about running into civilians. He and the Other would have privacy for this latest battle in the secret war between their two peoples.

Judging by the Other's speed, he knew Jarvis was closing in on him. Good. Panic made for poor judgment and wasted effort.

Keeping below the crest of the hill, Jarvis shoved through the underbrush as quietly as he could. Any element of surprise was better than none. Maybe he could get ahead of his quarry and stage a nice little ambush for him.

At the edge of a clearing Jarvis picked up his pace, loping through the grass and wishing he had some backup. Even one of the regular guards would have been welcome, but that wasn't going to happen.

Turning back in the direction he'd last seen the Other, he paused just inside the treeline. All he could hear was his own ragged breathing. Even the cicadas were quiet. Should he risk another few steps? What choice did he have? Some innocent local would pay the price if he didn't track the murderous son of a bitch down and skewer him. Drawing on his last store of energy, he stalked through the woods with his sword out to the side.

A twig snapped off to his left just as the air stirred behind him. With the instincts born of years of fighting, Jarvis brought up his sword and swung to kill.

The Other jerked back out of range, avoiding being gutted by blind luck. He took off running, pounding downhill toward the river with Jarvis right on his heels. The Other, dressed in Kalith black, was a living shadow as he darted between the trees.

Jarvis didn't slow down, knowing this was his last chance to catch his enemy. If he failed now, the Other would blend into the darkness and disappear until a trail of human death led the Paladins straight to him. That wasn't going to happen on Jarvis's watch.

He flung himself to the ground to slide down the steep slope in a controlled fall. Bruises didn't matter but a broken bone would leave him vulnerable to attack. He reached the bottom and pulled himself to his feet.

When the Other went splashing across the river, Jarvis charged in right after him, coming out only a few feet from his enemy. The Other finally turned to challenge him, his pale eyes crazed and gleaming in the failing light.

"You know you're going to die if we fight. Why don't you come along like a good little freak, and I'll shove you back across the barrier to your own world." Jarvis kept his voice reasonable, not sure why he was offering the bastard another chance at life.

Maybe because he was soul-sick with all the killing he'd done, and with no end of it in sight. But not once in all his years as a Paladin had an Other accepted his offer of clemency.

This one was just like the rest. He'd drawn his own sword and stood waiting for the fatal dance to begin. At the last second, his eyes flicked past Jarvis to focus just behind him. Oh, fuck no!

A sword hummed through the heavy evening air from behind Jarvis. He spun to block the blow, only to see at least two Others moving in to surround him. Even at full strength, he would've had a hard time taking on that many at once.

Bringing up his sword, he screamed out his rage

and prepared to die—again. Well, hell had room for a few Others, too. He might be fighting a losing battle, but he'd take his enemies with him.

An eerie howl broke the early evening quiet, startling Gwen out of the romance novel she'd stolen a few minutes to read. She stuck a scrap of paper in the book to keep her place and listened, waiting for a repeat performance. It wasn't long in coming, and then a second voice joined in the ballad, making her frown.

Larry, her brother's coonhound, was a young dog who'd bay at anything that moved in the woods, but Dozer usually showed more sense. Often as not, Larry treed some poor critter and just wanted someone to come admire his handiwork. Dozer spent most of his time sleeping on the porch or tagging along behind Gwen when she worked outside, but right now he sounded pretty darned upset. She pocketed her cell phone and got up to see what had them so worked up.

Dozer let loose with another long howl as she picked up a flashlight and grabbed the loaded twenty-two by the mudroom door. She followed the path toward the small river that ran through the woods bordering her property to the east. The dogs met her at the edge of the trees, looking worried and wagging their tails in obvious relief.

"Come on, boys, let's go see what you've found."

She offered Dozer the comfort of her touch while Larry ran on ahead, circling back occasionally as if to hurry her along. Despite the cloying heat of the evening air, a chill snaked down her spine.

Dozer crowded closer to her legs and this time, when Larry circled back, he stayed with her. Their unusual behavior was definitely worrisome. Maybe she should have called the dogs into the house and locked the door rather than charging out on her own—especially without telling Chase where she was going.

She shone the flashlight in a wide arc, but its glow extended only a few yards. Dozer whined again and took a few steps forward before looking back at her and slowly wagging his tail. Larry might not have a lick of sense, but she trusted Dozer not to lead her into danger.

"All right, boy, I'm coming." She rested the barrel of the twenty-two back over her shoulder and hurried after the anxious dogs.

A short distance ahead, Dozer stopped again, this time to raise his head and howl. Larry lay down beside the older dog and trembled. Gwen shined the flashlight on the path ahead of them but didn't see anything. Then she swung it down toward the river. Just a short distance from the path, she could just make out the shape of something lying half in the water.

It looked like a log, but that wouldn't have riled up the dogs—unless it had injured an animal when it went down. She never liked killing wild things, but neither would she let some poor animal suffer if she could help it.

Watching out for snakes, she made her way down to the river's edge, only to realize that the dark lump wasn't a log at all, but a man.

"Hey, mister, are you all right?" She had to ask even though it was obvious from the way he lay sprawled across the rocks that he wasn't. "I don't want to spook you, mister, but these woods are no place to be at night. You shouldn't be here." And maybe she should listen to her own advice.

The dogs crowded closer to the limp body, risking a quick sniff now that she was there to protect them. Larry gave the stranger's face a tentative lick, which got no reaction at all. Either the man had ironclad control over his reflexes or else he was unconscious. She refused to think he might actually be dead.

Her heart in her throat, she knelt at his side and pressed two shaky fingers against the side of his neck. His skin was cool and clammy, but she felt a faint pulse. What to do next? She used the flashlight to catalog the stranger's injuries.

He looked as if he'd tangled with the wrong end of a buzz saw, with deep cuts along his arms. She reached out to touch his shoulder and her hand came away wet—but not with water. Dear God, his shirt was soaked through with blood! She gagged as her stomach roiled.

Quickly rinsing her hand in the water, she tried not to think about the possible infections his blood might carry. Who or what had done this to him?

But she wouldn't be any good to either of them if she gave in to panic. She started to reach for her cell phone to dial 911, then froze and blinked her eyes to make sure she was seeing straight.

Unless she'd taken leave of her senses, one of the shallow cuts on his face had all but disappeared while she watched. She peeled off the chambray shirt she wore over her T-shirt and dipped it in the river. Using the damp cloth, she wiped more of the mud and blood off his face and the closest arm to study his injuries. After a few seconds she reached for the phone again, but this time she called the house and waited for her brother to answer.

"Chase, I'm down by the river with an injured man. Bring the garden cart and some old towels. And don't tell anyone." She disconnected before her brother could ask any questions.

In all her years, she'd seen only one other person heal that quickly: Chase, her half-brother. If this man had that same ability, he wouldn't appreciate being at the mercy of the local medical authorities. If he didn't, well, then she'd call for help as soon as they got to the house.

But maybe, just maybe, she and Chase would finally have some answers about his peculiar gift.

It took considerable pushing and shoving to get the garden cart through the door of the guest room, but they'd finally managed. Gwen quickly stripped the blankets down to the foot of the bed and spread out an old shower curtain to protect the mattress until they got the stranger cleaned up.

"On a count of three, we'll heave him up onto the bed."

Chase nodded and took the stranger's feet while she worked her hands under his armpits. She counted aloud to three, then strained to muscle his deadweight up and onto the bed. It worried her a great deal that the wounded man hadn't even whimpered, no matter how much they jostled him. It had to hurt, even though his wounds continued to heal before their eyes.

"Who do you think he is?" Chase stared down at the man, worry and curiosity an equal mix in his expression.

"No idea. I've never seen him before." Despite all the grime, he was a strikingly handsome man, one who'd be hard to forget. "We can look for his identification after we get him out of those wet clothes. He's starting to look a bit blue."

When she started tugging at the man's wet

shoes, Chase frowned and reached out a hand to stop her. "Maybe I should be the one to strip him."

Although Chase was almost ten years younger than she was, he'd recently developed a protective streak a mile wide. He was several inches over six feet and starting to pack on some muscle, yet she still had a hard time seeing him as anything other than her little brother.

"I need to check his injuries, Chase. You put the cart back outside and then grab the first aid kit. I'll get warm water, soap, and towels."

"But . . ." He started to protest again.

She already felt half guilty about not calling for an ambulance; the least they could do was get him cleaned up and comfortable as quickly as possible. "Chase, let's just get this over with. Please."

He grumbled about her stubbornness under his breath, but she let it pass. When Chase left, she started peeling off the stranger's wet socks and jeans. She left his boxers in place, figuring the soft cotton would dry fairly quickly. His T-shirt was a goner, though, so she cut it off with scissors.

Despite his goose-bumpy skin and streaks of mud, it was impossible not to admire all those well-defined muscles. Judging by the way he filled up the old double bed, he had to be at least Chase's height, well over six feet tall. She noted the calluses on his hands and feet, the kind common to those dedicated to martial arts.

Could he be in the military or law enforcement? Or was he some sort of criminal, left to die by his fellow thieves or injured in a heist gone bad? She wouldn't go there. For the moment, he was helpless and in need of care.

She filled a bowl with warm water, then carried it to the bedside table so she could wash away the dirt and blood to check his injuries. More for Chase's sake than her patient's modesty, she draped a clean towel over the center of his groin and set to work.

It was a relief to see that most of his wounds were already closing up and healing. A couple, though, were quite deep and caked with mud. Judging by the number of battle scars on his body, this wasn't the first time he'd been in this shape. What kind of life did he lead?

Shoving that thought onto the back burner, she began the delicate task of cleaning the filth out of the few deeper cuts. What on earth had he tangled with that would do such damage? It was almost as if he'd been in a knife fight, but it had to be a hell of a big blade to cause such damage.

When Chase finally returned with the first aid kit, his mouth was set in a straight line and his blue eyes darkened in disapproval. He placed the kit within easy reach before bending down to pick up the sodden jeans she'd tossed on the floor.

"Did you check his ID?"

"Not yet. I left that for you."

Chase pulled out a trifold wallet and carried it over to the lamp to see better. When he pulled out a wad of money, a foil packet fell onto the table. Gwen pretended not to see it while her brother blushed and hastily stuffed it back in the wallet.

"Doesn't look like he was robbed." He studied the driver's license. "His name is Jarvis Donahue, and he has a St. Louis address. How do you think he ended up in our woods?"

"We'll have to ask him when he wakes up." She dried the last cut and carefully taped a gauze pad over it with surgical tape. "If he's like you, he'll sleep through the night while his body heals. Come morning, though, we should get some answers."

Chase crowded closer to the bed. "He really is like me." The boy's voice cracked, a sign of how intensely the discovery affected him.

"It would appear so. Do you want to be there when I question him?"

"Yes." Then Chase shook his head. "No, you do it after I leave for work. You can tell me what he said when I get home."

"But . . ." she started to argue, but changed her mind. As volatile as Chase's temper had been lately, there was no telling how he'd react to his problems being discussed with a total stranger.

Gwen stretched her weary back, then gave her brother a weary smile. "Let's get this mess cleaned up and throw his wet things in the washer. I had to cut his shirt off, so he'll need something to wear in the morning. Can you toss one of your shirts downstairs when you go up to bed? You're pretty close in size."

Chase nodded as he stooped to pick up the jeans and dirty towels and headed for the mudroom. "I'll set his shoes on the dryer, too."

"Good idea. Oh, and one other thing. When you come back, bring that rope from the cabinet over the washer."

Chase's head jerked around. "Rope? What are you going to do with that?"

"I'm going to tie him to the bed, once I've got him under the covers."

Chase returned to study the stranger. "Why? If you're that worried, maybe we ought to call the sheriff."

"That's part of it, but mainly I'm afraid he'll thrash around when he starts waking up. Last time you fractured your arm, you almost broke my jaw when I leaned over to check how you were doing. I'd guess he outweighs you by a good thirty pounds, with most of it muscle."

Chase flushed with embarrassment. That hadn't been the only time he'd hurt her when he was in the throes of healing. He couldn't help himself; it was just the way things were for him. She'd learned to approach him with great care.

"Can you roll him to one side for me while I get rid of the shower curtain? Lying on that plastic won't be comfortable."

Chase set down the wet clothes and towels and turned the stranger on his side while she tugged the curtain out from beneath him. Then they pulled the blankets up to cover him and put a pillow under his head.

"Thanks, Chase. If you'll start the washer, I'll put the clothes in the dryer later. Once you've done that and gotten me the rope, go on up to bed. I'm going to stay down here tonight."

"I can take a shift. What if he gets loose?"

Gwen mustered a reassuring smile. "I'll bring the dogs in to sleep by my chair. They'll sound the alarm if he tries anything. I'll be fine."

Chase didn't like it, but he left to do as she asked.

She checked her patient one more time. His skin was warmer to the touch, and his color had improved considerably since they'd brought him into the house. The unhealthy blue tone to his skin was gone, and his face had relaxed into peaceful sleep. She was pretty sure she'd made the right choice in bringing him home instead of turning him over to the authorities.

She could only imagine what the local emergency room doctors would have done when his cuts and bruises disappeared right before their eyes. He'd be lucky if he didn't end up the object of some highly classified medical experiments. She shuddered at the thought.

After letting in the dogs, she restrained their guest with the rope. She felt a little guilty, but she wouldn't risk him hurting her or her brother. In the morning, she would untie him—*if* he gave her a believable explanation for how he'd come to be in that condition in her woods.

If she didn't like what he had to say, she would call the sheriff, although she'd have to come up with some excuse for not calling him in the first place. But she really, really hoped that this man had answers for all the questions she had about her younger brother.

She tugged a chair closer to the bed, then settled in for a long night.

Consciousness came burning back, jerking Jarvis out of the deep sleep his body demanded for healing. With it came the familiar surge of anger, coupled with a heightened awareness of being alive. His skin burned and hurt, as if it were too small to contain him any longer. Old habits had him twisting and turning to break free of his bonds; he hated being tied down, and hated the need for it even more.

But something was different. Waking up unable to move was hardly a new experience, but he was used to the cold chill of stainless steel under his back, not soft, sun-dried sheets. He tried to move his sword arm, but couldn't budge it more than an inch or two. Same with his left.

His legs were bound, too—but with rope rather than the security straps and chains his Handlers used. What was going on? Keeping his eyes shut, he reached out with his other senses.

There were other heartbeats in the room, two of which weren't human. The good news was that they weren't Others. The third heartbeat was definitely human, and from the faint scent of floral perfume, it was most likely a woman's.

Where the hell was he, if he wasn't dead and he wasn't in the lab?

His last clear memory was the nightmare realization that he was about to die at the hands of a rogue mob of Others. Everything after that was a complete blank.

He opened one eye to assess his situation. A ceiling fan whirred softly overhead.

To the right was an old-fashioned oak dresser and a wall covered in floral striped wallpaper. Careful not to make any sudden moves, he slowly looked to his other side and hit pay dirt.

A woman lay sprawled in a chair in the corner. She couldn't possibly be comfortable with her neck bent like that, but it clearly hadn't interfered with her ability to sleep. Who was she?

He'd always been a sucker for redheads, especially the ones with fair skin and a few freckles thrown in for extra interest. He grinned, willing to bet she hated each and every one of them.

He studied her face, liking what he saw. What color were her eyes? He was betting on green, or maybe a rich chocolate brown. Her hands looked strong and capable, and she wasn't wearing a wedding ring—although that didn't always mean anything. Not that it mattered. Once she cut him free, he'd leave, never to darken her doorway again. And that was a damn shame. He definitely wouldn't mind a romp in this bed with her.

Then he noted the rifle within easy reach of her chair. She'd been smart enough to tie him down, and he bet she knew how to use that gun. A bullet from a twenty-two wouldn't kill him, but it would hurt like hell. And if she hit a vital spot, it would definitely slow him down.

He shifted slightly, causing the bed to creak. Immediately there was the sound of claws scrabbling on a wooden floor, and two furry heads popped up over the edge of the bed. The dogs were well mannered enough not to jump up with him, but they whined and looked back at their owner as if trying to figure out what to do next.

The woman went from sound asleep to wide awake in a heartbeat. She jerked upright, her eyes wide and a little scared. Then she reached out to reassure her guardians.

"Down, boys. He doesn't need you in his face."
The animals immediately disappeared from view.

If she'd been pretty while asleep, she was stunning wide awake. And he'd been right the first time:
her eyes were a bright green with flecks of gold in
them. Right now they were focused on him with
sharp intelligence.

"Good morning, Mr. Donahue."

How the hell did she know his name? Then he
spied his wallet on the small table next to the chair.
She'd rifled through his things?

He let a little temper show in his words. "You
seem to have me at a disadvantage, Mrs. . . ."

"Gwen. Gwen Mosely, and it's Miss."

That pleased him far more than it should. "I
would offer to shake your hand, but I'm a bit tied
up at the moment."

When she made no move to untie him, he tried
again. "I won't hurt you, Miss Mosely. If you'll just
untie me, I'll leave and never bother you again."

Preferably without answering any of the questions she was likely to start asking, ones he couldn't
answer.

"My dogs found you last night, and my brother
and I brought you up to the house."

He could imagine what shape he'd been in when
they found him. After a fierce fight, he'd managed
to escape from the Others, but he hadn't expected
to live through the night.

"Thank you."

"You were a bloody mess." Her eyes darkened. "I don't suppose you'll tell me how you came to be in that condition."

"You suppose right." With the toll healing took on his body, he simply didn't have the energy to think up a believable lie. "You don't want to know the details."

"Well, yes, actually I do." She leaned forward, as if to encourage him to start talking.

He went on the attack. "Why didn't you call the authorities? Or are you in the habit of taking in wounded strangers and tying them up?"

Her fair skin flushed. "I thought about calling Sheriff Cooper, but he would have insisted on calling an ambulance. I didn't think you'd want the local medical authorities to get their hands on you. A man with your particular abilities could end up as a lab rat somewhere."

His stomach clenched. She was right—but her reaction to his ability to heal didn't make sense. Unless she knew more about Paladin physiology than any civilian had business knowing.

"I would have survived the experience." Short of a head shot or amputation, he could survive almost anything, but she didn't know that. Or shouldn't.

"My mistake, then. Next time I find you cut to shreds and half-drowned, I'll save myself a lot of work and call nine-one-one." She had a redhead's temper, all right.

He tried his most winning smile. "Did I forget to thank you? This is a far more pleasant wake-up than I expected to have."

She wasn't buying it. "Save the charm for someone who might fall for it, Mr. Donahue."

He couldn't help laughing. "Okay, but the gratitude was sincere. I really do appreciate what you did for me." He tugged at his ropes again. "Now, can you cut me loose?"

She gave him a slow nod. "On one condition. You stay for breakfast and meet my brother."

That seemed like a simple enough request, but was it? What difference did it make if he met her brother or not? Maybe he should find out.

"Deal."

She smiled. "Good." She began working on the ropes before she spoke again. "There's a bathroom down the hall on the right. I'll lay out towels and a toothbrush for you. Your clothes are clean—well, your jeans and socks are. I'm afraid your shirt was beyond salvaging. My brother is about your size, though, so you can wear one of his."

So her brother was full-grown. If he was an adult, though, why would he let his sister stand guard rather than do it himself? They had no way of knowing whether Jarvis was a good guy or a bad guy, and he'd give her brother an earful on the subject.

He remained still until she finished untying him, not wanting to startle her with any sudden moves.

When she stepped away from the bed with her two dogs flanking her, he slowly sat up. Other than a few sore spots, he was well on his way to mending.

When he swung his legs over the side of the bed, she actually blushed and backed farther away. He grabbed the sheet to cover himself up. In the lab, he was used to waking up stark naked with a serious woody and thinking nothing of it. But from the way she kept her gaze strictly on his face, she wasn't used to strange men walking around her house in their underwear, aroused or otherwise.

"I, um, I'll go get your things." She beat a hasty retreat.

Once she left the room, he picked up his cell phone from next to his wallet and called headquarters to check in. They sounded relieved to hear from him, but he didn't fool himself that they really cared. His permanent death might even come as a relief to some of the Regents, considering how often he was in their face over how they treated the local Paladins.

The good news was that the barrier had finally stabilized during the night. The mop-up campaign was nearly complete, and everyone had orders to stand down for the next couple of days.

Jarvis hung up, then headed down the hallway to the bathroom. After a hot shower, he'd ask his hostess a few pointed questions of his own.

Chapter 2

*G*wen heard the shower shut off. She flipped the pancakes on the griddle and decided she should make half a dozen more. Chase ate like a bottomless pit lately, and Jarvis Donahue was coming off a night of intense healing. Cooking three times the normal number of pancakes, scrambling a dozen eggs, and frying a pound of bacon should be enough. Maybe.

If not, there was always cold cereal. The coffee-pot stopped perking, and a pitcher of orange juice was already sitting on the table. She wiped her hands on a dish towel, then caught herself patting her hair to make sure it was tidy.

What was she thinking? Granted, this guy was definitely good-looking, but he wasn't the kind of man for a woman like her. Even if he did make her hormones sit up and take notice.

It had been a long time since she'd enjoyed the company of a man, in bed or out of it. She'd been responsible for raising her brother ever since she was twenty and he was ten. Keeping a roof over their heads and meals on the table had taken most of her energy; she'd had very little leftover for something as frivolous as a boyfriend.

Keeping the farm had been a wise choice; now it offered Chase a sanctuary from the outside world that sometimes felt too small and confining for him. He was becoming increasingly aggressive and short-tempered, especially around boys his own age. Keeping him buried under a stack of chores all summer had drastically reduced the number of complaints about his behavior, but she dreaded what would happen when school started up again.

She listened to the sound of her unexpected guest moving around in the bathroom. For the first time, she might find some answers to the question of what made Chase that way. Since this stranger shared Chase's ability to heal, maybe he shared some of the other characteristics, as well. If he'd found a way to master his volatile nature, then there was hope for her brother.

The footsteps overhead meant Chase was up and moving, too. Good. It would be interesting to see how the two males reacted to each other.

When the bathroom door opened, she quickly

added the pancakes to the stack from the oven. Then she set the warm platter on the table.

Jarvis walked into the kitchen and instantly the room seemed to shrink in size. Although there was no aggression in his stance, it was like watching a large predator establishing its territory. He had to still be hurting from the worst of his injuries, but there was no sign of it in the flex and play of his muscles under Chase's shirt. And boy, Jarvis filled out that T-shirt in a *whole* different way than her brother did.

Had the temperature in the room just jumped up twenty degrees?

Jarvis came to an abrupt stop when he saw the table. His dark eyes lit up, and his mouth curved up in a slow grin. "Maybe I *did* die and go to heaven. Tell me you didn't go to all that trouble for me? Although I'm not complaining a bit."

"I have a teenager in the house, Mr. Donahue. Cooking for him is almost a full-time job." Still, his reaction pleased her no end. Chase blindly ate anything that she set in front of him; having a more appreciative audience was an experience to be savored.

"Please have a seat while I pour the coffee."

He pulled out the nearest chair and sank down into it, moving a little gingerly.

"Would you like a couple of aspirin or something?"

"No, I'm better off without taking anything. I should be back to normal in another day or so." He added three teaspoons of sugar to his coffee before taking a big gulp of the scalding liquid.

"Go ahead and serve yourself. Chase should be along shortly."

"Aren't you going to sit down, too?"

He made no move eat until she took the seat opposite him. She'd chosen it because it was the farthest away from Jarvis, not trusting the way she was reacting to his proximity, but now she had no choice but to look straight across the table at him.

He was already pouring a generous amount of maple syrup over the huge stack of pancakes on his plate. Adding a sizeable serving of eggs and several strips of bacon, he looked like man intent on doing some serious eating after a long, lean period.

The two of them ate in a companionable silence for several minutes until Chase came pounding down the stairs. When he entered, Jarvis stopped chewing and stared at the teenager with something like shock before he quickly schooled his features to a more neutral look.

He definitely knew something, and she wasn't going to let him get by with keeping it to himself.

"Chase, this is Jarvis Donahue. Mr. Donahue, my brother Chase."

Jarvis immediately set down his fork and stood up. He held out his hand to Chase and smiled. "Make it just plain Jarvis. I've already thanked your sister for taking me in last night, but I know she couldn't have done it without your help. I appreciate it."

Chase's eyes flickered in her direction, waiting for her slight nod before accepting Jarvis's outstretched hand. "You look a helluva lot better this morning than you did last night."

Jarvis grinned. "I'm sure those hounds of yours have dragged in better-looking specimens than me." He sat down and picked up his fork again. "Sorry for starting without you, Chase, but it's been a long time since I've had home cooking."

He was a charmer all right, but his remark still pleased her. Once again silence descended on the table as the two males concentrated on stuffing their faces. Oddly, it felt very comfortable to have this total stranger join them for a meal.

As usual, Chase was the first one done eating. He pushed his plate away and stood up. "Nice meeting you, Jarvis. Glad you lived."

She sighed. "Chase, I swear one of these days . . ."

He just grinned. "See you later, Sis. We'll talk later, but I promised Mr. James I'd help him load the hay in the back field today."

"Okay. Be home for dinner by six."

"Will do." Then he whistled for the dogs and tore out of the house, letting the door slam shut behind him.

She loved her brother dearly and enjoyed having him around. However, that didn't mean she wasn't grateful that he'd found part-time work with the neighbor for the summer. It kept him in spending money and gave him something constructive to do with his time and overabundance of energy.

Jarvis finished his own meal. "That was terrific, Miss Mosely. If I ate like that every day, I wouldn't be able to fit through the door."

"Please call me Gwen."

He nodded as he picked up his plate and headed for the sink.

"I can clean up in here later. Please sit down."

"Let me earn my keep, Gwen. It won't kill me to do a few dishes."

He cleared the table with quick efficiency, leaving her nothing to do but sip her coffee and enjoy the view. The man did a great job filling out those jeans.

He hoped Gwen never took up poker for a living. She'd starve to death, because every thought was right there on her expressive face. Right now, she was working herself up to ask him something important.

When he'd been in the shower, he'd tried to figure out why she hadn't gone to the police when she'd found a half-dead stranger in the woods. Especially one whose wounds had closed up and healed in a matter of hours.

But one look at her younger brother had answered that question. He was a dead ringer for a Paladin who'd served in the area just about the time Chase would have been born. Chase might not know it, but one day soon he'd be picking up a sword and learning to fight. If he didn't, his life would be hell, and his pretty sister would suffer right along with him. It was obvious that the two siblings were close, and Gwen wouldn't like hearing her brother was a born warrior destined to die over and over again, fighting the same secret war that Jarvis did.

It was a bitch of a way to live, but it was written in their blood and their bones. Somewhere in their past, alien beings the Paladins called Others had crossed from a dark world known as Kalithia into this one and left their mark on the human gene pool. It was ironic that those distant ancestors had helped create the Paladins, whose job was to drive the Others back into the darkness of their own world.

While Jarvis kept his hands busy drying dishes, he tried to decide how much he could safely tell Gwen about her brother. Not much. He would also have to insinuate himself into their lives long enough to get Chase started on the path to becoming a fully trained Paladin, without his sister realizing what he was up to.

Being around Gwen certainly wouldn't be any

hardship. The problem would be to avoid any messy emotional entanglements. He was too old, too tired, and too close to the end to get involved with a woman, no matter how tempted he was to find out if she had freckles all over that luscious, creamy skin. The mere thought made him harden.

Great—how was he supposed to hide his erection now? He turned away from the sink and dried his hands on the dish towel, keeping the terrycloth in front of him until he was safely seated at the table. Stretching out his legs, he leaned back and waited for the inquisition to begin.

It didn't take long.

Gwen's green eyes looked troubled. "You were hurt pretty badly last night," she began.

"Yeah, I was."

"Bloody and cut to pieces." She worried her lower lip with her teeth while she waited for him to respond.

"I don't remember much about it, but I'll take your word for it." He wasn't about to tell her that he'd been fighting a pack of ravening monsters within spitting distance of her backyard.

"Yet here you are, no more than twelve hours later, with barely a scratch on you."

"True." He reached behind him to snag the coffeepot and refilled his mug. "Want some?"

There was a small flash of temper in the way she shook her head. She suspected he was toying with her, and she was right. Maybe he should just answer the question she was dancing around.

"You and your brother had different fathers, didn't you?" He dumped sugar into his coffee and stirred it.

She looked puzzled. "Yes, but how did you know that? Other than hair color, we have many common features."

"Because Chase is the very image of an old acquaintance of mine. He had that same black hair and bright blue eyes. And I'd guess when Chase finishes filling out that frame of his, he'll be as big as his daddy was."

Just as he'd intended, he'd shocked her.

"What did your mother tell you about Chase's dad?" he asked.

Sadness settled on Gwen's shoulders. "Not much. She never told us even who he was, but he hurt her pretty badly. I was just shy of ten when she met him. For the first time since my father died, she seemed happy. She would get all dressed up and go out to meet him somewhere, so I never even saw him. Then all of a sudden, Mom quit going anywhere. She'd just stare at the phone as if willing it to ring, but it never did. Then a few months later, she gave birth to Chase."

The dates fit. "His name was Harvey Fletcher, and he was a good man. It wasn't that he didn't want to call your mother; he couldn't. He died almost exactly eighteen years ago."

To his horror, Gwen's eyes filled with tears. "I wish someone would've let my mother know. At least she could've grieved for his passing, rather than spending the last years of her life waiting for him to walk back through the door."

"I'm sorry, too. I'd guess no one knew about your mother's involvement with Harvey. But from what I remember about him, he would never have willingly abandoned his son." He leaned over and put his hand over hers in comfort.

She stared at their hands. "Did this Harvey person heal like you do? Like Chase does?"

There was no use in denying it. "Yes, Harvey had that same ability."

She nodded as if she'd already guessed that would be the answer. "Were you and he related?"

Now there was a question. He couldn't very well tell her that they shared alien DNA. "Only very distantly."

She ran her hand over the table, smoothing a couple of wrinkles in the tablecloth. Evidently she had another question but wasn't sure how to go about asking it.

"Gwen, just spit it out, whatever it is."

"Chase gets into a lot of fights, especially with boys his own age. The trouble is, he's so much bigger than most of them that folks are afraid he's going to kill somebody one of these days. It's better in the summer when he's not shut up in school all day, but he's getting less able to tolerate crowds of any kind."

Boy, did that sound familiar. If the Regents hadn't found Jarvis when they did and brought him into the Paladin organization, he had little doubt that he would have ended up in prison. Chase's sister was smart to realize the boy needed help.

"Have you thought about getting him involved in martial arts? The discipline helped me learn self-control." Coupled with weapons training, the Regents had honed his innate urge to fight into a lethal combination designed solely for killing Others.

"Is it expensive?"

Here was his in with the family. "To get him started, just to see if he likes the sport, I'd be glad to work with him."

She considered the idea for all of two seconds before shaking her head. "I couldn't ask that of you, but thank you for offering."

"Why not?"

Her fair skin flushed with embarrassment. "Because I can't afford to pay you, and charity doesn't set well with me."

Pride was something he could understand, even if it was misplaced. "I wasn't asking for money, Gwen. Someone did the same thing for me when I was about Chase's age. It saved my sanity, so I'm just passing along the favor."

Pursing her lips, she slowly nodded. "All right, I'll talk to him and see if he's interested. If he is, how can I get in touch with you?"

"I'll give you my cell phone number. It's good day or night."

At least he'd planted the seeds. If they didn't take, he'd have to think of some other excuse to return to the Mosely farm. A new Paladin wasn't something to be wasted; there were too few of them as it was. He had a duty to the Regents organization to recruit a new warrior. It had nothing to do with the boy's sister, much less her red hair and those adorable freckles.

Yeah, right.

"Get the hell away from me with those damn needles. Why don't you just slit my wrist and bleed me dry? It'd be faster and hurt less!"

At the sound of Jake's irate voice, Jarvis poked his head through the lab door and grinned. "Hey, buddy, how goes it?"

The look his friend aimed in his direction was only slightly less irritated than the one he'd been giving the poor tech who was still waiting to draw his blood.

"I'll be fine when these bozos realize I'm a Paladin, not a damned pincushion." He begrudgingly held out his arm and let the tech apply a tourniquet.

Jarvis thought maybe Jake could use a distraction. He held out Jake's favorite laptop as a peace offering, knowing Jake spent most of his free time perfecting his dragon computer game. "Got time to do some research for me?"

Jake winced as the needle went in, keeping his eyes firmly on Jarvis. "Got nothing but time. Doc Crosby says I'll be here at least two more days until my legs are back in one piece. Why? What do you need?"

Jarvis waited until the tech had left the room. Then he handed Jake the computer, snagged a chair, and straddled it, resting his arms on the back.

"You might be too young to remember, but there used to be a Paladin here named Harvey Fletcher. He died about eighteen years ago. I need everything you can ferret out about him. No rush, though," he added, noting the gray cast to Jake's face.

"Any special reason?" Jake let his head sag back against the pillow as if the effort to support it was too much. Having been dead the day before had that effect on a man.

"I'm pretty sure that I found his son."

The announcement brought new life to Jake's expression. "I'll be damned. I thought you were out on mop-up."

"I was. Damned near ended up a permanent

casualty, too. I thought I was facing one Other, but he'd brought along his fan club."

"Bad luck, that." Jake didn't need the details to know that it had been rough. "So how did you go from almost dying to finding a new recruit?"

"A pair of dogs found me and raised hell until their owner came to investigate. She and her brother hauled me out of the river and up to their house. I woke up there this morning, tied down to the bed and all patched up."

"She?" Jake managed a half-hearted leer. "You have all the luck Jarvis. I wake up here getting poked with needles, while you have some beautiful woman fussing over you."

"I never said she was beautiful." Although she definitely was.

"She had to be better looking than Doc Crosby." Jake frowned. "Wait a minute. How did she know to tie you down?"

"I think she was going to call the sheriff when she found me, but saw my wounds starting to close up. She's seen her brother do the same thing and knew I might not come back in control of myself. She took me in for the night to get some answers about the problems she's been having with him."

Jake nodded. "It's bad enough when you know what's happening. I'll bet it's hell watching someone you love struggling to control untrained aggression. You gonna bring him in?"

"Eventually. For now, I offered to start teaching the boy martial arts. I figure the sister doesn't need to know that includes weapons training."

"So what do you want me to research? Seems like you've already got everything on track."

"I thought the boy might eventually like to know something about his father. Maybe even a picture if you can find one, something to help him feel connected to his father's legacy. Their mother evidently took it pretty hard when Harvey disappeared, especially when she turned up pregnant and no man in sight."

"How old is the sister?"

Jarvis pictured Gwen's face in his mind. "I'd guess she's got about ten years on her brother." Which made her fifteen years younger than himself—and way too innocent for the dark violence that made up the world he lived in.

What a damn shame.

Something in his expression must have given his thoughts away because Jake was looking at him skeptically. "So you're doing all of this for the brother, right?"

Jarvis gave in and smiled. "That's my story and I'm sticking to it."

Jake laughed and then winced. "Damn, I keep forgetting how badly cracked ribs hurt. When are you going to see the boy again?"

"Maybe in a couple of days. First I'm going to

crash for a solid twenty-four hours before I set foot out of this place again."

The doors behind them swung open and their Handler walked in. "Ah, Mr. Donahue. I was wondering when I'd see you. I understand that you had a rough time of it."

"A few cuts and scratches, nothing too serious." Anything short of dead wasn't too bad.

The doctor looked at him over the top of his reading glasses. "Right. Well, you hop right up there on the table next to Jake's and let me be the judge of that."

Aw, hell. But there was no arguing with the medical staff. If he didn't willingly offer himself up for the doctor's inspection, the Handler would call for the guards to force the issue.

Ignoring Jake's smirk, Jarvis yanked off Chase's shirt and let the doctor run through a cursory examination.

"Someone did a good job cleaning up those cuts."

Jarvis gritted his teeth when the doctor hit a couple of sore spots. "I'll pass along your compliments."

"Do that. Now go get some rest, and check back in a couple of days to make sure those two deep ones have healed up cleanly."

"Will do." He hopped back down and pulled his shirt back on. "Hey, Doc, did you know a Paladin named Harvey Fletcher? Died about eighteen years ago?"

The Handler frowned and then nodded. "Now there's a name I haven't thought of in a long time. He was a good man. Why do you ask?"

"Someone mentioned his name the other day. I hadn't been here all that long when he died."

Dr. Crosby stared up at the ceiling. "If I recall, he was permanently killed in some woods near here. I had just come on board as a Handler, but I remember everybody being pretty upset about his death. No one could figure out how it had happened."

He checked Jake's chart. "I'm going to kick you out of here, Jarvis. Jake needs to sleep, and he won't as long as you're here. He doesn't like to admit how close we came to losing him altogether."

Doc Crosby reached over and confiscated Jake's laptop. "I'll be keeping this until you look less like death warmed over."

Jake put up a token resistance. "Jarvis, remind me to program the dragon to eat the Doc."

"Careful, buddy. Remember those rusty needles Doc keeps for special occasions."

Jake frowned, but his eyes were already starting to close.

Jarvis nodded. "Thanks for everything, Doc."

After Dr. Crosby disappeared into his office, Jarvis leaned down to whisper to his friend, "Jake, do you need anything?"

Jake popped one eye back open. "By tomorrow I'll be bored out of my wits. Come by if you get a chance, so I can beat you at chess."

"In your dreams, buddy, but it's a deal. I might even sneak in some decent food."

"I heard that!" Dr. Crosby poked his head back out. "Make sure there's enough for me, too, or I'll restrict his diet and eat it anyway. Jake's not the only one who gets tired of the stuff they serve around here."

"Will do, Doc. See you tomorrow, Jake."

"I'll try to have something for you by then."

"Thanks. I appreciate it."

Once he had Jake's research and time to wash Chase's shirt, he'd have all the excuse he needed to pay another call on the Moselys.

Snapping beans allowed Gwen an excuse to sit on the screened-in porch for a much needed rest. She settled into her grandmother's old rocker as Dozer flopped down in his favorite spot right under the ceiling fan. She smiled and reached out with her bare toes to rub his back. He groaned and rolled over to give her better access to his belly.

"Silly dog. I've got better things to do than pet you."

That was true, but it didn't stop her from giving him a good scratch and rub. He rewarded her with a quick slurp of his tongue before settling in for his afternoon nap.

The dog had the right idea. It was too hot and muggy to do much moving around. She eyed the book she'd set on the table, then the bowl of beans. The vegetables won, but only barely. After finishing the beans, she would put them on to simmer and fix herself another glass of iced tea. Then she'd settle into the rocker and read. She could water the vegetable garden later.

She fell into the easy rhythm of snapping the beans as she rocked. The fan kept the air moving enough to keep the heat bearable. Other than the beans, she'd planned a cold dinner of leftover fried chicken, potato salad, and sliced fruit.

A few minutes later, Dozer lifted his head and sniffed the air. He whined and lumbered to his feet. After pushing the screen door open with his nose, he headed up the driveway toward the road. What had caught his attention?

Larry came charging out of the barn to take up position next to the older dog. Both stood stock still, except for the slow wag of their tails.

They seemed curious, but not worried. Setting the bowl aside again, she walked outside onto the steps. The low rumble of a powerful engine approached, and she waited to see who was paying her a visit.

Seconds later, a muscle car eased down the last

stretch of the driveway. The driver was wisely taking it slowly. If she had a car like that, she would have parked it up on the road rather than risk its paint job and undercarriage on a stretch of gravel that had more ruts than flat spots.

It wasn't a friend of Chase's; if one of his few friends drove something that hot, he would have mentioned it. The car was all about power and speed. She thought about the pickup she and Chase shared—banged-up, rusty in spots, and all too practical—and sighed with envy.

The car nosed off to the side of the driveway and stopped by the barn. The glare of the sun off the windshield made it impossible to make out the driver, but when the door opened, her heart stuttered. Jarvis Donahue was back.

It had been almost a week since he'd walked out the door and, she'd thought, out of her life. But there he was, petting Dozer and taking the time to throw a stick for Larry before heading for her.

Lord, the way that man moved, he was all grace and lean strength. His jeans were obviously old favorites, worn at the knee and frayed at the hem. His dark blue sports shirt was unbuttoned over a white T-shirt that outlined all those well-defined muscles. Seriously yum.

"You're looking healthier than the last time you showed up." She regretted the bit of a bite in her comment, but he could have called first. There he was looking fine, and she had her hair pinned up in a sloppy knot to keep it up off her neck. Her clothes were clean, but that was all she could say about them.

He smiled as he rocked back on his heels. "Yeah, I haven't been chewed up and spat out in a few days now. I'm thirsty, though."

Where were her manners? Short-circuited by her unruly hormones no doubt. "Come up on the porch and sit a spell. Lemonade or iced tea?"

"Tea sounds good."

"Sweet or plain?"

He pulled a chair closer to her rocker and sat down, looking as if he planned to be there awhile. "Sweet would hit the spot."

She laughed as she headed inside. "I should have guessed that, after seeing how much sugar you dumped in your coffee."

Inside the house, she decided to run a brush through her hair. She considered a quick change of clothes, but that would have been too obvious.

After filling a couple of glasses with ice and tea, she set them on a tray, then she added a plate of homemade cookies before carrying it out to the table between the two rockers.

"Help yourself to the cookies."

He didn't hesitate, grabbing three in one hand and the tea in the other. "Thank you, Gwen. It's already been a long, hot day."

"Did you come all the way from St. Louis?"

He looked surprised. "St. Louis?"

"That's what the address on your driver's license said." She blushed, even though they'd had a legitimate reason to pry into his privacy at the time.

His eyes crinkled in the corners. "I forgot you and Chase snooped through my wallet."

Now she was both embarrassed and outraged. "You were unconscious! We were only—"

He grinned and held up a hand to stop her. "I was just teasing, Gwen. You had every right to do some checking. But to answer your question, I'm spending the summer with some friends. They live just a little east and south of here."

"Oh."

He gave her an odd look before turning his attention toward the dogs rolling in the dust near his car. It took her a second to realize that she was rocking as if her life depended on it. She slowed down and wished her pulse would do the same.

"So what brought you down this way?" To keep her hands busy, she reached for the beans and started snapping them again.

"I had expected you to call. When you didn't, I decided it was a nice day for a drive. Did you talk to Chase about the lessons?"

No, she hadn't. She'd planned to, but kept finding one excuse after another to avoid bringing up the subject. The worst thing was that she didn't even know why. Knowing she couldn't afford to pay for lessons was part of it, but not the real reason. Her nights had been filled with restless dreams about Jarvis Donahue.

"He's been so busy working, I didn't want to take away what free time he has."

Jarvis took another cookie. "It's going to get worse for him, Gwen. The aggression, the need to fight."

"You don't know that."

He reached across the table to put his warm hand on her arm. "Yeah, I do. How about if I talk to him myself? If he's not interested, fine. But I know how it is for a boy like Chase. He reminds me a lot of me."

She looked at him levelly. "And who *are* you, Jarvis? You've never explained how you came to be in my woods, much less who left you in that condition."

"No. I haven't because I can't." His mouth was a hard slash and his dark eyes turned chilly.

"Can't or won't?" She finished the beans and set them aside, wishing she had something else to do.

"Both, actually, but I won't let anything hurt you or Chase."

She believed him; maybe even trusted him, although she wasn't sure she should. "He'll be home in an hour. If you're willing to take potluck, why don't you stay for dinner? That'll give him a chance to get to know you. Once we see how that goes, we can broach the subject to him."

"I'd be a fool to turn down more of your cooking." He snagged the last cookie and ate it.

Wasn't there an old saying that the way to a man's heart was through his stomach? Not that she was interested in his heart. But just in case, she'd bring out more cookies.

Gwen was antsy. Every few seconds, she'd look at the clock and then out the window. Jarvis pretended not to notice, but Chase was forty-five minutes late and that definitely worried his big sister. Maybe he could distract her. He walked over to where Gwen stood watching out the window.

"Can I do something to help? Maybe set the table?"

She jumped about a foot. "What?"

He hid the urge to smile. "I didn't mean to scare you. I just asked if I could help you set the table."

She blinked a couple of times, pulling her attention back to him. "I can do it."

He didn't argue, figuring she needed something to keep her mind occupied. He added ice cubes to the glasses and then filled them with tea. After Gwen got out plates and silverware, he took them from her hands and set them on the table.

"Napkins?"

She pointed toward the paper towel roll on the counter. "We use those."

Now he was out of ideas, and she was back to worrying. He eased up next to her, trying not to startle her again.

"If something was wrong, wouldn't the farmer he's working for have called?"

"You'd think so. If my brother doesn't show up in the next ten minutes, I'll give Mr. James a ring. Chase hates it when I hover."

Jarvis fought the temptation to wrap his arms around her, though he wanted nothing more than to offer her the comfort of his touch. He hated seeing her look so alone and frazzled. How many nights had she stood at that same window and worried about her brother?

Probably too many.

Then he heard something. It was too distant for normal human hearing to pick up, but a car or pickup was slowing down near the turnoff to the driveway. He waited until he was sure before saying anything.

"He's home."

"How do you know?" The relief in her eyes was painful to watch.

Before he could explain, the truck rolled into sight. She quickly hurried away from the window and started hauling food out of the refrigerator. She probably didn't want her brother to see her watching for him.

Chase parked the truck near the barn and made a beeline for Jarvis's car. He walked all around it, bending to check it out from all different angles. When he'd completed the circuit, he headed straight for the house.

Charging into the kitchen, he hollered, "Hey, Sis, whose car is that? It's totally sick!"

Then he spotted Jarvis and stopped, looking a bit flustered. "Must be yours."

"It is." Jarvis leaned against the counter and crossed his feet at the ankles. Recognizing a male in throes of serious car envy, he waited for the barrage of questions.

"What year is it? I bet it has an engine that really rips down these country roads. Can I have a ride in it?"

"It's a '69 Chevelle SS. She corners like a dream, and has a monster of an engine that eats these twisting roads for lunch. And yes, you can." He glanced toward Gwen. "If your sister says it's okay, I might even let you drive it sometime."

Gwen grinned. "Let's eat before he questions you to death. After dinner, we can all go out and ooh and aah over the car. Chase, get washed up. You're late enough as it is."

"My bad. We only had a little more hay to mow, so we finished it up."

Jarvis straightened up. "You should've called.

Your sister doesn't want you to know, but she worries. That's not fair to her."

Gwen started to object, but he cut her off with a quick shake of the head. "Do you understand, Chase?"

The boy, almost a man, met Jarvis's gaze for a second or two before looking at his sister. "Sorry, Gwen. Guess I wasn't thinking."

"Try to next time, Chase. Now go on, so we can all eat."

When he left the room, she turned on Jarvis. "I appreciate your concern, Mr. Donahue, but he's my responsibility."

"True, but he's almost eighteen years old, and it's time he starts taking responsibility for his actions. If he doesn't, it will only make it harder for him down the road. If you want him to act like a man, treat him like one."

He softened his words with a smile. "And he's going to need to take orders from me as his martial arts instructor."

"We haven't agreed to the lessons."

"No, but eventually you'll have to. He needs the control they'll give him."

And the Regents needed a new Paladin. Once the boy knew what he was and understood what it meant, the two of them would figure out how much to tell Gwen. As little as possible, if it were up to

Jarvis. She'd been more of a mother than a sister to Chase, and she would fight to keep him from picking up a sword, even in defense of the world.

Not only that, she would see Jarvis as the enemy—and he'd hate that a hell of a lot.

Chapter 3

Jordan, one of Chase's friends, stopped by after dinner. All three males abandoned Gwen while they examined Jarvis's car from stem to stern and back again. She'd already learned more than she'd ever wanted to about rebuilding a classic car. It was fun, though, watching Chase repeat word for word everything Jarvis had told him earlier.

It was obvious that Jarvis might be good for Chase. How had she missed realizing how grown-up her brother had become? It seemed like only yesterday that he was a skinny little kid running all over the farm with Dozer at his heels. Now the dog had grown gray around his muzzle, and Chase had to shave twice a day if he had plans for the evening.

Jarvis separated himself from the boys and wandered back toward Gwen. Chase wasn't the only one with a serious case of hero worship. Dozer and

Larry were tripping over each other as they vied for Jarvis's attention. He stopped to give each of them a thorough ear scratch before joining her on the porch.

"I told the boys I'd take them for a quick spin, if that's all right with you."

"Sure, but you'll be creating a monster, you know." She forced her gaze away from Jarvis and back to his car. "I can see it all now. Chase will lord it over his other friends, and you'll spend the rest of the summer chauffeuring a bunch of high school boys all over the county."

The look on Jarvis's face was priceless. Obviously his experience with teenage boys was limited. She decided to show mercy. "Don't sweat it, big guy. Chase doesn't have that many friends, and you can always charge them for gas."

He laughed. "I might, at that. I love my car, but not as much as she loves gas stations." He leaned against the porch rail. "I'll give them a few more minutes to drool over her engine and then give them their thrill for the evening."

"Hey, Jarvis, come here for a minute." Chase's voice was muffled because his head was under the hood.

Jarvis left with a wry grin. "I'll be back."

She tried to keep her eyes on her book, she really did. But it was a losing battle, especially when Jarvis leaned over to point out some bit of engine lore to the two boys. The way that man filled out those jeans ought to come with a warning label—"Caution: Not responsible for hormones raging out of control!"

Unfortunately, he glanced back in her direction and caught her staring. If she hadn't immediately blushed, he might have thought she was keeping an eye on the two boys. There was definitely a knowing twinkle in his eyes when he looked away.

Lord, she hadn't been caught admiring a man's butt since she was Chase's age. An adult woman should have more control.

She went inside, leaving the three males to enjoy the heady fumes of gasoline, oil, and testosterone. If any of them noticed her absence, they gave no sign of it. As she folded a load of towels, she tried to convince herself that was a good thing. After all, Jarvis was here for Chase.

It was all Jarvis could do not to hand Chase the keys to the Chevelle and tell him he could have the car for an hour or two. But he had no right to be thinking the kind of thoughts he was having about Gwen Mosely. She was sweet, good, and far more innocent than a woman her age should be.

Most women, even those who claimed to be only looking for a good time, wanted a man who could be depended on to show up when he said he would. Over the years, with the instability of the barrier in this region, he'd broken far more promises than he'd ever kept. Then there was the little problem that he hadn't aged perceptibly since his early thirties. No matter how dim the light in any bar, a woman was bound to notice eventually.

He hated always lying, and after a while all those lies ran together, making it impossible to keep the excuses straight. He'd been called away on a family crisis; his car had broken down; his company had sent him out of town on business. But if women had a hard time believing the lies, they'd never buy the truth.

Sorry, honey, I was too dead to pick up the phone and call. Or, I couldn't get the bloodstains out of my jeans and didn't want to gross you out.

But Gwen was different in one important way. She already knew part of his truth and wasn't bothered by it, even if only because he could answer her questions about Chase. Too bad he could tell the whole truth only to Chase, while teaching him to lie to everybody, including his sister. Damn, he hated this.

The time for admiring his car was over. He needed the rush of the big engine screaming down the road, running from everything but the sweet feel of the Chevelle eating up the miles.

"Come on, boys, let's see what she'll do."

Jordan climbed into the backseat and buckled

in while Chase took the place of honor, riding shot-gun. Jarvis carefully maneuvered around the worst of the ruts in the driveway and pulled out onto the deserted two-lane road.

"Hold on!" he warned the boys as he floored the gas pedal, going from zero to sixty in a handful of seconds.

Chase and Jordan screamed out their approval as Jarvis put her through her paces, showing off for the hell of it. It would give the two boys bragging rights with their friends, and make Chase want to spend more time in Jarvis's company.

Which was, after all, the whole purpose for this visit. The fact that he'd rather have Gwen next to him as he tore through the twisting turns was some-thing he couldn't afford to think about.

Gwen managed to keep herself busy without much trouble. The chores were never done on a farm, even one as small as theirs. There were weeds to pull, animals to feed, and dust bunnies to be hunted down and caught. An hour after the sound of the Chevelle's engine faded away, she was still at it, dragging the last of the little critters out from under the bed in the guest room. Some of them de-served a place in the Dust Bunny Hall of Fame.

The distant sound of a powerful engine caught her attention, and she hustled back to the kitchen to stow the cleaning supplies, then dashed for the bathroom to make sure she didn't have dirt on her nose and that her braid was still tidy.

Not that she was trying to impress anybody. Absolutely not. She just didn't want to embarrass her brother in front of his friends. She walked out to the porch and down the steps as her brother climbed out of the passenger door with a wide grin on his face.

"Aw, Sis, you have *got* to go for a ride in this baby!" He trailed his fingers along the long curve of the quarter panel, careful not to scratch it. "It was amazing!"

"I'm glad you had a good time, Chase." She looked past him to Jordan. "Hey, kiddo, your mom phoned wondering where you were. I told her you'd call as soon as you got back."

"Thanks, Gwen." Jordan charged past her into the house.

"Chase, you go with him after you thank Jarvis."

"Yeah, Jarvis, that was cool! Thanks for taking us." For once her brother's gratitude sounded sincere instead of just good manners.

Leaving the engine running, Jarvis got out of the car and came a few steps toward her.

"He's right, you know." He stuck his hands in his hip pockets and gave her a slow smile that was all temptation. "You really do need to go for a ride with me."

And why did the way he said that make her

think he meant far more than a quick spin down the road? Her heart fluttered. "Haven't you had enough of the Mosely clan for one day?"

"Maybe one of them, but not nearly enough of the other." He came closer, causing her to back up a step before she decided to hold her ground.

"I've got a strong hankering," he said, coming a half step closer and lowering his voice, "for a banana split with all the toppings. But ice cream isn't much fun for one person."

Lord, he'd tempt a nun. And she definitely wasn't a nun.

She grinned. "Let's go!"

He snagged her hand and pulled her toward the car.

"Wait, I need to tell Chase that I'm leaving."

Jarvis opened the passenger door and tucked her inside before she could protest. "I'll tell him."

He loped over to the front door and yelled in, "Hey, Chase, I'll bring your sister back eventually."

Then the two of them were flying down the highway, with a classic rock station blasting on the radio. The heady combination of loud music and speed filled her senses, leaving no room for second thoughts or doubts. Gwen leaned back and let the powerful car and its handsome owner carry her away.

• • •

What was Gwen thinking about? Definitely something good, judging by the soft smile and dreamy look in her eyes. Jarvis had taken the long way to the small drive-in restaurant where there was a banana split waiting with his name on it. As content as she looked, he almost hated to stop.

But he'd promised her ice cream, and he wanted her to trust him on the small things so she'd think he was a man of his word. That way, when he did need to lie to her, she might not notice as fast. She'd eventually find out, which was a damn shame, but he knew that Gwen wasn't going to like his real motive for mentoring her brother. Until that moment arrived, though, he was going to enjoy cruising the Ozark highways with a beautiful woman.

As they crested the next hill, he spotted the giant rotating ice cream cone ahead on the left. He slowed down and eased the Chevelle into the gravel parking lot, wincing when he hit a chuckhole.

Gwen giggled. "If you keep driving on gravel, you're going to need a new paint job."

"Yeah, this beauty is always wanting something. Last month it was a new exhaust system." He shook his head in mock disgust as he parked. "She's always had expensive tastes."

Gwen arched an eyebrow. "So I take it that the two of you have been an item for a long time?"

He patted the steering wheel. "We've been

through an engine rebuild, a new interior, and a couple of paint jobs. Nothing is too good for my girl."

"Sounds expensive."

"Some things are worth it." He raised his eyebrows in mock horror. "I actually had a friend who suggested I could have owned two or three boring beige sedans for what I have tied up in her. What fun is that? Besides, if I bought another car, it would hurt her feelings."

"I can see how that could happen." Gwen's green eyes crinkled in amusement.

"Now, about that ice cream. What do you say we eat at one of the picnic tables? There's a nice breeze, now that the sun's going down."

"Sounds good." She opened the door and walked around to meet him at the front of the car. "Besides, I'd live in terror of dripping chocolate on the upholstery and having to walk back home."

"I'd never make you walk." He put his hand on the small of her back as they walked up to the window to order, and liked that she didn't pull away. "Of course, you'd have to ride home in the trunk."

She gave him an arch look. "Just try it and see if I invite you for dinner again."

"We can't have that, can we?" So she was already thinking ahead to the next time—good.

The clerk came to the window. "Can I take your order?"

"I'll have a banana split with all the works. What sounds good to you, Gwen?"

He watched her nibble on her lower lip as she considered the options, and the small gesture had him wanting to kiss her.

"I'll have a chocolate cone—two scoops, please."

When they had their ice cream, Gwen led the way to the rustic picnic tables. The small voice of his conscience warned Jarvis that sitting across from her might be the safer choice, but he ignored it and slid in beside her. She stiffened briefly, but relaxed when he stopped short of touching her.

"This will hit the spot." He spooned up a big bite of the ice cream and savored it.

Gwen eyed the three scoops and piles of toppings in his bowl. "If I ate something that big, I'd have to run all the way home to burn off the calories." She shook her head sadly. "It's not fair that both you and Chase can eat like that without gaining an ounce."

"I hear it catches up with men later."

Purely human men, anyway. Part of the Paladin package was a higher metabolic rate, but few of them lived long enough to see if that would eventually change. The oldest known Paladin was Devlin Bane in Seattle, and he still looked to be in his late thirties.

"So one of these days, you're going to be walking along and all those calories are going to blow you up like a balloon? Now that's something I'd pay to watch." She held her cone close to her mouth and her tongue darted out to catch a drip.

The sudden tightness in the fit of his jeans had nothing to do with the ice cream, and everything to do with watching her lick her cone with such sensuous pleasure. Right then, he'd give almost anything to be a double scoop of chocolate.

She nodded toward his bowl. "Your ice cream is melting."

"I'll have to eat faster."

Maybe that would keep him focused on something other than the growing urge to kiss her. From the way she was watching him out of the corner of her eye, she still felt skittish around him. But damn, there went that tongue again. It was definitely time to steer the conversation to a safer topic.

"So I've been meaning to ask about those beasties in the pasture out behind your barn. They look a little small for llamas."

"That's because they're not llamas. They're alpacas. I'm a breeder. We sell the offspring, and keep the rest for their fiber. I usually get enough of that to sell to people who spin their own yarn, although I keep a fair amount for my own use. Thanks to the Internet, I've built up a steady clientele for my yarn and for what I weave and knit."

"How long have you been doing that?"

She scrunched up her nose as she thought. "Must be close to seven years now. My mom left enough insurance to pay off the farm, but it never was a moneymaking proposition. I was away at school when she died, and came home to take care of Chase."

For the next few seconds, she seemed lost in the past. When a large drip threatened to run down the side of her cone, he captured her hand in his and stole a big lick of her ice cream.

"Hey!" she protested, pulling free. "You have your own."

"My intentions were strictly honorable. My quick action saved you from being the victim of a nasty drip." He tried to look put upon, but couldn't keep from grinning. "So you were telling me about your critters."

"I needed a way to make the farm profitable, and decided that breeding alpacas would be a good choice for the two of us. I invested in some good-quality breeding stock and slowly built up my herd. I sell a few off each year, which provides the bulk of my income. The rest is gravy."

"That must have been hard, giving up your college plans and taking on the job of raising your brother." He doubted many young women would have done so.

She shook her head. "It wasn't any sacrifice. We're family, and that's what family does."

"Then Chase is a lucky young man," he murmured, thinking how different his friend Trahern's life would have been if he'd had a loving sister to take him in. Blake had been living on the streets when he'd been years younger than Chase was now. Jarvis's own situation had been a little better, but having an unstable Paladin for a father was no picnic.

Gwen ducked her head and blushed. "Thank you for saying so. We're not exactly rolling in the dough, but I've never doubted that it was the right decision for both our sakes. I could never have abandoned him to the foster system just so I could finish school."

Jarvis gently pried her cone from her fingers and set it down in his bowl, letting the chocolate mix with the pool of vanilla. She had to know what was coming, and didn't protest as he cupped her face to tilt her mouth to just the perfect angle.

But he owed her the right to make the final decision. "Tell me to stop and I will." Even if it killed him.

"Now why would I do something so foolish?" Her eyes drifted half shut as her mouth softened in invitation.

Their lips met on a sigh, then he tasted the sweetness of her chocolate-flavored kiss.

The world narrowed down to the solid strength of Jarvis's arms wrapped around her shoulders as he plundered her mouth. Gwen hung on to those broad shoulders, loving the play of his muscles and the warmth of his body next to hers.

When he teased the corners of her mouth, asking for entry, she smiled and opened to him. His tongue swirled in and out, coaxing her to surrender to him. It was hard to hold back, even though this was hardly the place to do more than kiss.

Jarvis slowly withdrew, using the gentle brush of his fingertips along the column of her throat to say he was doing so only reluctantly. She stared into his dark eyes, gradually regaining awareness of their surroundings. The warmth of the setting sun. The rough surface of the picnic table. The faint scent of aftershave mixed with the tang of male sweat. The sound of a car going by on the road. How cold she felt when he moved a few inches away.

"Wow," she breathed.

Jarvis smiled. "Totally."

What to do next? Their ice cream had melted into a big blob. She identified with it all too well. She had to do something besides stare moon-eyed at him. "I'll throw this away so we can get going."

When she headed for the garbage can, he thoughtfully avoided crowding her by walking over to open the car door for her. She used the few seconds of separation to bring her badly rattled nerves back under control. Although it was only a kiss, she'd never been kissed that way before, as if they had all day to enjoy it.

Feeling a bit shy, she approached the car and

Jarvis. He stepped around the open door to stand in front of her again, looking as confused as she felt. Finally, he brushed a stray lock of her hair back from her face.

"I have to tell you that I've been wanting to do that since I woke up in your house."

"Was it worth the wait?" she asked bravely.

His mouth curved up in that sexy smile that set her pulse racing. "Oh, yeah."

Gwen smiled back and then, feeling daring, rose up on her toes and kissed him again. "Next time, don't wait so long."

The flicker of headlights turning into the driveway meant they were finally back. A few seconds later, the Chevelle rumbled down the driveway and stopped outside the barn. When Gwen got out of Jarvis's car, Chase turned away from the window, not wanting her to think he was spying on them.

They'd been gone for almost two hours, and he wasn't sure what he thought about that. On the one hand, it was about time she had a life of her own. Between taking care of him and the farm since Mom died, Gwen had rarely had time to breathe, much less hang with her friends.

But seeing her with Jarvis reminded him that she was more than just his older sister. She was an attractive woman, even if he forgot that most of the time. Jarvis seemed like an okay guy, but

Gwen needed someone who'd be willing to stick around. According to his driver's license, Jarvis lived up near St. Louis. What had he been doing in their woods that had left him cut up and half dead?

And why was he hanging around their farm now? Chase had a feeling that returning a worn T-shirt had been just an excuse. Maybe he should have a talk with Jarvis the next time he came back. If he came back.

He went into the living room and turned on the ball game, keeping the television muted until he heard Jarvis's car start up again. Then he turned up the sound, to look as normal as possible when Gwen came in. For the time being, any questions he had were for Jarvis. After he had his answers, he'd decide what to tell his sister, if anything.

He suddenly realized he was holding the remote so hard that his knuckles were white. Ever since the phone call from his football coach after Gwen left, he'd been prowling the house looking for a handy target for his anger. He fought the urge to heave the remote across the room, not wanting to upset his sister any more than necessary.

He and Gwen both knew that it was getting harder and harder for him to keep his cool, no matter how he tried. He did his best to stay busy, working himself into near exhaustion to help maintain control. But he worried that one of these days he'd explode, and that Gwen would get caught in the fallout if he hurt someone. Or worse yet, her. That would be some payback for everything she'd done for him.

The back door opened and he forced himself to relax, using the techniques from that book Gwen had ordered online. They helped some, at least taking the edge off. He muted the television again as she walked into the room.

"So, did you have a good time with Jarvis?" Darn, he wished he'd worded that differently. "Did you like the car?"

Was she blushing? Yeah, she was. What was up with that?

"Yes, I loved the car. Did Jarvis tell you that he'd rebuilt the engine and did most of the restoration on the car himself?"

"Yeah, he did. That's pretty cool. I'd like to try doing something similar." He gave her a hopeful look. "Maybe I could practice on our truck."

"Have at it, big guy. However, while our only means of transportation is in bits and pieces, you're the one who gets to hitch a couple of the alpacas up to a cart to get groceries. It's only about ten miles to town, so it won't take you more than a few hours each way. Think Jordan will think that's as cool as riding in the Chevelle?"

He laughed. "Yeah, and think of all the hotties who'd be lining up to admire my sick new wheels."

"Hey, it could start a whole new fad when school starts up again. Though I doubt the football coach would appreciate his field being used for a pasture."

Chase turned to face the television to avoid his sister's eagle eyes. "Speaking of football, I'm kinda worried about going out for the team. Last year I didn't always handle being tackled very well."

Admitting that was hard, but the coach's call had been a warning that if there was any more trouble, Chase wouldn't make the first cut despite his size and speed.

Before he could tell her about the call, Gwen dropped down beside him. "I've been meaning to talk to you about something. You know Jarvis has the same ability to heal that you do."

Chase nodded.

"He said he had some of the same problems when he was your age—the temper and things. He offered to teach you martial arts because they helped him learn control."

Chase stiffened. "What else have you been telling him about me?"

"I didn't tell him much of anything. He wanted to know why we didn't call the authorities when we found him, and I told him that we didn't think he'd want them to see how fast he healed. And that morning, he recognized you without me telling him anything."

"What do you mean, he recognized me? We'd never met before."

Gwen drew a deep breath. "He knew your father. He said you look just like him."

Chapter 4

*C*hase lurched up off the couch and glared down at her, his body vibrating with anger or hurt. It was impossible to tell from the stony expression on his face.

"I'm sorry, Chase. I should have told you sooner, but I didn't know how." She looked her brother straight in the eyes. "And this was obviously the wrong way to go about it."

"You've known for over a *week*, Gwen. In all that time, you couldn't have found a way to tell me something as important as this? What did you think would happen when you told me? That I'd run off with Jarvis to hunt down my long-lost daddy?"

"No, that's not what I thought." She gentled her voice. "Your father died before you were born. That's why he never came back." She reached out to touch his arm.

Some of his fury melted away. "How did he die?"

She shook her head. "Jarvis didn't say how, just that he had. He also said your father wasn't the kind of a man who would have abandoned his child."

Chase sank back down on the couch. "How come Mom never knew what happened to him?"

"Jarvis's best guess is that no one knew they were involved." She took a seat across the room, figuring she'd crowded Chase enough for one evening.

"What else did Jarvis tell you?"

"I was too stunned to ask more. Maybe you should take it up with him yourself—although he may not know much more than your father's name. If the man died eighteen years ago, Jarvis would have been a boy at the time. He said they were only distantly related."

Chase sat in silence for a minute.

"So what *was* his name? My father, I mean."

She smacked herself on the forehead. "God, what a dunce I'm being. His name was Harvey. Harvey Fletcher."

Chase grunted, obviously not ready to let go of all of his anger. "It's no biggie. This Harvey guy obviously didn't care enough about Mom to tell his friends about her."

There was no easy answer to that. "If you decide you want to know more about him, call Jarvis. I've told you everything I can."

After a few seconds of uneasy silence, Chase asked, "And what's this about Jarvis teaching me martial arts?"

The crisis had passed, at least for the moment. "Like I said, Jarvis admitted that he had some of the same problems when he was your age, but that someone taught him martial arts to help him focus and maintain control. He's willing to do the same for you, if you're interested."

"Do we have the bucks for it?"

Gwen knew her brother wouldn't like charity any better than she did. "He said he'd do it for free, at least until you find out if you like it or not. After that, we'll work it out somehow."

"I'll think on it."

She dredged up a smile. "Good. I have his cell phone number if you want to talk to him."

"Word. I'll let you know what I decide."

It was time to leave him to his own thoughts. Even though Harvey Fletcher might never be more than a name to her brother, it was more of his father than he'd ever had.

"I'm going to bed."

"See you in the morning, Sis."

She paused in the doorway. "And I am sorry I handled this so badly, Chase."

He ignored the apology. "I may be gone before you're up in the morning. Mr. James wants to get an early start, before it gets too hot. I should be home in time to help with afternoon chores, but I'll call if I'm going to be late."

"Sounds good." It also sounded like Jarvis's pointed remark might have done some good. Maybe spending some time with him *would* be good for her brother.

Honesty made her admit that having Jarvis around would definitely be good for *her*. Her lips tingled, remembering his kiss. But Jarvis had a life, a job, things to do. If he was willing to spend part of his time with one of the Moselys, it was best spent with her brother.

Feeling more tired than ever, she headed upstairs to her lonely bed.

Jake looked up from his computer when Jarvis walked into the medical lab. "Where have you been all evening?"

Rather than answer, Jarvis studied the screen over his friend's shoulder. "How has the barrier been tonight?"

"Quiet, but you knew that. If it had gone down, you would have felt it, too. Which reminds me, did you ever find your sword?"

"No, but I haven't exactly been looking for it."

"Found something better to do with your time?" Jake turned around to face Jarvis directly. "So how is the delectable Gwen Mosely?"

"What makes you think she's delectable?" Jarvis pretended an interest in a stack of printouts on the table, though he knew his friend wouldn't back off. Once Jake decided to pursue something, there was no stopping him.

"I've seen her picture." Jake gave him a snarky smile. "When I was checking into Harvey Fletcher's past, I decided to look into the Moselys' background, too. The boy's aggression is definitely causing him problems at school, but that's no surprise. And it seems Ms. Gwen Mosely has earned some awards for her knitting and design." He rooted through a pile of folders, pulled one out, then handed it to Jarvis. "I printed out the newspaper reports, including a couple with her picture. Love the freckles."

"Go to hell, Jake," Jarvis muttered with no real heat. As usual, his friend had done a thorough job. "What did you find out about Fletcher? Anything safe to share with the boy?"

"It's all there, too. I couldn't find much, even when I hacked into the Regents' main computer files. You know they keep any records of us to the minimum."

Yeah, and he knew there were good reasons for the secrecy. But how many countless Paladins had lived and died, passing through this world without even their names being remembered? He tried not to think about it too much, but sometimes the whole damned system pissed him off.

"I owe you for this, Jake."

"How about that game of chess you promised, and we'll call it even?"

"Okay, one game. The doc gave me strict orders not to wear you out."

Jake rolled his eyes as he set up the board on the bedside table. "Yeah, lying here and being waited on hand and foot is just so exhausting."

"He just wants you out of here as fast as possible." He moved his pawn. "They always do."

Anything to get them back out in the caves, where they could die all over again. "Your move."

Jake countered. "So when are you going to see them again?"

"After I figure out the best way to approach the boy. Gwen was going to let him make the decision about martial arts." He kept his eyes firmly on the board. "He definitely needs the discipline training will give him."

"How will the sister react?"

"She's worried about the cost, but understands the need."

"So how much are you charging her? Or are you willing to take it out in trade?"

Jarvis's vision turned red and his hands shot out to squeeze his friend's neck. *"Don't ever say anything like that again! Understand?"*

He loosened his hold long enough for Jake to gasp, "Oh, yeah, I understand."

Jarvis dropped his hands and slouched back in his chair, pretending he hadn't just attacked a friend, all over a woman he'd met only twice. And kissed once, which made all the difference.

Instead of being angry, though, Jake grinned at him even as he rubbed the red marks Jarvis had left on his throat.

His temper flashed hot again. "Damn it, you did that deliberately, didn't you?"

"Yeah, but only to make a point."

"And what's that?" Although Jarvis already knew.

"I believe that you're worried about Chase Mosely needing help in becoming a Paladin." He reached down to capture Jarvis's knight. "But if you think that he's the only one you're interested in, you're lying to yourself."

Rather than acknowledge his friend's direct hit, Jarvis studied the board. He'd better start paying more attention to the game because his queen was in danger. Forcing himself to put Gwen Mosely out of his thoughts, he countered Jake's move and went on the attack. The sooner they finished this game, the sooner he could escape his friend's knowing looks.

The chess match had ended in a draw. The two of them were evenly matched, and normally Jarvis enjoyed the challenge of trying to best Jake. But he'd been relieved when Jake had said he was tired and ready to crash for a while.

Jarvis let himself out of Jake's room and took the file on the two Moselys and good old Harvey back to his quarters. Once he'd decided how much to tell Chase and how much to hide from Gwen, he'd wrangle another invitation to dinner.

On the way, he'd check out the woods to see if he could recover his sword. Besides it being one of his favorites, he didn't want to risk having Chase or Gwen stumble across it. So far, neither of them had asked many questions about how he'd come to be cut up in their woods. Chase was probably used to letting his sister do most of the worrying for them both, but Jarvis was surprised that she'd all but ignored the issue of his injuries.

He'd like to think it was because she trusted him, but it probably had more to do with turning a blind eye to the situation because of the possibility of getting some help for her brother. Maybe she'd even managed to convince herself that he'd been the victim of an accident rather than an attack. But if one of the dogs led her to the sword, she'd be in his face about it.

The Regents wouldn't be at all happy about a civilian getting involved in Paladin business, but that wasn't Jarvis's problem. If the bastards staffed the local sector adequately, he wouldn't have been out in the woods hunting an Other all by himself. Considering the fact that there'd been a pack of those crazed killers running loose, the Regents were lucky not to have lost Jarvis permanently.

When he passed through the cave that revealed the largest stretch of the barrier, he paused to study its condition. For the moment it appeared to be stable, but that could change from one second to the next. He'd defended his world with steel and with blood too many times to count, and he'd continue to do so until he lost the battle to hold on to his humanity.

It wasn't much of a future to offer Chase Mosely, but facing his choices head-on was a damn sight better than always fighting against his true nature. With help, Chase would learn to manage his temper and strength, funneling all of that aggression against an appropriate target.

The barrier shimmered and thinned. Son of a bitch—it was on the verge of going down! Jarvis hit the alarm button on the wall to summon the troops. Running to grab his sword in his room, he tossed the file on his bed, sending the papers flying everywhere. There'd be time to clean the mess up after the battle—if he lived through it.

"Jarvis isn't answering his cell." Chase dropped the phone in its cradle with almost enough force to break it. "I've been trying for three days already."

"I don't know what to tell you, Chase. That's the

number he gave me." Gwen studied the sweater she'd been working on and decided that the new pattern was working out. If it turned out as well as she expected it to, she'd make a tidy profit on marketing the design. "He said he was staying in the area for the summer, but maybe he got called back to St. Louis for some reason."

"Maybe, but that doesn't explain why he's not answering his cell phone. That's the whole reason people carry them, so they can be reached anywhere, anytime."

Deciding she'd done enough knitting for one evening, she set the project aside, then stretched her arms and flexed her fingers to get the kinks out. "He doesn't seem like the kind of man who would go back on his word. He promised to teach you, so I have to think he will."

"Yeah, well, how much do we know really know about him?" Chase paced the floor, his long legs eating up the distance in jerky steps. "We never did find out who cut him up that night."

"If you're that worried about it, ask him."

She was so not in the mood for this, wishing Jarvis were right there in front of her so she could give him a piece of her mind. If he'd changed his mind about helping Chase, all he had to do was call. As disappointed as she and Chase would be, at least they wouldn't be jumping every time the phone rang, hoping to hear Jarvis's voice.

"I'm going to bed."

"Good night."

"Yeah, whatever."

Chase clicked off the television and stomped out of the room. She didn't need his attitude, but right now she didn't have the energy to deal with it. Even if he did have a legitimate gripe with Jarvis, he shouldn't take it out on her.

She needed to lose herself in some mindless television before facing her bed. Alone. As the opening music for the nightly news came on, she realized that it wasn't just Jarvis's broken promise about the martial arts that had her upset. No, it was the promise of that single kiss that hurt the most. As handsome as he was, Jarvis probably had women lined up from here to St. Louis and back, all wanting a piece of his action.

It hurt to think that the kiss that had curled her toes and fried her brain had meant so little to him. Common sense and any handy mirror should have warned her that she was out of his class. A small-town farm girl probably held little appeal for a man like Jarvis.

The worried look on the newscaster's face caught her attention, breaking up her pity party. She caught the tail end of his spiel, delivered in a suitably somber manner.

" . . . *the shallow earthquakes have been rolling through the boot-heel region of the state and down into northern Arkansas and western Tennessee and Kentucky for the past three days. These cluster quakes finally slowed to a stop earlier this evening and show no immediate sign of resuming. Experts tell us that the quakes are too slight for most humans to notice, although there have been reports of animals exhibiting some skittish behavior in the areas surrounding the epicenter of this seismic activity.*"

He paused to take a breath and pasted on a bright smile before continuing. "*And how about them Cards today? We'll be back with all the top sports stories after this commercial.*"

No wonder the alpacas had been restless. Normally they were placid creatures, happy to graze and hang out with their herd. But for the past couple of days, they'd spent most of their time clustered together in one corner of the pasture, grazing only intermittently. It was a relief to have a reasonable explanation. If their odd behavior had continued for another day, she would've called the vet out, an expense she could ill afford when nothing was obviously wrong.

She started flipping channels, looking for something to hold her interest. She finally picked a repeat of an old detective show, figuring since she knew how it turned out, she wouldn't have to concentrate much. The minutes slipped by as she watched the star of the show pull together the right answer to the mystery again, the way he did every week.

Wouldn't life be simpler if she could wrap up every problem that she'd ever faced in sixty minutes, with time out for commercials? Of course, if she was going to live out her life in a television series, she didn't want to do it in a rumpled suit, looking at crime scenes.

But as far as she knew, they'd never made a show about a woman who raised alpacas, spent her evening hours knitting, and had no social life at all. Who'd want to watch it? It was boring enough to live it.

Obviously her pity party was back in full swing. She'd be better off going to bed and reading herself to sleep. After turning off the television, she checked the doors. When she looked out on the porch, both dogs were asleep. Dozer lifted his head briefly, thumping his tail before going back to sleep.

She turned out the lights and trudged upstairs, wishing she had something more exciting waiting for her than a stack of unread books.

Jarvis stumbled out of bed, feeling more hungover than rested. Before he'd taken his second step, something sharp jabbed into his big toe.

"Damn it, what idiot left all this crap all over the floor?"

Stupid question. This was his room, therefore it was his mess, making him the idiot. As brain dead as he was feeling, it was a pretty accurate assessment of his mental capacity. He blinked his bleary eyes, trying to make sense of the papers scattered on the carpet. When he spotted the black-and-white picture of Gwen Mosely, it all came rushing back. He'd tossed the folder of information from Jake on the bed six days ago. Six *long* days ago.

God, he hurt all over. Too much to bend over to pick it all up. Maybe after a shower his brain and body would function well enough to do that without keeling over. Twelve hours of sleep hadn't come close to making up for day upon day of nonstop fighting.

At least nobody from his side of the barrier had died this time. Toward the end, even Jake had been well enough to join the party. It had felt damn good to have his friend back. They were used to fighting together, instinctively knowing what the other would do in any situation.

The Regents had finally brought in some replacements just as the earthquakes had come to an abrupt stop as inexplicably as they'd started. The new guys hadn't gotten into the fight, but at least they could stand guard, allowing the locals time to mend and catch up on their sleep.

He'd have still been in bed if his body hadn't woken him up screaming for a bathroom and food, in that order. Which reminded him, his toe was still hurting. He looked at it and spotted a staple sticking into it. After plucking it out, he headed to the bathroom, knowing the small wound would heal by the time he got out of the shower.

Twenty minutes later, he was dressed and feeling better for the shower and shave. It was early yet, with an entire day stretched out before him with nothing to do that involved picking up a sword. Sweet!

Back in his bedroom, he gathered up all the papers and shoved them back into their folder. Once he had breakfast in front of him, he could take his time sorting through the papers. He couldn't wait to see what Jake had managed to dig out.

When he picked up his cell phone, he noticed it was dead. He dug out the charger and plugged it in. The screen lit up, showing a bunch of missed calls. He scanned the list and one number immediately caught his eye. Son of a bitch, Chase Mosely had been trying to call him for days. Or maybe it had been Gwen, but that didn't feel right.

He suspected she was old-fashioned enough to want the guy to do the calling, at least at the beginning of a relationship—not that they had one. He checked the voice messages. Just as he'd suspected, the boy had called. He'd left a couple of messages, his voice sounding more uncertain on the third one; by the fourth his temper was showing.

The last one consisted of a couple of words that Gwen probably wouldn't have appreciated her brother using, but Jarvis didn't take it personally. He'd ended the call with a pissed-off "Oh, just forget it."

Shit! Jarvis tossed the phone down on the dresser, resisting the urge to take his foul mood out on an innocent piece of electronics. No wonder Chase was angry. Jarvis had told Gwen his cell number was good day or night. He'd forgotten to mention that he might be too busy killing to answer right away.

He slammed out of the room with the folder, wondering what lie would convince the Moselys he hadn't ignored their calls. Where could he have been for six days where he didn't get cell phone service? "In hell" was hardly an answer that either of them would believe, much less understand.

He was known as a problem solver, but the lack of caffeine and food was definitely affecting his ability to think rationally. Maybe after he got a meal and about a gallon of coffee under his belt he could figure out what to do next.

The cafeteria was mostly empty, but he was glad to spot Jake sitting by himself in the far corner. After piling a tray high with eggs, bacon, and hash browns, he snagged a full pot of coffee and carried it all to the table.

Jake acknowledged him with a weary nod, but

didn't speak. For the next fifteen minutes the two of them quietly shoveled in their breakfast, punctuating every few bites with a swig of coffee. Jarvis gradually started to feel better, although he still didn't have more than the minimal energy it took to lift a fork.

Jake held out his cup for a refill. "You're looking a little gray around the edges there, boss."

"I feel like a truck ran over me and then backed up for a second run. If the barrier doesn't stay up for at least a week, I may impale myself on my own sword just to get some rest."

His friend snickered. "Doc Crosby said if he saw me around the lab again anytime soon, he was going to quit. I guess I wasn't the best of company."

"He'll probably tell the Regents that two broken legs, some cracked ribs, and a few bone-deep sword cuts shouldn't be enough to keep a fine Paladin like you down."

"And that's probably true, except for the whole being dead part. As much as I like to think I'm as tough as they come, I seem to need a pulse to function."

"Wuss."

"And proud of it."

The dark humor helped to restore Jarvis's equilibrium. He held out his coffee cup and clinked against Jake's as a toast. "To us wusses, and to a job well done."

Jake finally pushed his plate aside, then nodded toward the file tucked under Jarvis's tray. "I assume you've been too busy to read that yet."

"Yeah, I'd forgotten about it until this morning. I'll read through it after I finish breakfast." Then he frowned. "I had told the boy to call me anytime. He's been trying to reach me for days."

Jake set his cup down and leaned back in his chair. "So what are you going to tell him?"

"I haven't figured that out yet. It needs to be simple and believable. Even if he's too young to ask a lot of questions, his sister isn't."

"How about the truth? The boy's going to have to hear it eventually."

"I hadn't planned on telling him anything about us until we had a chance to work on martial arts together. Once we start weapons training, I was going to bring him in gradually, especially considering he's underage."

"Sounds like a plan. As long as you keep the sister out of the loop, it won't be hard to convince Chase to sign up." Jake's smile looked a bit tarnished around the edges. "I can almost remember when I was young enough to think all of this was noble. I couldn't wait to save the world."

A world that had no idea how much it owed to a handful of men who sacrificed their bodies and their minds for the good of mankind. Jarvis understood the need for secrecy, but a little appreciation from those who did know what the Paladins did would be nice.

"Keeping Gwen out of the loop isn't going to be easy. I suspect the two of them are closer than most siblings. After all, she's been as much a mother to the boy as an older sister. No matter how I break it to her that her baby brother is a born warrior, she isn't going to like it."

"Worried that she'll kill the messenger?"

Jarvis hated the sympathy in his friend's eyes. He hungered for more of Gwen's kisses and a whole lot more, and knew that wasn't going to happen anytime soon—or maybe ever.

"I'm worried that now she won't trust me alone with him long enough to even tell him, especially if *she's* as mad as *he* sounded. The boy is getting too volatile to tolerate even that much frustration. I've got to come up with a plausible explanation of where I've been, where I couldn't make a phone call. Any suggestions?"

"Tell them that you work for a classified government agency, one that requires you to be on call twenty-four/seven." Jake leaned back in his chair and smiled. "With everything on the news these days about homeland security, who's to argue?"

"Not bad." Jarvis looked at the idea from every angle he could think of. "But what could I be doing where I couldn't make any phone calls?"

"Security, my man, security. No news in, no news out until the crisis is past."

"Hell, that's even the truth. Works for me." He picked up the file. "I'll go give this stuff a quick read and then make the call. If you hear an explosion coming from my quarters, you'll know things didn't go well."

"If that happens, I'll deliver the pieces to Doc Cosby. Now that the barrier is stable, he'll need a victim to work on to keep his skills sharp. After spending some time with you, he'll realize what a joy I am."

Jarvis laughed and walked away, feeling a helluva lot better. On his way back to his room, he stopped to check on the barrier and to see if the new guys were doing their job. They were scattered around the main cavern, looking pretty much at home. Good.

He hoped that the Regents made a few of the transfers permanent. With all that had happened in the past few months, both in Missouri and out on the coast in Seattle, the organization was due for a major shake-up. Two Regents had been killed, one who deserved it and one who didn't. And that wasn't all. Although it would be interesting to see how it all played out, it was their problem. He had his own.

Inside his room, he pulled a soda out of the small refrigerator and flopped down on the bed. It didn't take him long to hit the high points in the file. Harvey had been well liked, considered a leader among the locals. One fact leaped off the page: he'd been killed permanently in some woods a bit west of the installation. Could that have been along the same stretch of river where Jarvis himself had run into the group of Others? That bore checking into.

He set the Harvey papers aside to give to Chase someday, when the boy was ready to hear it. For now, he'd give Gwen a picture of Harvey for her brother to keep.

Jarvis eyed his cell phone, feeling like it was a guilty conscience poking and prodding at him. He guzzled the rest of his soda, wishing it would take away the bad taste that having to lie to Gwen Mosely left in his mouth. His first loyalty was to the Regents and his fellow Paladins. He knew his duty and he'd do it.

That didn't mean he liked it. He reached for his phone and started to punch in Chase's number—to hell with it. At this point the boy was more likely to hang up on Jarvis than listen to reason. Despite Chase's size, he wasn't strong enough to physically throw Jarvis off their farm, no matter how mad he was.

Seeing Gwen again was just icing on the cake, a sweet temptation he wasn't strong enough to resist without some help. He hit Jake's number on the speed dial to invite him along for the ride. Jake was closer to Chase's age by a good fifteen years, and if they started lessons, it might help to have a second person to demonstrate the different moves.

Jake would also serve as a buffer between Jarvis and Gwen, helping him maintain a safe distance from her pretty green eyes and those tantalizing freckles.

"Jake, meet me out front. You're going with me." He disconnected the call before his friend could respond, figuring Jake would have plenty of time to give him grief in the car.

Chapter 5

*G*wen lost herself in the soothing rhythm of carding a bag of alpaca fiber. If she finished in time, she'd start spinning it into yarn. Here in the sanctuary of her workroom, which took up half of their small barn, she was safe from all the aggravations and anger that awaited her right outside the door.

She wasn't sure who she was more upset with, but Chase and Jarvis Donahue were definitely at the top of her list. Her brother had stormed out of the house an hour ago, pausing only long enough to whistle for Larry to join him before disappearing into the woods. He'd left without saying where he was going, how long he was going to be gone, and without doing his chores.

She'd watched him leave, wishing there was something she could have done, short of dumping a bucket of cold water over his head, that would have cooled his raging temper. Granted, it didn't take much these days to set him off, but getting sent home early from football practice hadn't helped. The coach had called her before Chase had time to get back home to warn her there'd been a problem. Evidently Chase had gotten frustrated and thrown his helmet. The only thing that had saved him from getting kicked off the team for good was that he'd hurled it away from the people clustered on the field. Even so, Chase was officially on probation now. One more problem and he was off the team.

Although she'd spent much of last season on pins and needles, worried that Chase would hurt someone, she would hate to see him humiliated that way, even if it was his own fault. Which led her right to the other man she was definitely not happy with. If Jarvis hadn't been serious about helping Chase, or even if something had changed and he couldn't, the least he could have done was answer her brother's phone calls. Damn the man!

There was only one male in her life who was still in her good graces: Dozer. She leaned down to scratch his ears.

"It's just you and me, big boy." She smiled when he leaned in closer for more. "If your buddy Chase doesn't straighten out, you'll be the one eating a pork chop for dinner tonight, and he'll be eating kibble with Larry. How does that sound?"

Dozer looked up at her with worshipful brown

eyes and thumped his tail. At least he was smart enough to appreciate her efforts. When she resumed her carding, he lay back down with a sigh. But before his eyes had time to close, his head jerked back up off the floor and he lurched to his feet. He shook briefly, rattling the tags on his collar, before walking over to sniff at the door.

Gwen watched and waited. He only seemed curious, making her wonder what he was hearing that she wasn't. She set her carding aside before following Dozer's lead and opening the door. As soon as she saw the car coming down the driveway, she considered ducking back inside and locking the door.

It was bad enough that she was mad at Jarvis, but once again he'd given her no warning. With her luck, he'd be wearing something right out of *GQ*, and here she was in cutoffs and one of Chase's old T-shirts. And to top it all off, there was a second man in the car. Just great.

She waited until the Chevelle rolled to a stop, then she stepped out into the sunshine, using her hand to shade her eyes. When Jarvis didn't immediately climb out of the car, she wondered if he was a little unsure of his welcome. Her temper softened, but only a little. He had some serious explaining to do before she'd roll out the red carpet.

The passenger door opened first and a young man climbed out. He was as tall as Jarvis, and built along the same lean lines. He gave her a tentative smile and started toward her. She crossed her arms over her chest and waited to see what he had to say for himself.

"Hi. I'm Jake Beck, a friend of Jarvis's. You must be Gwen Mosely."

"I am." She looked past him toward the car. "Your friend afraid I'll take his head off if he sticks it out of the car?"

Jake smothered a laugh. "Something like that. Seriously, Jarvis wants a chance to explain, but he'll turn around and leave if that's what you want. Or I can act as a go-between." He dropped his voice. "He's been beating himself up pretty badly all the way here. Will you at least listen to what he has to say?"

That did it—she couldn't send them packing without giving Jarvis a fair hearing. She always was a soft touch; just ask every stray cat and dog in the county.

"Tell him I'll listen, but if I don't like what I hear, the two of you will be driving right back to wherever you came from. Have a seat on the porch. I'll be out in a few minutes."

Jake's smile widened. "Thank you. You won't regret it."

She had her doubts about that, considering her dog had just forsaken her and was sitting beside Jarvis's door, begging for his attention. Rather than call the furry traitor away from his hero, she walked with great dignity into the house and closed the door. In the kitchen, she sagged against the counter, fighting to bring her pulse under control. Jarvis was back. She'd like to think that her excitement was because of how badly Chase needed what Jarvis could teach him, but that would be a lie.

If she was going to meet him on equal ground, she needed to change clothes and collect her thoughts. Jarvis and his buddy could just cool their heels for a few minutes while she went upstairs. Was her green sundress ironed?

Not that she wanted to impress Jake and his lily-livered friend. Nope, not one bit.

Sitting on the porch felt only a degree or two cooler than hell, but at least Gwen hadn't run for her rifle when he pulled in. He'd take this stifling heat over skulking back to the Center with his tail between his legs anyday. Although that might still happen, at least Gwen was willing to give him a chance to explain.

Seeing her again had hit him hard. Judging by the sideways glances Jake was giving him, he wasn't hiding it very well either. Maybe it hadn't been such a smart idea to bring his friend with him.

"Are those the woods where she found your sorry ass?" Jake nodded toward the tree-covered hills out past the pasture.

"Must be, but I didn't think to ask."

Jake snickered. "If I'd come back from the dead looking at her, I wouldn't have been thinking about my sword either. At least not the one I fight with anyway."

Jarvis groaned, and looked to make sure the door was still closed. "Speaking of that, I still need to go out there and look for my sword. It would be bad enough if either of the Moselys found it, but can you imagine the ruckus if someone else stumbled across a bloody sword? Every cop within fifty miles would be out searching for a dead body. That's all we'd need."

Jake sat up straighter in the rocker. "The Regents would have a cow if we caused a cleanup mission of that size right now. With all that's happened here lately, and especially in Seattle, heads would roll. I plan on keeping a low profile until the dust settles." Jake shot Jarvis a worried look. "If the barrier stays stable, maybe the two of us can backtrack from the Center and see if we can find it."

"I'd planned on doing exactly that, but with the barrier thinking it's a damn yo-yo, there hasn't been time." He had to warn his friend. "I don't want you in the line of fire if all hell does break loose around here. I figure I'm at the top of the Regents' shit list. They don't much like the way I get in their faces about how they understaff, underfund, and under-everything-else around here. Then there's the little matter of letting Trahern bring Brenna inside without clearance, not to mention two dead cops and a Regent."

He gave Jake a rueful smile. "So unless you want to serve on some desert island with only me for company, you might want to start distancing yourself to avoid the fallout."

Jake's expression turned hard. "Not going to happen."

Before Jarvis could argue the point, the door behind them opened. He jumped to his feet to open the screen door for Gwen, looking cool in a dress that emphasized her red hair and green eyes. God, he hoped he wasn't drooling.

She might not be happy with him right now, but that hadn't stopped her from bringing out iced tea for them.

Jake took the tray from her and set it down. "Thank you, ma'am. Something cold will hit the spot." He gave her a winning smile.

Son of a bitch, he'd brought Jake along because he was closer to Chase's age. He hadn't stopped to think that made him about Gwen's age. How stupid could he have been?

"Here, take my seat." Jarvis motioned her toward the rocker. "I can sit on the floor."

Gwen arched an eyebrow. "You really are here to grovel, aren't you? Good—you should be."

Jarvis's *former* friend laughed. "Miss Mosely, would you mind if I took a glass of tea and went to look at your alpacas? I've never seen one up close."

"Call me Gwen." She handed him a glass. "Go ahead and say hi to them. Contrary to popular opinion, they don't spit, not unless you do something stupid and provoke them. They've been skittish this past week, maybe because of those earthquakes in the area. Did you hear about them?"

"Yeah, I heard." He took a long drink of the tea. "Thanks for the drink and for the warning. I'll be sure and watch my manners." He left the porch and strolled out toward the pasture.

Dozer seemed torn between following Jake and staying close to Gwen. Family loyalty won out and he flopped down on the porch, but positioned himself to keep an eye on the interesting new stranger. Gwen stood with her back to Jarvis, watching Jake.

Jarvis had thought Gwen looked damned cute earlier in those snug shorts and her oversized shirt. But the dress she had on now made him want to drag her back into the house, if only to keep Jake away from her. His friend wasn't one to poach, but Jarvis had no real claim on her, either. And at the moment, she seemed to find Jake more interesting than she did him.

Which really pissed him off. He moved closer, knowing he shouldn't crowd her, but he couldn't help himself. He wanted to lean down and kiss the small spray of freckles on her shoulder so badly he could taste it. Time for explanations.

"Look, I'm sorry I didn't return Chase's calls. I didn't get the messages until last night, when it was too late to call. Sometimes my job gets pretty intense. When that happens, I can't focus on anything else."

She still wouldn't look at him, but the hum of tension in her stance made it clear that she was listening. "So intense that you couldn't find five minutes in six whole days to make one call? What kind of job gets that intense?"

He *had* to touch her; he couldn't help himself. Gently, so she wouldn't feel threatened, he tugged her around to face him. "I have the kind of job that I can't talk about. And before you ask, I can't predict when things will all go to hell like they did. This week has been a bitch, but you'll have to take my word on that. Or not."

Gwen looked him dead in the eye, looking for what, he didn't know. Hoping she found it, he continued. "I don't know if it means anything, but given my druthers, I would have been here for Chase." Then he risked a light kiss on her lips. "And for you."

She didn't kiss him back, but at least she didn't move away. "That night in the woods, you were working, weren't you?" It wasn't really a question. "Is it always that dangerous?"

There was no way she'd believe him if he denied it; she'd been the one to drag him in from the woods. He hedged his bets. "Not always."

"But often enough." Her pretty eyes looked sad. "I saw faint scars on your body when I . . ." Her cheeks flushed with color.

Jarvis shushed her with a finger across her lips. "Yes, I've been hurt before and will be again. But you already know how well I heal, so don't let that freak you out."

She opened her mouth to reply, but the sound of a dog barking made her step back to put some space between them, almost tripping over Dozer. Jarvis reached out to steady her, then immediately dropped his hand. Obviously she didn't want Chase to get any wrong ideas.

"I'm not the one who needs to hear your explanations." She watched Chase come strolling out of the woods. "By the way, he holds a mean grudge."

Fine. He'd go talk to Chase. He shoved his way out the screen door, not caring how it slammed behind him. The noise carried far enough to make both Jake and Chase look in his direction. Damn it, this wasn't going well. But he could only put out one fire at a time.

Chase had stopped just short of where Jake stood, his body language clear that he wasn't all that happy to see either of them. Jarvis made his approach slow and steady, not wanting to spook the boy into running. Dozer plodded alongside him, his tongue lolling out of the side of his mouth.

When Jarvis got within speaking distance, he

stopped. "I understand you've been trying to reach me."

"I quit trying." The boy knelt down beside Larry and patted his thigh, calling Dozer to join them.

This wasn't going to be easy. Jarvis cast around for a way to get past the boy's anger. Maybe he'd start by distracting him. "Chase, this is my friend Jake Beck. Jake, Chase Mosley."

Chase may have wanted to ignore the introduction, but his sister had definitely brought him up better than that. He stood up when Jake started toward him, hand extended. "Nice to meet you."

"My friend here tells me you're interested in learning martial arts." Jake nodded in Jarvis's direction. "He's the best instructor I know."

"Yeah, well, I was thinking about it a few days ago." His *but not now* was unspoken but clear.

"Chase, when I gave Gwen my number, I didn't tell her that sometimes my job demands all of my attention. I can't talk about what I do for a living. But when it all goes to hell, I haven't got time to breathe, much less dial a phone. I came as soon as I got the message."

Jake backed him up. "He did, Chase. When he realized that you'd been calling for the past few days, he was seriously pissed that he'd missed talking to you."

Chase looked from Jake back to Jarvis, weighing their statements. "You two work together?"

Jarvis nodded. "Have for years. I taught him all he knows."

His friend snickered. "Not hardly. You've gotten your fair share of bruises from me."

That caught Chase's attention. "Does he heal like I . . . like you . . .?" He looked to Jarvis for an answer.

"Yeah, he does. That's one reason I asked him along today. I wanted you to know that there are more than just you and me with that ability."

The boy mulled that one over for a few seconds. "You really couldn't call?"

"I wouldn't lie to you about that, Chase. And you can count on it happening again with no warning. I can't help that, but I do promise to call you beforehand if I can. If that isn't possible, I'll call you as soon as things let up." He caught Jake's eye. "And if for some reason, I have to discontinue your lessons, even temporarily, Jake will take over."

The boy clearly wanted to give in, but still had some anger he needed to get out. "You're just blowing me off."

He started for the house, but Jarvis caught his arm. "Okay, hard-ass, what's with you? You've never screwed up?"

Chase jerked his arm free. "Yeah, I have. You think just saying you're sorry is enough, but when I do something, I get put on probation!"

"Are you talking juvie?" Surely Gwen would have mentioned it if Chase had gotten arrested.

Chase blanched. "Hell, no. Nothing that bad. I threw my helmet at football practice, and the coach called me on it in front of everybody. One more screwup and I'm off the team." He pinned his gaze on the ground, refusing to meet Jarvis's eyes. "That sucks."

Damn, he felt for the boy. Paladin tempers were a bitch to live with. "Yeah, it does suck—and that's all the more reason for you to start working out with Jake and me. I guarantee you'll gain more control from it. Once you've got some moves down, I'll take you to a gym to practice with some other guys. They all know different disciplines, so you'll learn from some of the best."

"We're always looking for fresh meat." Jake's grin was wicked, coaxing a tentative smile from Chase. "If you work hard, you'll be able to hold your own in no time. And if you lose it with us, at least we'll understand."

"Sounds good." Chase shuffled his feet a bit. "I've got to do something about my temper. Gwen worries too much as it is."

She'd worry even more once they brought Chase into the organization—and hate Jarvis for doing it. He wasn't the one who threw the dice that cast Chase's lot in with the Paladins, but that wouldn't matter to her. All he could do was make the transition from civilian to Paladin go as smoothly as possible for the boy.

"Do you think your sister will object if we use the barn for a dojo?"

"Half of it is her workshop, but we should be able to use the other side. When can we start?" There was a note of excitement in his voice. Both dogs picked up on it and were dancing around his feet, tails wagging.

"Now, if you'd like. Jake and I brought some workout clothes. We'll change in the barn."

Just that quickly, the shadows haunting Chase's eyes faded. "I'll go change and be right back." He took off toward the house with both dogs at his heels.

Jarvis watched him go. "That went better than I'd hoped."

"You're doing the right thing for him." Jake moved up to stand beside him. "You know that, don't you?"

"For him, yeah. And for the organization, because we're stretched so damn thin everywhere." He stared at the kitchen window, where he could see Gwen talking to her brother. "But try telling that to her."

The muffled sounds of male bonding fueled with heavy doses of testosterone seeped through the wall separating her workroom from the makeshift gym that the two men had helped Chase set up. They'd carried his weight set down from his room and hung up a heavy punching bag from the rafters. Jarvis had assured her that it was an old one that the gym he normally worked out in was getting rid of. It had some sizable patches of duct tape on it, so maybe he was telling the truth.

But it didn't matter. She was prepared to turn a blind eye to a little charity if it helped Chase. From the occasional burst of laughter next door, whatever they were doing was working. Every so often, the connecting wall rattled and shook, but she did her best to ignore the noise.

She finished packing up the orders she needed to take to the shipping office the next time she went into town. After setting the boxes by the door, she cast around for something else to do—something that would keep her wayward mind from thinking too much about the glimpse she'd gotten of Jarvis when they'd been carrying things into the barn.

Seeing him without his shirt on, his sleek muscles shiny with sweat! Jake wasn't half bad either, but there was no comparison.

Another thud against the wall startled her.

"Sorry, Gwen! Didn't mean to shake the rafters that hard!"

It was at least the sixth apology the three guys had called out. She smiled as she approached the wall, well aware that it was Jarvis standing so close to the thin wall. "That's okay. Just give me some warning if you think the barn's going to collapse."

"You okay in there?" His voice had dropped, making the question sound more intimate than he probably realized.

"I'm fine." She put her hand on the wall, as if she could feel his warmth through the wood and drywall. "How's it going?"

Silence. Then Chase's boom box began spewing out music loud enough to scare the bejeezus out of the alpacas.

After a second or two, she made herself walk away, intent on getting back to business. Then the door to her workshop opened and Jarvis stood in the doorway, asking without words if he was welcome in her private sanctuary.

"Come on in and look around."

As he closed the door, she began straightening the bins of yarn that were already in perfect order. Anything to keep her mind off the gorgeous hunk of manhood behind her. She fumbled for a topic of conversation and pounced on the obvious. "How is Chase doing?"

"Great. He's a natural, just as I expected him to be." Jarvis's voice came from right behind her, his breath sending a chill dancing down her spine.

She closed her eyes, trying to string together a coherent thought. "That's, um, real good. Nice."

He laughed. "Am I making you nervous, Gwen?"

He was now close enough that she could feel his body heat all along her back. Would that make any woman with a pulse nervous? Heck, yeah.

"What makes you think that?"

"Because it makes me nervous. I'd hate to think I'm the only one wondering if we're ever going to kiss again." His big hands slid up and down her arms, sending more shivers through her.

She ought to step away, out of his reach. But when she moved, it was to face him. His smile was crooked, his dark eyes warm.

"That dress is driving me crazy. Ever since that first morning when you were sleeping in the chair, I've been dying to see all the rest of your freckles." He fingered the edge of the fabric at her shoulder. "The way this is cut just makes it worse, because it teases with hints and glimpses as you move."

She'd always hated her tendency to freckle, and he was making them sound like a gift from above. "They get worse in the summer."

His face lit up. "Really? Tell me, do you have them . . . everywhere?"

She nodded. He groaned and closed his eyes.

He leaned in close and whispered, "I would give anything to get the chance to count them all. I can't sleep nights, for thinking about it."

Lord have mercy, the images that flowed

through her mind: the two of them in her bed, his big body sliding over hers, in hers . . . Her hand came up to rest on his chest, unable to resist touching all that warm strength.

"Kiss me."

She skimmed her hands up the expanse of his shoulders to the back of his neck, enjoying the journey. Then she raised up on her toes to close the distance between them and pressed her lips against his.

She tasted every bit as good as he remembered. Gwen filled his arms perfectly, matching her feminine curves against him. His loose gym shorts did nothing to disguise the effect she was having on him, but she didn't seem to mind. On the contrary, when he splayed his hands on the sweet curve of her backside and pulled her up against the evidence, she made a sexy little noise in the back of her throat as if asking for more.

He yearned to take her someplace private and get her naked *now*. It was damn hard to be noble with her in his arms.

Her hands stroked his back, her nails scraping lightly over his skin. He wanted to purr or roar, warning everyone to stay the hell away from them. He pushed the soft cotton fabric of her dress to the side, wanting to taste a few of those freckles he'd noticed on her shoulders. He flicked his tongue over her damp skin, loving the rich flavor that belonged solely to her.

She arched her neck to the side, giving him better access, and he growled his approval as he nibbled along her collarbone. At the same time, he reached down to catch the hem of her dress, sliding it up as he enjoyed the satin feel of her thigh. When his hand reached the leg of her panties, he hesitated. How far did they dare go?

Gwen wasn't trying to stop him, but . . . this wasn't the time or the place. She must have sensed his reluctance because she froze. Silence hung between them except for their ragged breathing and the staccato beat of his pulse.

At least she wasn't running for the door or shoving him back on his ass. He wanted to yank her right back into his arms.

"Whew, those freckles ought to come with warning labels—they've got some serious mojo going!" He kissed the tip of her nose, right on the freckles. "We could get company any minute, so I figured we'd better slow it down a bit."

Her gaze immediately went to the door. When she realized they were still alone, she slumped slightly and laid her head against his shoulder.

"It could have gotten a bit awkward if Chase came charging in here to show you his moves."

She giggled. "He might be more interested in the ones you've been showing *me*. Especially where your hand is right now."

It took him a moment to realize that, contrary

to his direct orders to stop, his fingers had slipped past the flimsy barrier of Gwen's panties and were busy caressing the treasures within. Even now, he could barely muster the strength to stop.

"I'd say I'm sorry, but that would be a lie." He slowly withdrew his hand and tugged her skirt down where it belonged, although it damn near killed him.

Gwen didn't look upset. "I'd have some of my own explaining to do." Then she patted his backside—from within his gym shorts.

A chuckle bubbled up from deep inside him and turned into a full-blown belly laugh. He leaned against the wall while he struggled for control. Gwen's own sense of the ridiculous caught up with her, and the two of them laughed until their sides hurt.

"Must have been one heck of a joke." Jake came in, with Chase right behind him. "I don't suppose you want to share it."

"No, you had to be there. Or better yet, not."

Jarvis's answer set Gwen off again, and the other two rolled their eyes in disgust. When he was laughed out, Jarvis looked at Jake and Chase. "How did the rest of the lesson go?"

"Great!" Chase answered. "I tossed him on his"—his eyes flickered over to his sister and back before he continued—"uh, butt. That was fun."

Jake punched the boy in the arm. "Everybody

gets lucky once in a while, so don't let it go to your head. Don't they, Jarvis?"

Jake always did see too much. "How about we get cleaned up, pile in the Chevelle, and head into town for a pizza fest?"

"I call shotgun!" Chase yelled.

No way. The only Mosely he wanted sitting next to him was the cute redhead. As the four of them filed out of the barn, Jarvis held out his hand to Gwen and smiled when she took it.

Chapter 6

The car purred down the road out of town, carrying them all back to the farm. They had only a few more miles to go before she and Chase would climb out of the Chevelle and the two men would head off to wherever they lived. Another puzzle she had yet to solve. She glanced over at Jarvis, whose profile was highlighted by the dash lights. There was so much strength in his face, but so few answers.

As if feeling her gaze, he reached over and squeezed her hand. She squeezed back before withdrawing her hand from his. The stereo was playing classic southern rock, filling the easy silence that had settled over the four of them after a long evening together.

Dinner had been fun. The three guys had carried most of the conversation. It had been such a relief to see Chase so relaxed and happy that she had been content to sit quietly and let him argue sports with Jarvis and his friend. They all had differing, usually very vocal, opinions on this year's pennant races, but it had all been done in good fun.

In between, Jarvis shot hot looks her way whenever he thought Chase wouldn't notice. When they first arrived, he slid in next to her in the booth, taking up far more than his fair share of the seat. For her brother's sake she'd tried to leave enough room between her and Jarvis to make it clear that the two men were there for him, not her.

The trouble was, Jarvis wasn't letting her get by with it. He'd moved over until his thigh was right next to hers. And after a while, he'd ever so casually draped his right arm across the back of the seat behind her. Soon his hand was lightly resting on her shoulder. Every so often he'd mumble a few numbers and touch her skin as if he were really counting her freckles. How was she supposed to ignore something like that?

But she couldn't seem to resist him on any level. There were so many things she should be asking him. They still didn't know how he'd come to be so cut up and bloody in her woods. Then there was the whole question of what he really did for a living. Now that she'd met Jake, it was easy to see that Jarvis was used to being the one making the important decisions. Jake was no weakling himself, but when there was a question, he often looked to Jarvis before answering.

If they were in the military, much of what she'd observed about the pair of them made sense—especially if their assignment was top secret. Still, something about that scenario didn't feel right. What kind of mission could he have been on in the Ozark woods that would have ended up with him getting cut to pieces without others of his unit looking for him? Her mind raced with possibilities: undercover cop, FBI, ATF, CIA—the whole alphabet soup.

Chase's welfare was first and foremost in her life, and she was trusting these two almost-strangers to help him. Maybe she was sticking her head in the sand, but her instincts were telling her that Jarvis was a man of his word. If he said he could help Chase, she believed him.

Their driveway was just ahead on the right. "Why don't you let us out up here?"

Jarvis slowed the car and eased down the driveway. "Nope, but thanks for worrying about my car. She appreciates it."

He pulled up in front of the barn and turned off the engine, then he twisted around to look at Jake. "Why don't you grab us a couple of sodas for the road."

"I'm not thirsty," Jake said.

"I am." Jarvis met his friend's gaze in the rearview mirror. "And since you've got to get out of the car anyway, you can go inside with Chase and get me a drink."

Gwen started to open her door to get out but Jarvis's hand shot out to stop her. "Not yet. I need to talk to you." He gave her another one of those looks that melted her bones. "Privately."

Then he climbed out of the car so that Chase and Jake could get out of the backseat. Her brother shot Gwen a questioning look over his shoulder as he followed Jake inside. Meanwhile, Jarvis had walked around her side of the car and opened her door.

"I needed to give you something that I didn't want Chase to see yet." He held out a large brown envelope.

She opened it, her hands fumbling a bit. Something in his expression warned her that whatever the envelope contained was important. She drew out a single piece of paper, a photocopied picture of a man. One look at the face and she didn't need to ask who it was. The blue eyes and black hair and something about that stubborn-looking chin looked awfully familiar.

"This is Chase's father, isn't it?" She studied Harvey Fletcher's face in the yellow glow of the security lights over the barn door.

"Yes. Jake looked it up for me, but I didn't want to give it to Chase without letting you decide if he was ready. Neither of us will say anything until you give it to him."

"This will mean a great deal to Chase. It's been hard on him never to know even his father's name." She traced Harvey's jaw with her finger. "He was handsome. I can see why Mom was attracted to him."

"By all reports, he was well respected, too. There might be a chance I can track down someone who actually knew Harvey. Chase might like to talk to somebody with firsthand knowledge."

"I'll leave that up to my brother, but this was awfully nice of you and Jake to do." She put the picture back in the envelope. "I think I'll give this to him later. He's had enough excitement for one day."

"And how about you, Gwen? Got time for a little more excitement?" Jarvis sidled in close. "The picture wasn't the only reason I wanted a little private time with you."

The other reason was there in the dark gleam in his eyes and the way his smile had suddenly turned predatory. Before she could respond, he kissed her hard and fast. He tasted of pepperoni and hot male, suddenly her favorite flavor for kisses.

The squeak of the screen door registered dimly in the back of her mind. Pinned against the door of the car, she pushed at Jarvis's chest. Reluctantly, he pulled back. At least this time their hands hadn't gone exploring. Much.

Jake hovered near the porch, not wanting to interrupt them.

"I know you're there, Jake." Jarvis didn't even glance toward the house. "And yes, I know we need to be going."

He dropped his voice. "I forgot to mark my place when I was counting those freckles. I'm going to have to start all over. I like to be accurate . . . and thorough."

Heat flashed through her, shorting out her ability to think or even walk. The no-good rascal knew exactly what he'd done, too. He wrapped his arm around her and walked her to the door.

"I've told Chase that I'm busy tomorrow, but I'll be back on Saturday. I'll work with him in the afternoon, but I'd like to take you out for dinner after that. Just the two of us."

What could she say to that? "I'll look forward to it. And thank you and Jake for today. It was great."

"You're welcome." He brushed the pad of his thumb over her lips. "And thank you, too."

Then he walked off.

Jarvis paused to wipe the sweat off his forehead. It was only a little before ten o'clock in the morning, but the day was well on its way to being a scorcher. So far they'd had no luck finding his sword. As he stuffed his handkerchief in his hip pocket, he spotted something that made his blood run cold. "Son of a bitch! Will you look at that!"

Jarvis knelt down to study the tracks along the riverbank. Jake joined him, squatting down at his side. One glance at the ground and his friend let out a low whistle.

"These look old enough to be from that night." He traced the outline of a couple with his fingers.

Jarvis shook his head as he studied the surrounding terrain. "There's no way to know if they all came through here at once or over several days. Either way, there's been a damned parade of Others walking along this stretch of the river."

That was a scary thought. If the Others had found a new way to escape their home, how the hell could the Paladins protect the barrier and prowl the countryside at the same time?

Jake stood up, his hand sliding inside his jacket to grip his gun. "You'd think if they'd been using this route for a while, there'd be something in the news about unexplained violent deaths."

"Yeah, you'd think." Jarvis looked around, trying to gauge how far he was from where Gwen's dogs had found him. Not nearly far enough for his comfort. He didn't like knowing how close a bunch of crazies had come to her small farm.

"Let's see how far we can trace these." He drew his automatic and attached its silencer. The woods were quiet except for the usual background noises. Cicadas droned away as a few birds flitted in the tree branches overhead. If someone else was moving around in the woods, their ability to move silently beat anything he'd ever encountered.

About a quarter of a mile downriver the ground grew rockier, making it harder to follow the tracks, until they disappeared altogether. Where were the bastards heading?

He told Jake, "I'm going to cross over to see if I can pick up anything. Why don't you climb higher up and see if they left the river?"

Jake snapped the strap over his gun to keep it from falling out while he was climbing. "Other than tracks, should I be watching for anything else?"

"Maybe broken saplings. I remember sliding down toward the river, chasing the Other I'd been tracking. But I have no idea where all of his buddies came from, so watch your back."

Jake sighed. "If you manage to get me killed again this soon, Doc is not going to be happy." He started working his way uphill, cutting across the slope at an angle.

"Meet you back here in twenty." Jarvis checked his watch. "That's about ten-thirty."

"Will do." Jake was already sweating with the strain.

Hopping from rock to rock, Jarvis succeeded in crossing the narrow bend in the river without getting his shoes wet. He backtracked upstream, looking for any evidence that the Others had changed directions. No such luck.

He returned, walking about ten feet up from the riverbank, sweeping his gaze from left to right. His efforts paid off about fifty yards farther downstream. The grass was trampled, and there were splashes of dried blood on the grass. He could collect samples, but there was no need, since a lot of it was probably his. There were a couple of clear imprints of his own tracks.

The only question was how he had started off here, fighting against impossible odds, only to be found half dead in the river downstream. Why hadn't the Others finished the job? He circled the area, studying the ground for some hint of what had happened.

There. He bent down to brush a few leaves out of his way.

"I'll be damned."

"Probably." Jake came splashing back across the river. "What'd you find?"

"I've been wondering why I survived the other night, when it was obvious that I shouldn't have." He pointed to the ground. "Paw prints. I guess I owe Chase's furry friends some sirloin. Gotta wonder if the Others have ever seen anything like Dozer and Larry before."

Jake laughed. "I doubt it. A couple of good-sized dogs in full temper could put the fear of God in anyone."

"At least until they figured out that those two

would be more likely to lick somebody to death." Jarvis stood up, brushing his hands on his pants. "If my sword is anywhere to be found, it should be near here."

The two of them fanned out, walking in ever widening circles. Though he wanted to find his lost weapon, the real mission was to find out where the Others had gone to ground. Even if the dogs had driven them off, the pale-eyed crazies had had enough presence of mind to stick to the rockiest ground. It was as if they'd disappeared into thin air.

At least they hadn't gone on a bloody rampage, killing everyone who'd cross their path. If they had, the story would have been splashed across all the regional newspapers and networks.

"Hey, Jarvis! Come here!"

Jake stood at the edge of the river, staring down at the water. When Jarvis reached his side, Jake pointed at something shiny glinting in the deep side of the river.

"Crap, that water has to be at least eight or nine feet deep." Jarvis glanced at Jake. "I don't suppose you . . ."

"You suppose right. Ain't no way I'm going diving for your sword. I have no desire to ride all the way back to headquarters in wet jeans. The good news is that there's no one here but you and me. If you want to go skinny-dipping, I won't tell."

The sparkle in his eyes told the real truth. Ten

minutes after they got back, it would be all over headquarters. Jarvis would be lucky if Jake didn't use his phone to take pictures of Jarvis's bare ass to post online for their friends' enjoyment. He'd have done the same to Jake—what's the use of having close friends if you couldn't heap abuse on their heads once in a while?

"Fine. But remember, my friend, payback can be a bitch." He peeled off his shirt and then his jeans. His socks and shoes joined the pile on the ground. At least the day was hot enough to keep anything important from shriveling.

The river, however, was another matter. He braced himself for the jolt and waded in. Going slow would only prolong the misery, so as soon as the rocky riverbed dropped off sharply, he pushed off and swam the short distance to the other side.

The cool water actually felt good. He stroked the length of the deep pool several times before stopping to tread water.

"You should try it, Jake. It feels great."

"Maybe next time." Jake sat on a boulder, his gun out and his eyes scanning the area for intruders.

Time to get down to business. Jarvis took a deep breath, then dove straight down to where his sword rested on the bottom.

He missed it the first time, but managed to latch on to the pommel on his second dive. It was firmly stuck. He swam back up to take another breath.

After half a dozen hard yanks and some mental cursing, he finally freed the sword from where the current had wedged it under a log. He broke for the surface, dragging the heavy weapon behind him, and swam to where he could stand up.

"Here, take this damn thing before I drop it again." When Jake didn't immediately relieve him of the sword, his first reaction was irritation. Then he saw the worry in his friend's expression.

"What's wrong?" He waded out of the water, and looked across the river to see what had Jake's attention.

They weren't alone. Luckily, the new arrival was of the four-legged variety. Unfortunately, there was no way to know if Larry was prowling the woods by himself, or if one of his owners was close behind.

Jarvis dropped the sword and jumped behind the cover of some brush to yank on his clothes. The last thing he wanted to do was try to explain what he was doing here in the woods, since he'd told both Moselys that he wouldn't be in the area until tomorrow.

Jeans were a bitch to pull on over damp skin, but he managed it without damaging anything important. After yanking them on, he worked on his shoes and socks. There. He was decently dressed, although only Larry had put in an appearance so far.

Jake joined him at the river's edge. "Could be he's out by himself."

"Maybe, but the way my luck runs in these woods, I wouldn't count on it." He studied the hillside, looking for any sign of movement, but didn't spot any. "At least we've got the sword. Time to get out of here."

"Sure thing, boss."

Larry trailed along with them from the other side of the river, pausing every so often to whine and wag his tail.

"Go home, Larry!" It felt just plain stupid to be pleading with a dog, especially one as intellectually challenged as Larry appeared to be. "Chase and Gwen will have my hide if you get lost following me."

Larry's tail speeded up as he gave Jarvis his best doggy smile. Jake's laughter didn't improve Jarvis's mood.

"You think it so damn funny, you get rid of him." He marched off upriver.

He hadn't gone more than a handful of steps when Larry's whine changed to a low growl. Jarvis whipped around. "What's up?"

"Larry's sensing something." Jake had already drawn his weapon, staring deeper into the woods on their side of the river. "Whatever it is, the dog's not happy about it being there."

A chill rode up his spine. Jarvis switched the sword to his left hand and drew his gun.

"Larry, stay!" He wasn't sure the dog would

obey the command, but he didn't want to endanger Chase's pet.

"Let's go, Jake."

The two of them moved slowly, scanning the limited distance they could see clearly. He heard a splash and a few seconds later, Larry caught up with them, water dripping from his coat. For once the dog was all business, his nose to the ground as he ran a zigzag pattern a few steps ahead of the two men.

Jake leaned in closer to whisper, "I'm going to skin that dog if all we end up with is a bad case of chiggers."

Jarvis laughed softly. "Or if he corners a skunk for us."

"Thanks for that happy thought."

With the noonday sun directly overhead, the woods were sweltering. There wasn't a breath of air moving to ease the heat and humidity.

Larry disappeared over the rise ahead. Cursing, Jarvis kicked into high gear, not wanting the dumb dog to barge into something that would get it killed.

He and Jake reached the top at the same time. Larry was waiting for them, his tail wagging as if to thank them for joining in the chase.

"Damn you, dog, if I had the energy, I'd kick your butt all the way back to the farm." Jarvis leaned against a tree to catch his breath.

"Do you think it was nothing, or was he really on the trail of something that shouldn't have been here?" Jake looked at the rocky cliff that rose above them on two sides. "Nothing short of a goat could climb those walls that fast."

Jarvis did a slow three-sixty with no idea of what he was looking for. "I'd feel a damn sight better if it had been a raccoon. At least then we wouldn't wonder what we missed."

But they had to leave. Both were scheduled to be on duty in two hours.

"Come on, dog, let's head back."

Gwen pushed her favorite alpaca out of the way so she could go out the pasture gate. "Go on, girl. I've got work to do."

It was usually Chase's work, but she'd traded chores with him so that he'd have time to practice his moves before his early-morning football workout. Since she'd agreed to have dinner with Jarvis that evening, the switch in their normal routine worked out for both of them.

She'd gotten an early start on shoveling out the alpacas' pen, wanting to have that done long before Jarvis was due to show up. She didn't want to be wearing her pasture boots when he arrived.

Too late. He was already there, leaning against the fender of his car. As usual, Dozer was hanging with him, getting his ears scratched. Larry was rolling in the dirt, stirring up a cloud of dust a short distance away from the car.

"Hi."

The sun's warmth had nothing on the heat in Jarvis's smile. "Hi, yourself. I like the boots. Is that the latest style for the fashion-conscious alpaca herder?"

Gwen turned around slowly, letting him look his fill. "Yes, they go especially well with cutoff jeans and old T-shirts. It's not a look that everyone can pull off, but I'm workin' it."

"Believe me, I'd like you in nothing better."

She laughed, no longer feeling embarrassed by her attire. "Come on inside. Chase should come rolling in in half an hour or so."

He straightened up. "That long, huh?"

Why the sudden change in his expression? "Yeah, he usually gets home around noon. Why?"

"Because that means we're alone for the next half hour. I'd hate to waste the opportunity."

Jarvis sauntered toward her, leaving little doubt what he had in mind. She backed away.

"You do *not* want to get close to me until after I've cleaned up. I've been doing chores all morning."

"I could scrub your back for you."

Oh Lord. The thought of sharing their big old claw-foot tub with Jarvis melted her right there. The sensible part of her pointed out that sometimes football practice ended early. But the wild part was already racing ahead to start the water running.

"I'm not sure that's a good idea." Which they both knew wasn't exactly a definite "no."

"I could get an early start on my freckle hunt." He reached out to brush his knuckle down the side of her face.

"Jarvis, I . . ."

The rattles and squeaks of their old truck interrupted her, and though she should be relieved, she was disappointed. Jarvis gave her a crooked smile before turning away to greet her brother.

Chase pulled up next to the barn and shut the engine off, which rumbled on for a few seconds before finally clunking to a stop. He climbed out and headed straight for Jarvis.

"Sorry if I'm late. The coach wanted to talk to me."

Gwen's stomach lurched. "What happened?"

Her brother grinned. "Nothing. He wanted to thank me for a good practice. He said the last couple of days, he could see an improvement in my attitude."

Jarvis slapped Chase on the shoulder. "Nice job, Chase!"

Her brother basked in the warmth of his approval. "I'm still on probation, but I promised myself I'd really try not to piss him off so much."

"That truck sounds pretty ragged. How long since you've had it tuned up?" Jarvis asked.

Gwen answered, "I honestly can't remember, which probably means it's long overdue."

"Chase, why don't we get our practice out of the way, and then take a look under the hood? Judging by the sound, I'd guess it wouldn't take much more than points and plugs to get it running better. Want to work on it together?"

"Heck, yeah!"

She protested. "Jarvis, you don't have to spend your day off working on our old truck."

"It's not work. I find tearing engines apart relaxing."

She wasn't going to win this particular battle. "If you're sure, but I'm willing to pay for any parts you need."

He gave her another one of *those* looks. "I'm sure we can work out a payment plan we'll both be satisfied with."

Oh brother, she was melting again. "How about we start with lunch? A neighbor gave us an apple pie."

"Great! If you have some ice cream to go along with it, I'll throw in a free oil change."

"It's a deal—but first I'm going to shower."

She could feel Jarvis watching her all the way to the door. She would have put a little extra sway in her walk, but her brother was there. Besides, there was a limit to how hot a girl could look in pasture boots and cutoffs.

Chapter 7

"*T*ake it easy, Chase." Jarvis leaned against a bale of hay. "Slow down until you get it right. Then we'll go for speed."

So far, the boy was taking every correction and criticism well—not that Jarvis expected things to stay that way. Right now the exercises he was putting Chase through were new and fun. But somewhere around the hundredth repetition, tedium would set in, and with it a shorter fuse—if Chase followed the same course of behavior that Jarvis had himself, not to mention most of the young recruits he'd ever trained.

"Bring your fists up higher and snap that leg out to the side when you kick." He moved over to stand beside Chase to go through the motions with him. "That's it. Much better. Now once more from the top and we'll call it a day."

Chase groaned, letting his hands drop to his sides as his shoulders slumped. No doubt his energy level had taken a serious hit between his morning football practice and the regimen that Jarvis had put him through. The kid had gumption, though, because he immediately backed up, assumed position, and went through the entire routine without a single error.

"Jake's going to be jealous. It took him a lot longer to master that one. We'll knock off for now and see what we can do for the truck."

"I'll go snag us some cold drinks and be right back."

"Sounds good."

Chase took off at a slow jog. Considering how hot it was, Jarvis wasn't sure he could move that fast. He picked up his T-shirt and wiped his face before pulling it over his head. There wasn't much shade where the truck was parked, and he didn't want to risk getting fried.

Outside, he reached into his car for his sunglasses. Where was Gwen? He hadn't seen her since they'd finished lunch a couple of hours ago. He checked the time. Good, he should be able to work on the truck with Chase and still have time to get cleaned up before taking Gwen out to dinner.

Their first real date.

He knew better than to get mixed up with a woman like Gwen Mosely. He knew better than to get mixed up with *any* woman, but especially one with such innocence about her. She wasn't naïve, so maybe inexperienced was the better word. Regardless, she deserved better than a man whose career path had been bathed in blood and who could only look forward to more of the same. He didn't want her to end up like her mother, staring at the phone and wondering why it never rang.

Yet he couldn't resist the temptation of spending a little more time in her company. His worn and ragged soul basked in the warmth of her touch. And her kiss was nothing short of mind-bending. One taste or a dozen would never be enough for him—all the more reason to walk away for both their sakes. Jake could take over Chase's training for a few months until the boy turned eighteen, then the Regents could take a more direct approach in bringing Chase into the fold. Once the boy knew what it meant to be a Paladin, Jarvis could reestablish his relationship with him in secret.

That would work—even if it killed him.

Gwen stepped out of the house and headed straight for him, a glass of lemonade in her hand. Her red hair burned fire-bright in the afternoon sun, and her smile had a predictable effect on his anatomy. At least his shorts were baggy enough to hide it. Or maybe not, because her steps suddenly faltered, and her green eyes went all smoky as she got within reach.

How could he ever have the strength to walk away from all that beauty? "You looking forward to dinner tonight?"

"Yes, if you're not sick of spending all your free time with Chase and then me." She held out the drink. "Chase got a phone call. He said you needed this and that he'd be out in a few minutes."

Jarvis cast around for a safe topic of conversation, one that didn't include trying out that pile of hay in the barn. "We're about to start on the truck. Nothing like a little grease on a boy's hands to make him feel all manly."

"Something tells me that Chase isn't the only one who can't wait to get his hands dirty. Still, it's nice of you to do it. Chase has always been interested in learning stuff like that, but I'm useless in that department."

"You already have enough on your plate to deal with. And it'll be good for him to learn a few basics. If his first car is anything like the one I bought, he'll spend as much time under the hood as behind the wheel." He nodded toward the Chevelle. "That's how I learned how to restore her."

"And you've done an amazing job with that car. I really enjoy riding in it." She smothered a smile. "Oops, I meant to say *her*."

Jarvis grinned. "If you've enjoyed the front seat, you'll have to try out the backseat sometime."

Before she could respond, Chase came barging

out the door. "Sorry to keep you waiting. Are we ready to start on the truck?"

"Sure thing. Raise the hood and I'll be right there."

Gwen turned away. "I'll let you get busy. Yell if you want me for anything."

He couldn't help laughing. "Oh, honey, you already *know* the answer to that one."

"Get your mind out of the gutter, Donahue."

Then she walked away, her hips swinging.

She'd spent far too much time looking out the kitchen window. What were he and Chase laughing about so hard? Some man thing, no doubt.

Jarvis picked that moment to straighten up, which put him in the perfect position to catch her staring out the window. It was too much to hope that the sun was reflecting off the glass bright enough that he couldn't see her . . . No such luck, because he waved at her before turning his attention back to Chase.

Then he started for the house. She didn't bother pretending to be busy; he would only have laughed at her again. She opened the door and stepped out on the porch.

"Chase and I are going to run into town to pick up the parts we need. We'll get them installed in plenty of time for our date."

Now that was a loaded word. It would have been easier for her to think of it as a casual dinner between two friends. "Date" had a whole world of implications she wasn't ready to think about.

"Where we are going? So I know what to wear."

"That green dress was nice. I liked it a lot . . . for a whole bunch of reasons." That predatory smile was back in full force.

"Okay, I'll aim for nice, but casual and comfortable." She needed a cold drink. Now.

"I'll need to shower after we get done with the truck. Hope that's okay."

Jarvis naked in her shower was *so* okay. She resolutely blocked the image from her mind. "Considering you've been working all afternoon on our truck, I could hardly complain."

"Need anything while we're in town?"

"No, I'm fine."

That was a lie. She wasn't fine at all, not with her hormones eager for what Jarvis had to offer. While they were gone, she'd hunt through her wardrobe for something that would incite another freckle hunt.

Jarvis concentrated on the winding road. He let Chase pick the radio station, hoping the loud music would prevent the boy from asking the question he'd been working himself up to for the past hour. No such luck.

Chase reached over and turned the music down low, then sat tall, staring straight at Jarvis. "So you and my sister are going out for dinner tonight."

"Yep. You have a problem with that?"

"I don't know." After a bit, he added, "Maybe. It all depends."

He *really* did not want to be having this conversation with Gwen's brother. He'd outgrown being grilled by suspicious fathers close to twenty-five years ago. "On what?" he asked.

"Gwen doesn't date much."

"Maybe she's picky." He sort of liked that idea, considering she'd agreed to go out with him.

"It's more like most guys don't want much to do with a woman who comes saddled with a younger brother to raise." Chase shifted restlessly. "She should've been free to finish school and maybe marry some college guy. Instead, she spends all of her time taking care of alpacas and me."

"That was her choice, Chase. You have nothing to feel guilty about."

"I know that, but now that I'm almost out of school, she's going to be able to do more things for herself. She deserves some happiness." Chase shot him a determined look. "With a guy who's going to stick around."

Jarvis's stomach did a nosedive. "Whoa there, big guy. This is just a date. A *first* date, at that. Don't go listening for wedding bells."

"That's my point. She likes you a lot. She acts different when you're around." The boy's fists were clenched now. "You could hurt her bad if you're not careful."

Jarvis liked her a lot, too, more than any woman he'd ever met. And he certainly didn't want to hurt her. But he couldn't make himself walk away, especially since he still needed to spend time with Chase.

"It's just a casual date," he repeated. "I thought she might like a break from cooking. Now, where's the auto parts store?" He injected enough strength into the question to make it clear that their previous discussion was closed.

The door to the bathroom opened with a billow of steam. Gwen blinked twice and backed up a step. Seeing Jarvis step out of the mist was like a scene from some romantic thriller. Sort of like that new James Bond guy crossed with Russell Crowe. A charming smile, but with something lurking in his eyes that warned that the civilized behavior was only a veneer. Underneath all that polish was a warrior capable of both extreme violence and hot sex, whichever the moment called for.

Then the air cleared, and it was Jarvis standing there, her date for the evening. It occurred to her that the image that had flashed through her mind wasn't an illusion—not entirely anyway.

Despite his charm and the way he was trying to help Chase, she couldn't forget the way they'd met. Whatever he did for a living had almost cost him his life. He was dangerous on so many levels.

"Let me get my bag, and I'll be ready."

She walked over to the counter for her purse and keys. The need for a little excitement in her life was clearly stronger than she'd thought.

Her brother ambled into the kitchen, putting himself between her and Jarvis. He had an odd expression on his face, not quite anger, but he was clearly unhappy about something.

"Chase, is everything all right?"

His attention was solely on Jarvis. "Where are you going?"

Jarvis crossed his arms over his chest and widened his stance. "We haven't decided. It will depend on whether Gwen is in the mood for a good steak or for Italian."

"How late will you be?"

This time the edge of anger was more obvious. What on earth was wrong with Chase? Since when was it his job to interrogate her dates?

Jarvis wasn't helping much with his vague answers. "I'm not sure."

She stepped between them. "Chase, I'm a big girl. I'll be home when I get here."

"Fine, Gwen." He shot her a withering look. "Just know that I'll be waiting up."

"Why on earth would you do that? You know Jarvis will make sure I get home safely."

He glared over her head at the man in question. "See that you do."

He marched out of the room and up the stairs, leaving Gwen embarrassed and confused. "What brought that on?"

"He's protective of you, Gwen. You're a very attractive woman. He knows that, and he senses that I know it, too. He doesn't trust my intentions." He followed her onto the porch. "Can't fault his instincts."

She couldn't decide how to respond. Did she thank him for the compliment, or run for the hills because that gleam was back in his eyes? Or grab him and kiss him?

Jarvis opened her car door. "So what's it going to be? Steak or Italian?"

When he joined her in the car, she answered, "I love a good steak."

He nodded and started the engine.

As he drove, Jarvis stole another look at Gwen. That soft, sexy dress was creating all sorts of fantasies in his imagination. He needed to cool things down.

"Your brother did good work today. He has a solid feel for the precision needed to excel in martial arts. And with the truck, he already knew enough to identify most of the problems before we even raised the hood."

She smiled. "I could hear a huge difference after the two of you finished tuning the engine. I'd like to buy a new truck, but that will have to wait until I sell part of the herd next year or the year after."

Good. Another safe topic. "Is it hard, selling your animals?"

"It almost killed me the first time I sold a pair that I'd raised from birth, but it's gotten easier. The trick is to make sure that they are going to good homes. As long as I know they'll be well cared for, I can live with it. And I always make sure my customers know that I'll buy them back if it doesn't work out."

"Has that happened often?"

"Once or twice. Alpacas aren't always the best of pets, any more than a cow would be. But people take one look at those big eyes and think they have to have one. Trouble is, they're really herd animals and much happier hanging out with their own kind."

She gave him a challenging look. "But enough about me. You've already heard plenty about my boring little life. Tell me something about Jarvis Donahue."

What could he tell her? Certainly not what he did for a living.

When he didn't immediately answer, Gwen sat up straighter. "I'm sorry. I didn't mean to pry."

He contradicted her. "Yeah, you did, and you *should* be asking questions about me. I was trying to think of something interesting."

She laughed. "You don't need to worry about being interesting. You've got that nailed."

He liked the sound of that. "Why don't you ask me questions and I'll try to answer them?"

"Okay, what's your favorite color?"

"Green." Because it was the color of her eyes.

"What's your favorite sport?"

"Football, followed by baseball. Then basketball. Motor sports of all kinds are good, too." This was easier than he'd expected.

"Do you like to read? If so, what kind of books do you like best?"

They were definitely on a roll. "I read more than I used to. History, mostly. I just started a book on the Civil War here in Missouri."

"Did you grow up here in Missouri?"

That was a tricky one. "I wasn't born here, but I've spent the last twenty-seven years here, ever since I got out of high school." He waited for her to do the math.

Her eyes widened with shock. "Jarvis, that would make you forty-five!"

"Yeah, is that too old for you?" He wasn't surprised by her reaction to his real age. Paladins quit aging physically at around thirty.

"No, not at all. You look a lot younger than that,

though." Then she giggled. "I'd say it was due to clean living, but somehow I don't think that's the case."

How long would it take her to figure out his ability to heal and his apparent youth came from the same source? From there, it was only a hop, skip, and a jump to her realizing that her brother carried the same traits.

"So how old is Jake?"

She was already on the right track. Or the wrong one, considering the Paladins were supposed to keep their different nature secret. "Thirty, I think. Somewhere around there." Luckily, the restaurant was just ahead. "We're here. Hope you're hungry." For more than just a good steak dinner, too.

Halfway through dessert, Jarvis's cell phone rang. They'd been dawdling over peach cobbler and coffee, keeping the conversation light and easy. He ignored the first call after glancing at the number. When it immediately started ringing again, he cursed under his breath and gave her an apologetic look.

"I'm sorry, but I've got to take this." He got up and disappeared out the front door of the restaurant.

Whatever it was must be important . . . and secret, reminding her that she had no idea what Jarvis did for a living. The image of him lying in the river, cut and bloody, filled her mind, and she pushed her cobbler away, no longer hungry. She signaled the waitress. "Can we please have a couple of boxes for the cobbler?"

The young woman picked up the dessert plates. "Yes ma'am. I'll be right back with them and the check."

The waitress had come and gone, and Gwen's coffee had grown cold before Jarvis finally reappeared. His mouth was set in a grim slash, warning her that whatever the call had been about wasn't good news.

"I'm sorry to cut our evening short, but we've got to go. I've been called into work." He dropped a wad of bills on the table, then eyed the boxes. "Thanks for getting the desserts to go. Would Chase like mine? He's probably worked up quite an appetite, glaring at the door and watching the clock."

Jarvis's comments weren't exactly said in good humor, but she laughed anyway. "Maybe we shouldn't give him the cobbler. It's a mistake to reward bad behavior."

Jarvis looked disappointed. "I'm real sorry to hear that. I had some bad behavior in mind that I'm pretty sure you would have enjoyed. I know *I* would have."

At least he was smiling again. She looped her arm through his as they headed toward the door. As soon as she touched him, she could feel the tension thrumming through him.

By the time they reached the parking lot, she almost had to run to keep up with him.

"Jarvis?"

He realized what he was doing and came to an abrupt halt. "Sorry, Gwen, I didn't mean to drag you."

"That's okay. I know whatever is going on is important." She suspected it was also dangerous, but he'd drawn a pretty clear line cordoning off subjects he wouldn't discuss.

He cupped the side of her face. "I don't deserve you."

She didn't like the sound of that at all, but wasn't sure how to respond. "Don't make it complicated, Jarvis. Dinner was lovely, and the phone call wasn't your fault. There are a lot of jobs where people have to be on call all the time. You know, like doctors."

If anything, he looked even more grim. "I'm sure as hell not a doctor."

No, whatever he did for a living was a whole lot scarier than that.

"I know, but the idea's the same. Let's get me home so you can report in."

She intertwined her fingers with his and tugged him toward the car. When they got to where they'd parked in the shadows at the far end of the lot, he didn't immediately start the car. Instead, he scooted across the seat until he was close enough for her to feel his heat.

"I've been looking forward to this all day." He brushed his mouth gently across hers. "To heck with peach cobbler. *This* is the perfect dessert."

She didn't hesitate, parting her lips in invitation. "Don't be a tease. Kiss me like you mean it, Jarvis."

"Oh yeah."

Then his arms pulled her tight against his chest as he plundered her mouth with his tongue, plunging in and out. With each stroke he fanned the flames higher, making her ache for his touch. As if sensing what she wanted, he gently rubbed and kneaded each breast in turn.

That only made things worse, as her legs stirred restlessly, trying to ease the throbbing deep inside her. She fumbled with his shirt buttons, wanting to feel the sleek strength of his chest. He shifted back to give her room, while putting his hand on her leg and sliding it upward.

He kissed her mouth again, then rained quick little kisses down to the pulse point at the base of her neck. After nipping her gently, he followed the line of her jaw up to her ear.

"Come for me, Gwen," he whispered, his voice rough with heat. "I need you to come apart in my arms."

She could no more have resisted the promise in

his dark eyes than she could have given up breathing. He gently turned her until he was sitting between her legs, her dress rucked up around her waist. She held out her arms in welcome, loving the feel of him pressing down on her. The armrest was digging into her back, and the steering wheel kept him from having enough room to stretch out. But the second he tugged her panties down far enough to slip his hand inside, everything else ceased to matter.

She tangled her fingers in his hair and pulled him close for another kiss as he used his fingers and palm to slowly, surely drive her crazy. He gently brushed his fingertips over her slick folds before finally sliding one, and then two fingers deep inside her.

She whimpered. She felt him smile, and he moved his fingers in and out, driving her higher and higher. When she arched against him, hovering right at the precipice, he plunged them deep one more time. Her body shattered, taking her mind with it. All she knew was that the strength of this man's arms gave her something to hold on to, keeping her firmly anchored in this world.

Slowly, coherent thought returned. She nuzzled his neck, almost purring with contentment. "I wish we were someplace a lot more private."

"Me, too." He looked surprisingly satisfied, considering he'd been left out of that little party.

"I'm sorry you didn't get to—"

He shushed her with a kiss. "I've been dreaming about this since that first morning. Watching you was enough. I had to know, just this once."

She tried to puzzle out what he meant, as he helped her straighten her clothes.

"We'd better get going. I don't have much time."

His words sent a chill of dread through her, but she was determined make the few minutes left positive.

She felt around for the middle seat belt. "Mind if I sit closer?"

"I'd like that."

He kissed her again before starting the engine. Then they were hurtling down the Ozark highway, taking her back to her real world.

He walked her to the back door. "I really am sorry, Gwen."

"I know."

She also knew that he wasn't just talking about their date being cut short. The slight hint of good-bye in his voice shook her far more than it should have.

She stood on the first step so she could look him straight in the eyes. "I'll tell Chase you might not make it tomorrow."

"I wish . . . ah, hell, Gwen. I can't do this. It's too much, and you deserve better." He kissed her, then walked away without finishing his thought, but he didn't have to.

She already knew. When he did come back, it would be for Chase—but not for her.

Chapter 8

Jake took one look at Jarvis's expression and intelligently shut his mouth. He handed Jarvis his sword and fell into step beside him. It wasn't anybody's fault that the barrier was threatening to go down, but at the moment he was the closest target for Jarvis's bad mood. As long as he didn't speak, he might live long enough to fight the real enemy.

He made it as far as the elevator. "You know I'm sorry about calling you in, but they didn't give me any choice. Was Gwen mad?"

Jarvis frowned. Damn it, he should have known Jake would be unable to stay the hell out of his personal business. He leaned his sword against the wall, then he snagged a fistful of Jake's sweatshirt and slammed him back into the corner of the elevator.

"Don't. Say. Another. Fucking. Word." He punctuated each word with another shove. "Understand?"

Despite the choke hold Jarvis had on him, Jake managed to croak, "Yes."

Jarvis let go, picking up his sword. Silence continued until the elevator settled on the bottom floor and the doors slid open.

Jarvis stepped out first and glared across the cavern at the barrier. Sure enough, there were sickly green streaks flickering across the surface. He flexed his fingers on the pommel of his sword, anxious to get on with it.

Jake followed him across the floor. "Is everything okay?"

"No. But it's nothing killing a few dozen crazies won't help."

Jake gave him a concerned look. "That's not like you, Jarvis. Maybe you should sit this one out."

"Why the hell would I do that? The crazies ruined my evening. I figure on ruining theirs." He knew he was worrying his friend, but he couldn't help that.

"Come on, Jarvis. We both know you've never enjoyed killing."

"Maybe not. But it's what I'm good at, and all I'm good for."

The barrier flared in intensity, casting Jake's face in eerie colors. "So the evening went that well, huh?"

"The evening went fine. Too fine." He angled toward Jake, but kept a wary eye on the barrier.

"Gwen is . . . well, you've met her." There were no words.

"Yeah, she's special all right. So what happened? Did she get mad that you were called in?"

"No, she said she understood that some people are on call all the time, like doctors. I think she was hoping I'd admit to being something normal, something she could accept." He turned back toward the fading sheet of pure energy. "Even if it wasn't forbidden, I don't know that I could tell her what I am."

"If you told her you were a soldier, she'd understand that."

He sneered at his friend. "Yeah, right. Tell her that the guy who wants to put the moves on her is a killer who fights aliens for a living? She'd either die laughing or slam the door in my face."

Jarvis brought his sword up as the alarms sounded and Paladins began pouring into the cavern, weapons at the ready. Jake took his usual position to Jarvis's right and slightly behind his shoulder.

The idiot just wouldn't let it lie. "You're doing both of you a disservice, if you think that's true. Did you forget that she's already seen you after a bad day at work? That hasn't stopped her from looking at you like a birthday present she can't wait to unwrap."

"Shut up, Jake."

Jarvis couldn't let himself think like that. He was

too old, too close to dying for good to accept that there could be anything else for him but this.

A cold calm settled over him as the barrier flared bright and then died.

The first swarm of Others came crashing across, madness and death in their eyes. Jarvis smiled and welcomed them with his sword.

Heavy footsteps stalked her. It was too dark, too noisy to know whether she was sought by one or by many. No matter how hard she struggled to run, the living ground grabbed her feet and held on tight. Each time she managed to break one foot free, her other would be trapped by something that held on with claws and power. Her throat burned raw with the effort to force a scream past the fear. It was impossible to breathe, much less speak.

An animal howled, its voice echoing all around her. She shivered as another joined the chorus, a warning that evil was moving closer. Darkness like a living shadow swept over her, carrying her over the edge of rocky cliff. For a lifetime, she fell through the night, watching the ground race up to greet her.

Gwen shot upright in her bed, her breath coming in short gasps and her nightgown clinging to her sweaty skin. With a trembling hand, she reached over to turn on the bedside lamp, hoping to drive the shadows away and banish the fear.

It didn't help.

Maybe a cold drink would help. When she reached the bottom of the steps, Dozer howled out on the porch. As the mournful sound faded, Larry picked up where his buddy left off.

She flipped on the porch light to see what had the dogs all stirred up. She couldn't see anything, so she stepped outside. After pulling on her barn boots, she picked up her flashlight. The two dogs flanked her as she walked out toward the pasture.

It was unlikely that anything was threatening the alpacas, but she wouldn't be able to sleep until she knew they were all right. The dogs kept close by her side, occasionally ranging out in front of her, sniffing the ground as they walked.

Then Dozer froze midstep, his nose in the air, and growled low in his chest.

"What is it, boy?" She reached out to pat his head. "What's out there?"

He let loose with another long, mournful howl, and her skin prickled with goose bumps. She hurried over to the fence and scanned the pasture with the flashlight. The alpacas blinked in the bright light, but seemed fine.

The dogs, however, were still freaking out about something. Both of them stood facing the woods at the back of the property, whining softly. The only other time they'd acted this way was the night they'd found Jarvis. That time, they'd herded her out to where he lay, cut up and bloody. Now they stood between her and the treeline, clearly worried.

She hovered behind them, unsure of what to do. Surely if it were Jarvis out there, Dozer would go charging out to find him. There was no way she was going exploring in the darkness armed with only her flashlight. Before she set foot in the woods, she needed her rifle and cell phone.

As she turned back to the house, Dozer barked softly and followed her. Now his tail was wagging and Larry trotted up beside him, all signs of nervousness gone. Whatever had caught their attention was gone now. Relief washed over her as they rushed ahead to wait at the screen door.

"All right, you two idiots," she told them after patting both of them on the head. "I'm going back to bed. Please keep it quiet so I can sleep."

Dozer bumped into her on his way to his favorite spot. Larry turned three times and then flopped down on the floor with a sigh. She wished she could slough off the unease their reactions had caused her. It must have been coyotes, or maybe a couple of stray dogs passing by. But as much as she'd like that explanation, it didn't feel right.

Come morning, she'd head out with the dogs and her rifle and take a look around. If someone was up to no good in her woods, she'd call the sheriff and let him handle it.

• • •

God, he hurt, but it was mostly bruises and tired muscles. The few nicks and cuts would disappear with a few hours of rest. The fighting had been fast and furious, with no time to think beyond the need to defend himself and his friends. Jake had survived the fight in good condition, which pleased both of them. The barrier had finally been restored after six hours of sporadic fighting.

Doc Crosby would be busy for another few hours stitching up a few guys, but none would require more than a day to heal. All good stuff.

Jarvis unlocked his door and headed straight to the shower to wash off the stench from a battle fought well. He had stripped before he reached the bathroom door. After turning the water temperature to hot, he stood under the stinging spray, wishing he could wash regrets and missed chances down the drain along with the blood-tinged water.

As tired as he was, and as sick as he was of killing and death, he'd almost rather be back out there in the cavern swinging his sword than be alone with his thoughts.

Last night, it had taken every ounce of strength he had to walk away from Gwen Mosely. He'd stolen precious time from his duty to the Regents to hold Gwen in his arms, just to spend another handful of minutes with her. She'd burned hot and bright, just as he'd known she would.

But he wasn't being fair to her or the Regents. A man couldn't live balanced on a line between two different worlds, cheating them both in order to keep them separate. He should have answered Jake's phone call the first time it rang. Then he'd compounded his mistake by not leaving as soon as he heard the barrier was failing. He'd managed to get back only minutes before it had collapsed completely.

And finally, he shouldn't have given in to the temptation to spend an evening with Gwen, acting like he was a normal man out with an attractive woman. It was one thing to pick up a woman at a bar or club for an evening's fun, where they both knew the score going in. How many times had he spent a few hours in a stranger's arms, pretending it meant more than scratching an itch? But that attitude wouldn't work, not with Gwen.

He cocked his head to the side, listening hard. The phone was ringing in the other room. Not his cell, so it wasn't Gwen or Chase. Someone upstairs here in the complex wanted him. Once again, he was tempted to ignore the summons. But if he didn't respond, they'd send someone to pound on his door. If that failed, they'd use the master key to get in. One way or another, they'd find him.

He dunked his head under the spray, quickly

rinsing away the shampoo and soap. After shutting off the water, he snagged a towel and stomped out into the other room.

Grabbing the receiver, he snapped, "What?"

He listened for several seconds with growing anger. "Fine, sir. Leave the new schedule on my desk. I'll look at it after I've had a chance to get something to eat." He braced himself and asked one last question. "When are you sending them back?"

The answer burned like acid in his stomach. "Yes sir. Of course we should be grateful we had the extra help this long."

Then he gently set the receiver back down in the cradle. Staring at it, he considered what he should do next. Get dressed. Eat. No time to sleep. Yeah, that's the best he could do. Before that, though, there was one last thing to do.

Calmly picking up the phone, he yanked its cord out and heaved the damned thing at the wall. He kicked the shattered bits of wire and plastic out of his way while he got dressed.

Before leaving his room, he used his cell to call Jake. "Meet me in the cafeteria. We need to talk. Oh, and Jake? Would you tell maintenance that the phone in my room doesn't seem to be working?"

Jarvis stared down at the half-eaten pancakes on his plate, too wired to eat any more. Jake, on the other hand, had shoveled in his breakfast and was eyeing Jarvis's last strip of bacon with greedy eyes.

"For Pete's sake, take it if you want it that bad." He shoved the plate toward his friend.

Jake accepted with a grin. "What's put you off your feed?"

"They're pulling the extra men they brought in. They'll be gone after the end of the week." He didn't bother to keep the cold anger out of his voice. "They're scheduled to be assigned to Seattle."

Jake tossed his napkin on the table, clearly not any happier about the situation. The locals would barely have time to heal and rest before having to start pulling full duty again.

"Oh, and we're supposed to be grateful that they could lend a hand even for a few days." Jarvis clenched and unclenched his fists, trying to use up some of his anger. "One of these days . . ."

On some level, maybe the Regents were doing the best they could with limited resources—meaning the Paladins themselves. They tried to supplement their ranks with purely human guards, but they were a limited resource, too. And unfortunately, once guards died, they stayed that way.

Jake asked, "What's on our agenda for the day?"

"I need to check the cavern. I'm still trying to figure out where that Other got out when I tracked him to the woods by the Moselys' farm."

"Speaking of Gwen—"

"Which we weren't," Jarvis stated firmly, even knowing that nothing would stop Jake. The man was a bulldog when he latched on to something that caught his interest.

"Maybe not, but you were thinking about her. Are you going to call her?"

Leave it to Jake to cut straight to the point. "The only Mosely I'm interested in talking to is Chase. I need to let him know that I'll be stopping by for a few hours this afternoon."

"Want company?"

Jarvis considered the offer. "Better yet, why don't you go by yourself? Might as well let him get used to working with different teaching styles."

Jake laughed. "Oh, buddy, you've got it bad! I'd be glad to work with Chase, but I don't believe for one minute that you're sending me there for his benefit."

"Shut up, Jake."

"But you like her . . . maybe a little too much?"

"I said shut *up*, Jake." Jarvis had never hurt a friend bad enough to need medical care, but if Jake kept this up he'd make an exception.

Both of them were saved by the ring of Jarvis's cell phone. He gave his friend a nasty look and flipped his phone open. *Son of a bitch!*

Closing his eyes, he tried to banish all the morning's frustrations. "Good morning, Gwen. No, you're not interrupting anything important, but you're cutting in and out. Give me a few minutes and I'll call you back. The reception isn't good where I am."

He headed for the elevator to catch a ride up to ground level. Outside, he'd be safe from prying eyes and ears.

Gwen had the phone in a death grip, waiting for Jarvis to call her back. He'd probably think she was crazy, but she had to ask the question. She hadn't been able to sleep after coming back in from the pasture, worrying about what had stirred the dogs up so much. Even though neither of them had howled anymore, she'd heard Dozer whining every so often.

She'd finally given up on sleeping altogether and gotten up well before sunrise. After a small breakfast, she'd started on her chores, figuring on getting them done before the day's heat set in. But the whole time she'd been near the back pasture, the two dogs had ranged backed and forth between her and the woods, their dark eyes sensing something out there that they didn't like.

She considered herself to be a strong, capable woman, but something about this spooked her pretty badly. Would Jarvis scoff at the idea that there'd been something strange going on out in the woods? She really hoped so, because then she could laugh it off as the result of too little sleep. What was taking him so long to call her back?

To keep busy, she filled the sink with soapy water to wash the breakfast dishes. She was almost done by the time the phone rang. She wiped her hands on the dish towel and grabbed the phone.

"Hello? Jarvis?" She sounded breathless to her own ears, like she'd been running laps around the barn. "I'm sorry to have to bother you."

"Don't apologize, Gwen. I told you to call me anytime. What's up?"

He sounded distant to her, sort of cool, but that was probably her imagination. "I have something to ask you that's a little odd. Crazy, even."

There were a few seconds of silence. When he spoke, he sounded more like himself, a hint of laughter in his voice. "Don't stop now that you've piqued my interest."

How did she ask a man if he'd been roaming her woods? Especially since, the last time he'd done so, he'd almost died?

"Gwen, I won't bite. Ask me."

"Were you in my woods last night? You know, like you were the night we met?" It all came out in a rush, on one long breath.

"No, I wasn't. Why do you ask?"

The humor was gone, but she couldn't decide if he was angry or really interested in what she had to say.

"Last night the dogs started howling, like they did the night you were hurt. They were locked in on the porch, so I got up to see what was wrong. When the three of us walked out to the pasture with a flashlight to check on my animals, I didn't see anything out of the ordinary. But the whole time we were back by the pasture, both dogs kept watching the woods, as if someone was out there."

She leaned against the counter, her eyes closed as she tried to recall exactly what happened. "They whined and growled down low in their chests. Then just as quickly, it was over and they were back to normal." Now that she'd said it all out loud, it sounded stupid. Obviously she'd overreacted.

"How did the rest of the night go? Did the dogs act upset anymore?"

"Dozer whined some now and again. Other than that, it was quiet." She walked over to the door and stared out toward the pasture. The alpacas were all grazing or sleeping in the sun. She couldn't see Dozer anywhere, but Larry was rolling on his back over by the barn, kicking up his usual cloud of dust. Everything looked peaceful and normal.

Maybe the fear she'd felt had stemmed from her nightmare, but it hadn't felt that way. "I'm sorry to have bothered you, Jarvis. It was obviously nothing."

"It's no bother." He hesitated, "Look, I was going to call Chase to let him know that Jake would be by to practice with him today. I'll ask him to take a look around while he's there, if it's okay with you."

She ignored the flash of disappointment. Jake was a nice guy and all, but he wasn't Jarvis. Obviously she'd been right about his mood when he'd brought her home last night. Despite how right the evening had gone for her, something had gone wrong for him.

"Don't worry about it. Chase is working down at Mr. James's farm, but he's due home in an hour. Tell Jake that he's welcome anytime after that, but he doesn't need to waste his time hunting shadows out in the woods. I can do that myself."

"Gwen, I'd like to come myself but I . . ."

Oh, God, this was awful. "No, Jarvis, don't apologize. Like I said, I shouldn't have called."

She hung up before he could sense she was on the verge of tears.

Jarvis stared at the phone, thinking about what to do next. He wanted to drive like a maniac to Gwen's farm to make sure that she was all right. Next would be to order an all-out search of her woods, to make sure they hadn't let some Others escape last night.

He shuddered to think of her out in the middle of the night, armed with only a flashlight and a pair of coondogs against crazies armed with swords. He couldn't very well order her to stay inside at night until further notice. Oh yeah, that would go over well with her. He'd be lucky if she didn't come after him with her twenty-two or her cast iron skillet.

He started to punch in Jake's number. There were a few things that needed to get done before he could leave. As long as the sun was out, there was little danger that any Kalith running loose would leave the cover of the woods. Just in case, though, he'd send Jake to Gwen's to ward off any investigating she might do on her own.

He headed for his office to deal with whatever needed immediate attention on his desk. Hopefully that new schedule didn't include him or Jake for the next twenty-four hours. Once he had put out any fires, he'd follow the same path he'd taken before through the woods and look for fresh signs. If he didn't find any, so much the better.

If the Kalith crazies *had* been there again, he'd have to notify the Regents about this new peril. But regardless of what he found, he'd be spending the night in the woods near the farm. Something had spooked the dogs, and he wouldn't rest until he knew what it was.

He caught sight of Jake just as he turned the corner toward his office.

"Jake, we've got problems."

Chase sucked down half a bottle of water and then dumped the rest over his head. "I think every muscle in my body hurts."

Jake laughed. "And we're not done yet."

He held his hand out, offering a hand up off the floor, but Chase shook his head. He might feel like he'd been run down by an alpaca stampede, but he had his pride. If Jake still had the energy to continue, then so did he. He tossed the water bottle to the side and slowly climbed to his feet.

First, though, he had a question he'd been wanting to ask since Jake had arrived. "Where's Jarvis?"

Jake had delaying tactics of his own. He took his time finishing off his own bottle of water. "He's working today."

"And you're not?"

Jake's expression hardened. "I did my fair share."

"Of what? You're both pretty damned secretive about what you do for a living. When my dogs found your buddy cut up and half dead in our woods, Gwen thought he might have some answers about why I'm the way I am. She didn't call the police, but I'm thinking maybe she should have." He crossed his arms over his chest. "It's no skin off my ass what you and Jarvis are into, but I won't have Gwen hurt."

Jake sat down on a bale of hay. "How did you sleep last night?"

Chase fought for control, figuring losing his temper wouldn't get him anywhere with Jake. "What does that have to do with anything?"

"Just answer the question. It's important."

"I didn't. Not much, anyway. If Gwen hadn't been up wandering around herself, I would have taken the dogs out for a late walk. Why?"

Jake leaned forward, his eyes staring straight into Chase's. "Does that happen often? The urge to head toward the woods?"

"Often enough. I don't want Gwen to know, though. She'd have a fit if she knew I do that sometimes. I try not to worry her if I can help it."

"I don't doubt that."

Finally, Jake looked away, nodding perhaps over a decision he'd made. "You already know that Jarvis heals like you do. Like I do."

Chase nodded. Where was all this going?

"I can't tell you what we do, Chase, because it's not my place to do so. I will tell you that it's all tied together: the way we heal, what we do for a living, that powerful draw you sometimes feel but can't explain. When Jarvis can tell you everything, he will. Until then you'll have to trust us both, if you can."

"I'm not worried about me, Jake. It's Gwen. She acts differently around Jarvis than she has with any other guy she's ever dated. Excited, happier." He fought to find the right words. "Will these secrets you're both keeping hurt her?"

"I can tell you this: Jarvis is the best, most honorable man I've ever known. But whatever happens between him and your sister is their business. It will either work out or it won't, same as any other couple." He stood up. "Now let's finish our workout before we stiffen up."

Chase wanted to argue, but it was clear that Jake wasn't going to say any more on the subject. He would have been tempted to use his fists to get the answers he needed, but that wouldn't work with Jake or Jarvis. Both of them were more than capable of flattening him unless he got in a lucky punch.

But there was also something about the two men that made him want to trust them. Rather than admit that they couldn't answer all his questions, they could have made up a plausible lie. And Jake was right: he couldn't protect Gwen from life, any more than she could him, as much as she tried.

Time to get back to work. He assumed the beginning position and concentrated on getting the moves correct. At least that was something he could control.

Jarvis slapped his neck, trying to kill the damn mosquito that was plaguing him. His mood had been crappy to begin with, and the irritating buzz wasn't improving it any.

As far as he could tell, the only signs of Kalith warriors passing through these woods were the same ones he'd seen before with Jake. Of course, there was too much territory for one man to cover thoroughly, so he could be passing within a few feet of incontrovertible evidence and not even know it.

Pausing at the top of a small rise, he studied the surrounding woods. He was pretty sure that Gwen's farm was half a mile up ahead. The closer he got, the higher the risk that he'd run into her dogs or Gwen herself. That would be a major mistake on several levels.

First, he'd told her he was too busy to come, which was why he'd sent Jake in his place. If she caught him in a lie, she'd be angry. Second, it was time to put some emotional distance between her and himself. It would be too easy to let things get out of hand. Having her fly apart at his touch had set him on fire. And just the thought of burying himself deep in the welcoming heat of her body made him hard.

But there was no future for the two of them, and the more time they spent together, the worse the risk of her getting hurt badly. He'd vowed to protect her, and that included from himself—which really sucked.

But at the moment, protecting her from the Others was foremost. He started down the slope, heading for the farm. He needed to know that no Kaliths had come close enough to do her harm. As long as he was careful, he shouldn't get caught. Even if her dogs caught his scent, she'd have no way of knowing it was him and not some critter.

He started a zigzag pattern, widening his search

area. The ground was rocky with only a thin layer of topsoil, making it difficult to pick up any trace of someone passing through. He turned back to study his own trail and found that his tracks were almost impossible to see. At this rate, the only way he'd know if an Other had come through was if they actually crossed paths. That was extremely unlikely in broad daylight.

The trees thinned as he approached the edge of the woods. Slowing his steps, he moved from tree to tree, hoping the dappled shade would help disguise his presence.

Just his luck—Gwen was walking out of the pasture gate. As she turned to close it, she almost tripped over Dozer. She scolded the dog, patting him on the head at the same time. It was a sad state of affairs when he was jealous of a dog.

He needed to get away before the dog noticed him and started barking. Jarvis had almost made it into the deeper shadows when the sound of stealthy footsteps on his left made him spin around. He yanked his sword up and prepared to defend himself.

Chapter 9

*W*hen he saw who it was, he immediately dropped the sword back down to his side and cursed.

"Damn it, Jake, are you trying to get yourself killed again?" He closed the small distance between them, ready to rip into him, when he noticed Jake was looking past him and shaking his head.

Jarvis closed his eyes and prayed for deliverance. "We're not alone."

"Nope, we're not."

Jarvis turned to Chase, standing a short distance behind him. Could this get any worse?

Yeah, if it had been Gwen instead of her brother standing there.

"Hi, Chase. How'd your lesson go?"

The boy moved up next to Jake, his eyes glued to the sword in Jarvis's hand. "Fine. Is that thing real?"

"Yeah, it is." He held it out to Chase, pommel first. "Take a couple of practice swings, but be careful because it's sharp." As if Chase couldn't see that for himself. "Your sister will skin me alive if you whack off any important body parts with it."

Chase held it up in front of his face, studying the pommel, then ran a careful finger up the flat side of the blade. He looked all too right standing there in modern-day clothes and holding an ancient weapon. Jake reached over and adjusted the boy's grip a little before standing back to give him room to try a few maneuvers.

"This is cool. Heavy though." He reluctantly handed it back to Jarvis.

"You get used to the weight. Just like any other kind of weapons training, it takes practice to learn how to use swords correctly." And now wasn't the time to tell Chase just how much practice he'd be getting with one.

"What are you doing here? I thought you weren't coming today."

"Wait until we're closer to the river before we talk."

Jarvis led the way back toward the deep pool where he'd recovered his sword. Once they were safely out of Gwen's and Dozer's hearing, he stopped.

"I'm here because evidently your dogs heard something in the woods last night. Gwen didn't

want to worry you, but she thought they were acting like they did the night they stumbled across me
in the river."

Chase frowned. "Why did she tell you and not
me?"

"Because she wanted to know if I had been here
last night. Which I wasn't." How much should he
tell the boy? He'd stick to the truth as much as possible. "I offered to come take a look around, but she
didn't want to bother me. I decided what she didn't
know wouldn't hurt her. Jake did your lesson today
so I could do some scouting around."

"Did you see anything?"

Jarvis shot Jake a telling look. "Nothing I didn't
expect to. As far as I can tell, some animal must
have spooked the dogs."

Chase clearly wasn't buying it. "Is this one of
those situations like they joke about on television?
You know, 'I could tell you, but then I'd have to kill
you?' Because I'm getting pretty sick of half answers."

The boy's bullshit detector certainly worked
fine. "Yeah, it is, and I don't blame you for feeling
that way. I will gladly tell you everything you need
to know when I can."

"And when will that be?"

"It would be better if we waited until you're
out of school, but legally you'll be an adult on your
eighteenth birthday. We'll talk after that."

"That's a month from now. What if I don't want to wait that long?"

"Once you cross that line, there's no going back. Besides, you're still a minor and you do *not* want me to have to ask your sister's permission. I doubt she'd even give it. She's protective of you, and rightly so."

Chase pointed toward the sword. "If it involves me using one of those suckers, she'd definitely refuse. Either that or she'd come after you with those big shears she uses on the alpacas."

Jake snickered. "I assume she wouldn't be giving Jarvis a haircut with them."

The boy's grin was wicked. "Hell no, and she wouldn't sharpen them first, either."

Jake and Chase cracked up, but Jarvis didn't find it quite so funny.

"Go ahead and yuck it up, you two. Just remember: I don't get mad, and I don't get even. I get ahead." He walked away, calling back over his shoulder. "Don't forget—I was never here."

The knock on his office door was a welcome distraction. Jarvis closed the file he'd been reading and called out, "Come on in."

Jake stuck his head in the door, looking a bit sheepish. "Thought you'd want to know that I'm back."

"I expected you two hours ago." Not that they'd actually set a specific time.

"Gwen invited me to stay for dinner."

Jarvis gripped the arms of his chair to keep from lunging for his friend's throat. It wasn't Jake's fault that he'd spent the evening exactly where Jarvis wished he'd been. Instead, he'd eaten a cold sandwich while he read reports and tried to squeeze a few more dollars out of the budget.

"Did Chase say anything to her about running into me in the woods?"

"Nope. He kept his mouth shut." Jake came the rest of the way into the room. "I felt guilty letting her cook fried chicken for me . . ."

"As you should have." Damn it, if anyone should have been sitting in Gwen's kitchen eating her cooking, it was him.

Jake gave him a disgusted look. "Jarvis, my man, you need to quit feeling sorry for yourself. If you weren't running scared of how she makes you feel, you could've been there, too."

Propping his feet up on the other chair, he made himself comfortable. "But what I started to say was that she looked like hell. I'd be surprised if she slept two hours last night. I tried to talk her into letting me take them out for dinner, but she refused."

The idea of Gwen lying awake scared all night made Jarvis sick. "I checked as much of the area as I could alone. I'm going back tonight to see if anything stirs. To be honest, though, I don't expect to find anything. Even if there were Others in the woods last night, the barrier has been stable all day."

He tossed the file he'd been reading back in the stack. "I could be way off base here, but both last night and the night I ran into that mob of Kaliths followed right after a major failure in the barrier."

Jake steepled his fingers and stared at them. "Makes sense, but where could they be going?"

"No idea. We won't know much of anything until we know if this is a regular occurrence or just a fluke." He stood up to pace the floor. "It makes me crazy to know that there could be a parade of those bastards marching through the woods that close to Gwen."

He glanced at Jake, who had a big stupid grin on his face. "What's so damned funny?"

"You." Looking smug, he added, "I'm not saying that we shouldn't be concerned about the possibility of a leak. But the bottom line is, Gwen is making you crazy, period. That woman is on your mind day and night. Maybe especially at night."

Jarvis couldn't deny it. "She's a good woman, Jake."

"So? If anyone is long overdue for some goodness in his life, it's you."

"Jake, my latest test scores were at the high end of normal. My next death could very well be my last. Do you really want to explain to her that

I won't becoming back because I died once too often? She watched her mother pine for a man who never came back for just that reason."

He continued pacing, trying to burn off his anger. "Then there's the little matter of Chase being one of us. Even if I did decide to see what develops between me and Gwen, how do you think she's going to react when her brother signs on to fight the rest of his life? She probably has visions of him going to college and settling into a nice, normal job."

Jake shook his head. "I think you're underestimating Gwen. If you care that much for her, let *her* make the choice. Right now all you're doing is confusing both of you."

"Paladins are lousy husband material, and you know it."

"That's just an excuse." Jake pointed toward the phone. "Call your good buddy Trahern, and ask how he feels about Brenna Nichols. Think he regrets letting a good woman into his life? I sincerely doubt it. Trahern was right at the edge of being crazy when he last died. Without Brenna talking him back to life, he'd be buried now. And he isn't the only one because Devlin Bane is living with his Handler. The Regents might not like it, but it seems to be working for them."

"So?"

"So I'm saying maybe Gwen could do the same for you."

God, Jarvis wanted to believe that. "Maybe. But there's the matter of Chase."

"How do you think she'd react if he wanted to join the military? That's not much different, except we don't get to wear those cool uniforms or snazzy medals."

Jake's words made sense, but maybe that's because he wanted them to. "And if I hurt her? What then?"

"Maybe you won't. Either way, you're going to be spending some serious time around her because of Chase. Why not see where this takes you? It'd be good to see you get some happiness in your life."

Jake's cell rang. He checked the message and shoved the phone back in his pocket as he stood to go. "I'm needed. I'll see you later."

He opened the door. "And one more thing, Jarvis. I've known you through good times and bad, but I've never thought of you as a coward."

Then he was gone.

Jarvis sat down and picked up the next file in the stack—but before he even opened it; he set it down and reached for the phone.

Gwen had the fidgets. She couldn't seem to settle down and get anything done. Jarvis had called last night and asked if he could see her to talk about something important. She'd been so sure that he wouldn't be back, but now she didn't know what to think.

At least Chase wasn't home. His friend's parents had invited him along on a campout to give the boys a break in routine before school started up again. It meant extra chores for her, but hey, what else did she have to do?

She was trying not to get her hopes up, telling herself he wanted to talk more about the training he and Jake had been giving Chase. Though he could have done that by phone.

Was the minute hand on the clock even moving? It sure didn't seem like it.

Should she put on lipstick? No, Jarvis had seen her often enough to know that she didn't dress up to work on the farm. She'd settle for a little mascara. With the nice skirt and top, that was enough.

Was that him pulling into the driveway? She peeked out the kitchen window. Sure enough, that familiar blue car was in the driveway. Her heart fluttered as she scurried into the bathroom to check her appearance one last time. Maybe a little lipstick wouldn't hurt after all.

Satisfied, she straightened her shoulders and walked out to the porch, trying not to look *too* eager. But hot damn, he looked good. He was wearing black slacks and a dress shirt with the sleeves rolled up to reveal really great forearms. Yum! But he was awfully dressed up if he'd come to talk about Chase. The flutters were back in her stomach.

He peeled off his sunglasses and tossed them into the car before starting toward the house. The way that man moved ought to come with a warning label.

When he spotted her watching him, he smiled. "Thanks for seeing me."

She opened the screen door. "Come on in. There's a nice breeze if you'd like to sit outside, or if you prefer air-conditioning, we can go inside."

"Out here's fine." He chose his usual chair.

"Would you like a glass of fresh lemonade?"

"Sounds good, but don't go to any trouble."

"It's no trouble."

In the kitchen, she took a slow breath. He seemed tense. Was something wrong?

She poured the lemonade, then walked out onto the porch, with a smile.

He took a long drink. "Thanks, Gwen. That hit the spot."

"You're welcome." She settled into her chair, trying to appear relaxed.

When the silence dragged on, she set her drink aside. "There was something you wanted to talk about."

His smile was slow in coming and didn't reach his eyes. "Yeah, I do. I just don't know how to start."

"Is it about Chase's training?"

"That's part of it, but not everything." He ran his fingers through his hair, looking frustrated.

"I'm not that scary, am I?" she teased.

"No, and that's the problem, Gwen. You're anything but scary." He finally looked straight at her. "I want to keep seeing you for a lot of reasons, most of them purely selfish, but I want to be fair to you, too. Am I making any sense here?"

That little ember of hope she'd been nursing was starting to burn hotter. "Not really."

"Look, can we walk a bit?"

He rose to his feet and held out his hand. She let him tug her up out of the rocker and followed him down off the porch. They walked in silence out toward the pasture, where they stopped to watch the alpacas.

Finally, he sighed. "I'm a man with a lot of secrets, Gwen, ones I can't share with anyone outside of the group I work with. In the past, when I met a woman I was interested in seeing more than once, I either avoided talking about my job or lied about it if she pushed for details."

"That must be a hard way to live—not to mention trying to keep your story straight."

"You get used to it after a while, and lying came pretty easy to me. I figured if the woman never found out about the lies, no harm, no foul."

She tried to figure out how she felt about that. A little jealous of those nameless women in his past. But if one of them had really meant anything to him, he wouldn't be standing here with her. He might have secrets, but he was a man of honor. She'd bet her last dollar on that.

"You did that to protect them as much as yourself."

"That's a nice way to look at it. But I find that I don't want to lie to you." He kept his eyes firmly on the alpacas. "I enjoyed our dinner the other night." The corner of his eyes crinkled as he added, "And I *really* enjoyed what happened afterward."

"Not as much as I did," she admitted, even as her cheeks burned hot.

"So here's the problem. I can't tell you anything about what I do when I'm not here. Not now, maybe not ever. You already know my job is dangerous, but you wouldn't even know that much if your dogs hadn't found me that night."

He finally turned to face her directly, putting his big hands on her shoulders.

"I want to be here for you, Gwen, as long as you understand that I can't promise anything will come of it."

So he was offering her a good time while it lasted? That hurt, but he was clearly trying to be up-front about what he could and couldn't promise. The only question was whether it was worth the risk of being badly hurt. Because she very much feared she wouldn't be able to keep things light with him. Not only did she honestly like him, but she'd never felt this powerful attraction for anyone else.

But the situation stirred up memories of her mother's sorrow, which had shadowed the last years of her life. Gwen most certainly didn't want that for herself, and her logical mind told her to run from him, to protect herself at all costs.

Her heart, though, heard Jarvis's offer differently. It recognized that he was offering her as much of himself as he could give. It made her sad that he was forty-five years old and had never let himself get even this close to a woman before. How could she throw that back in his face? Especially because she'd never, ever felt this way about any man and might never again.

She mustered up a shaky smile. "Jarvis, I don't know where this will lead, either. But I don't want you to walk away from me one minute before you absolutely have to."

He smiled broadly, then wrapped his arms around her and leaned down to kiss her sweetly, a gentle wooing that melted every bone in her body. If not for his support, she would have collapsed on the ground. Any second thoughts were lost in his kiss.

Jarvis was afraid to stop kissing her, fearing her commonsense nature would remind her what a poor risk he was. The selfish part of him was doing cartwheels because she'd heard every word and still wanted him.

He slowly broke off the kiss but continued to hold her close. She seemed to need the embrace as much as he did because she made no move to step away. Then his stomach growled, reminding him how long it had been since lunch.

He felt the vibration of Gwen's laughter through his chest. "Hey, big boy, don't they feed you where you work?"

He tugged on her hair. "Just so you know, smarty, I planned on taking you out to dinner." Then he realized that he hadn't seen Chase yet. "Should we ask your brother to go with us?"

Gwen leaned back to smile up at him. "What's the matter? Feel like we need a chaperone? If so, we're in trouble. He's gone until the day after tomorrow. He was supposed to call you or Jake."

"He probably did, but I haven't checked my messages." Then the meaning of what she'd told him sank in: they were *alone*.

"If you're not set on going out for dinner, I've got leftover fried chicken and potato salad." Gwen slipped her arm around his waist as they started back toward the house.

Hot damn! "I'd be a fool to turn that down. Jake came back raving about your fried chicken."

She looked pleased. "Well, he didn't get any of the peach pie sitting on the counter right now, so you can lord that over him."

"Peach pie *and* fried chicken? Woman, where

have you been all my life?" He picked her up and twirled her around, loving the way she laughed.

"I'm so glad I found you—and not because you're a great cook. I also like your brother, and even your dogs."

She gave him an arch look. "As I recall, I found *you,* not the other way around."

"True enough." He kissed her again. "At least I was smart enough to end up half dead in the right river."

"I'm not sure 'smart' is the right word, but it's certainly worked out well." She led the way into the kitchen. "Lucky us, huh?"

Jarvis knew he was, but he wasn't so sure about her. He would make sure to treat her right, and maybe she'd remember that when she learned he was teaching her brother how to be a killer just like him.

Dinner was relaxed and casual, the conversation easy. They both loved westerns and fantasy novels. Gwen claimed not to be much of a sports fan, but had absorbed a lot of knowledge through her brother. It felt damned good to spend time with an attractive, funny woman that he didn't have be on his guard with the whole time.

When they'd both eaten their fill, she put away the leftovers. "Leave the dishes. I'll do them later.

Why don't you go put a movie in while I cut the pie?"

"Any preferences on the movie?"

"I like them all, except the ones on the left side. My brother's taste in movies isn't quite mine."

"What, you don't live for car chases and explosions?"

She laughed.

He skimmed the titles and decided on *The Fellowship of the Ring*, since she'd mentioned it being a particular favorite during dinner. After setting the DVD, he sank down in the corner of the sofa. Like everything else in Gwen's house, the furniture was chosen for comfort. He couldn't remember ever feeling as at home anywhere before.

When Gwen came into the room, she set a piece of pie and a glass of milk on the coffee table in front of him, then sat down as close to him as she could without being in his lap. He'd talk her into trying that later.

He clicked the button to start the movie. As soon as the credits started rolling, she gave a happy sigh. "I was hoping you'd pick this one. I loved the whole series, especially Aragorn. You've just got to love a man who swings a big sword!"

Jarvis choked on his milk, trying not to laugh or spray the milk out. It was a shame he couldn't offer to show her *his* sword.

She patted his back. "Are you all right?

"I'm okay," he gasped. "I just swallowed wrong."

As the movie played, Gwen cuddled in closer and he put his arm around her shoulders. Just holding her close felt damn good. When he started toying with her hair, she looked up and smiled. He couldn't resist the urge to kiss the freckles scattered across the top of her cheeks and nose.

"I still need to get back to counting, you know. I haven't forgotten."

Her eyes sparkled. "That's fine, as long as you don't tell me how many there are. I really don't want to know."

"But I like them. I've always been a sucker for a beautiful redhead, especially with green eyes and freckles."

"Yeah, right." But she wanted to believe him; he saw it there in the way she looked at him. "I bet you have a line like that for every hair color."

"Nope. And there's only one redhead who appeals to me." He shifted to lift her onto his lap. "She's blinded me to any other woman."

"Really."

She was still skeptical, so he kissed her, showing just how hot she made him burn with the slightest touch.

Her arms wound around his neck and her fingers tangled in his hair as she met his demands with a few of her own. Her kiss tasted of peaches and desirable woman, and the heat they generated settled right where she was sitting. If she had any doubts that he wanted her, she could feel the hard evidence.

He filled his palm with her breast and squeezed, loving the sounds she made when his touch pleased her, or when she demanded more of the same. And he liked that his Gwen didn't need much coaxing. She reached for his shirt buttons, undoing enough to allow her access to his bare chest. Her touch left fire in its wake.

He was skating the fine edge of taking her right there on the couch. It was definitely a step up from the front seat of his car, but she deserved better. "Gwen, honey, I need to slow down before I lose all control here."

Her sweet eyes studied his face for a heartbeat or two. "And if I want you to lose all control?"

He groaned. "Are you sure? Because I'm willing to wait until you're ready, even if it kills me." He hoped she didn't take him up on it, though.

Her smile was full of promises and heat, the kind of a smile that a man wanted his woman to keep just for him.

"My bedroom's upstairs. I think the light's better there for freckle counting." She slid off his lap and held out her hand.

With that look in her eyes, he would have followed her straight into hell. But as they climbed the stairs, he knew heaven was waiting for him at the top.

Chapter 10

*T*here was a skylight in the slanted ceiling over the queen-size bed, bathing it in the soft glow of the evening sky. The room matched the rest of the house, comfortable and welcoming. It suited Gwen perfectly, from the soft green of the walls to the bright-colored quilt that covered the bed.

As soon as they crossed the threshold, Gwen turned into his arms and smiled up at him. "Kiss me."

"Yes, ma'am."

He brushed his lips across hers before finally getting down to the serious business of making love to this woman who had invited him into her home, and then into her bed.

As he kissed her, he undid the last few buttons of his shirt and shrugged it off. Gwen murmured her approval as her hands skimmed over his back and shoulders. He toed off his shoes and kicked them out of the way while Gwen did the same.

She came up for air and stepped back. For the first time, her smile looked tentative as she unfastened the three buttons at the top of her shoulders and let her dress fall to the floor at her feet. Her underwear was plain, but the peach tone suited her coloring. He was sorely afraid his tongue was hanging out at all that luscious beauty.

When she started to unfasten her bra, he reached out to stop her. "Let me. I've been dreaming of this moment since that first morning."

Her hands dropped back down to her sides as she waited, now looking a little more sure of herself. Before he'd allow himself the privilege of touching her skin, he reached for the zipper of his slacks and shed them along with his socks. The rest could wait.

His fingers felt shaky as he eased a fingertip under the strap of her bra and slid it down over her shoulder. She shivered despite the heat that shimmered between them. The second strap slid out of the way, then he stepped behind her to undo the back clasp—and realized that they were standing in front of a full-length mirror. The bra fell to the floor and his heart almost stopped.

Her breasts were full and firm and tipped with rosy nipples that beaded up hard, begging for his attention. Holding her gaze in the mirror, her eyes wide with anticipation, he slowly brought his hands up to cup the lower curve of her breasts.

Her skin felt like woman-scented silk, just as he'd known it would. She arched back at his touch, leaning into his chest and twining her hands back behind his neck, offering herself up to him. Nuzzling her neck, he whispered heated promises and praise in between soft kisses.

Gwen had never experienced anything as wonderful as this slow dance of touches and sighs. How had she lived this long without knowing that watching a man's hands learn her body could be so seductive? Of course, she'd never known a man like Jarvis before, nor had she ever invited a man to climb the stairs to her bedroom until now.

His dark eyes met hers in the mirror, and he smiled. It should have seemed odd to be standing there with a man she'd known such a short time, both clad in only underwear and skin. But if she had to chose a perfect moment in her life, this would be it. They were headed for the bed that she had never shared with anyone else, and she couldn't wait.

"Jarvis, let's . . . ," she said as she tried to urge him in that direction.

"Not yet. I'm not done looking." His smile was a bit wolfish as one hand stayed busy kneading her breasts and the other caressed past the curve of her waist to pause at the narrow band of elastic of her panties.

Was he going to . . . oh Lord, yes. His fingertips slid inside the peach-colored cotton, down and
down. She closed her eyes, unable to watch something so incredible erotic. His hand stopped.

"Stay with me, Gwen. It's just me and you here."

At his insistence, she watched, not at all sure she
recognized the woman reflected in the mirror. He
continued his feather-light touches, brushing gentle
fingers across the curls hidden in her panties. Tension coiled tighter and tighter as she waited for that
first intimate touch where she ached for him.

As if reading her mind, he slowly slid his hands
back to her waist, leaving her feeling bereft until he
peeled her panties down to her feet. She put a hand
on his shoulder to keep her balance as she stepped
out of them.

When he stood up, she gave him his orders.
"Hands to your sides, because it's your turn, Mr.
Donahue."

She palmed his erection through the soft cotton
of his boxers, liking his soft gasp and the way his
eyes drifted half shut in pleasure. Feeling brazen
and a whole lot curious, she slowly dragged his boxers down his long, muscular legs.

"Like what you see?" he asked, his voice rough
as he kicked the boxers into a handy corner.

She looked up at him from where she knelt on
the floor. "I have to say, Mr. Donahue, that you sure
have a lot to offer a woman."

His laugh was rueful. "Gwen, you're killing me." He fisted his hands, showing what a struggle it was to keep them to himself.

She rewarded his efforts by cupping his sac and gently squeezing while she stroked him, loving the velvety hard feel of him. The second time she tried it, he broke.

In one swift motion, he swept her up in his arms and carried her to the bed. Then he was right where she wanted him, stretched out full length, half on her, half to the side, their legs and arms tangled together.

His kiss was hot, taking as much as he was giving as their tongues mated and danced, harbingers of what was to come—and she could only hope soon. She felt hollow, needing him to take her, to unite their bodies.

Then he stopped abruptly. "Damn, I didn't come prepared. Gwen, I'm so sorry. I didn't plan on this—on us . . . and we can't risk it." He rested his forehead on hers. "I'm sorry."

It pleased her that he hadn't expected to end up in her bed, that he'd given her the choice of when they would take their relationship this far. But really . . .

"Good news, big guy. I have a box of condoms in the drawer there. I bought them in case Chase ever had a girlfriend."

"Bless your foresight, woman." He grinned.

When he'd covered himself, he picked up where they'd left off. He seemed to find her breasts fascinating, paying a great deal of attention to each in turn.

She did a lot of exploring on her own, loving the steel-hard feel of his muscles as they flexed and moved under his skin. And the man's backside should have been up for an award.

Then he moved up and over her, banishing all thoughts except anticipation. She wrapped her legs up high over his hips, welcoming him into the cradle of her body. He pushed up on his arms, every inch of him straining and poised at the entrance of her body.

She flexed her hips, wanting him now. "Take me, Jarvis."

How could he refuse her? He bit his lower lip, trying not to lose all control as he thrust once, twice, and then three times before he was where he needed to be, buried deep inside Gwen's welcoming heat. For her sake he wanted to go slow, to give her time to adjust to his invasion, but he wasn't sure he could hold back.

Especially with her digging her nails into his ass, urging him on. When he was sure he wasn't hurting her, he let loose, showing her with his body and with his touch what he couldn't tell her in words.

That she mattered to him more than he could remember anyone ever meaning to him. That he wanted her with every breath he took. And that he wanted to please her, to wipe her memory clear of any other lover that she'd ever had. Because this moment in time, when his body was learning the beauty of hers, felt as if he'd gone back to the beginning of his life and had been reborn.

"Jarvis!" Gwen called his name as she arched beneath him, clearly hovering on the edge and needing that final push into oblivion.

He reached between them to caress that small nub at the juncture of her legs. He drove into her harder and deeper until he felt her fly apart, trembling underneath him as her inner muscles clasped him tight.

"Hold on, Gwen!" He shuddered as he rode out her climax and then his own. It seemed to last forever, a moment when everything was perfect and new.

After, he shifted to the side, giving her room to breathe as they both floated back down to earth. He kissed her mouth softly, then her cheek, and then her shoulder before tucking her in close. He reached down to snag the quilt that they'd kicked to the foot of the bed and pulled it up over them.

There weren't words for what they'd just shared, so he let the sweet sound of their racing heartbeats say it all.

Jarvis stared up at the stars through the skylight. He'd never felt this content in his life before. He'd enjoyed his share of good sex, but he'd never been one to stick around afterward to prolong the afterglow. Right now, he couldn't imagine ever wanting to leave this bed.

Gwen stirred and lifted her head off his shoulder. She looked a bit surprised to see him, and he suspected that she didn't often wake up to find a man in her bed. That idea pleased him immensely.

"Hi there." He brushed the hair back from her face as he moved in to kiss her.

Her fingers trailed over his cheek as she smiled against his mouth. "Hi there, yourself."

This time they let the heat build gradually. With soft touches, slow strokes, and low laughter, the passion rekindled until he pulled Gwen up to straddle his hips. Her eyes drifted shut as she rocked against him.

He loved watching the way her breasts bounced with each movement. Finally, he pulled her forward until he could capture one enticing peak with his teeth and tongue. Gwen leaned in closer, encouraging him to continue. While he suckled her hard, he cupped her bottom and thrust up against her damp core, loving the slight friction but wanting so much more.

At this rate he wasn't going to last long. With no warning he rolled her off to the side. She tried to push back, but he trapped her with the weight of his body. "Give me a minute, honey."

He reached for protection, but she took it from his hand and ripped open the packet. "Let me."

But instead of covering him, she decided to torment him a bit, and all he could do was fist his hands in the blanket and hold on for the ride. Who knew that Gwen could work such wicked magic with her fingers and tongue? In only seconds, she drove him half out of his mind with pleasure. If he hadn't begged for mercy, it would have all been over.

Finally, she surrendered the condom. Once he had it in place, he decided on a little revenge of his own. With no warning he flipped her onto her belly and pulled her hips up toward him. Then he slid his fingers between her legs, testing her readiness. Oh, yeah, she wanted him as much as he wanted her.

He positioned himself between her legs and thrust into her from behind. He held on to her hips as he slowly moved in and out, almost withdrawing before plunging back in again.

"Jarvis, quit teasing!"

She dropped her head down onto her arms, arching higher and deepening the angle between them, snapping his control. He rode her hard and fast, the bed shaking with the power of his thrusts. Then Gwen shattered beneath him as he shouted her name and climaxed in a burst of the thunder and lightning.

He withdrew from her body, too spent to do more than tug her down onto the bed beside him.

There would be time for words and kisses when his lungs remembered how to work properly. As their sweat-slick bodies cooled and their pulses returned to normal, he spooned against her back, his face buried at the nape of her neck.

A short while later, Gwen stirred. "Jarvis?"

"Hmmm?"

"Want to join me in a bath?"

Now there was an idea guaranteed to bring a man back to life. "If I can find the strength to move, I'd love to."

She giggled. "I keep forgetting what an old man you are. If you're not up to it . . ."

He might not be up for everything at the moment, but he'd make it to the tub or die trying.

"You go start the water. I'll be right behind you."

She moved toward the edge of the bed, giving him an excellent view of the elegant curve of her back. There was strength in this woman, both in her smooth muscles, no doubt from working the farm, but also inside, where it really counted. Gwen Mosely would face down the world as her man's full partner. He really hoped that someday she'd find someone to share her life with—a regular guy who didn't spend his working hours ankle-deep in blood. She deserved that kind of happiness.

And even though it wouldn't be him, he'd keep watch to make sure that guy treated her right—the lucky bastard.

"Jarvis, is something wrong?"

He realized he was glaring at the imaginary guy, his hands clenched in fists. With some effort, he managed a smile. "No, I'm fine."

"If you're sure . . ." She pulled the sheet up around her, looking a little uncomfortable.

"I'm sure." So maybe the smile was a bit ragged. He rolled to the other side of the bed to get up. "I'll scrub your back if you'll scrub mine."

"It's a deal."

The early morning sunshine cast her lover's face in stark relief. Lost in sleep, even with the dark hint of beard, he looked far younger than forty-five years. She couldn't think of a single reason that he would lie about such a thing, but it was hard to believe that he was seventeen years older than she was. And he sure hadn't acted that old during the long hours of the night, when they'd awakened twice more to make love.

The ticking of her alarm clock reminded her that it was time for her to get up, but she couldn't resist spending these last few minutes lying in Jarvis's arms. He looked so at peace with the world, with the shadows that never seemed far from his eyes gone for the moment. She admired the expanse of his chest and shoulders, left bare by the sheet bunched down around their hips. In the daylight it was easy to see the scars that marked his body, most of them only faint silver lines. Although she knew one or two had to be from the night she'd found him, the sheer number of them spoke of a lifetime of such injuries.

It hurt her to think of him being wounded and in such pain over and over again, although he'd probably downplay it if she were to ask him. He was definitely a man of secrets, but they didn't worry her. With the constant threat of violence in the world, she knew there were men and women who served the side of good in secret. Even if he couldn't talk about it, she knew Jarvis had to be one of them.

In a burst of fierce emotion, she wanted to strike back at everyone who had ever hurt him. Even if he did share her brother's ability to heal, that didn't make the pain they suffered any less. She'd like to get her hands on whoever put him in danger's way so callously.

"Now who's frowning?" Jarvis's eyes crinkled as he smiled sleepily. "Do I look that bad in the morning?"

"You look . . . cute," she whispered and brushed her fingers across his morning whiskers. "A bit scruffy, maybe, but still cute."

He frowned and touched where her waist curved out to her hip. She glanced down to see four faint streaks of red.

"Damn, was I too rough with you last night? Are

there any other bruises?" He sat up and threw back the covers as if to check her over from head to foot.

"No, you weren't at all rough with me. Besides, you'd have your own fair share if you didn't heal so fast." She caught his wandering hand in hers. "I might have a few twinges this morning, but that's because it's been a long time since I . . . you know." She stopped to kiss the palm of his hand. "But no one has ever made me feel as cherished as you did."

He drew her close for a kiss. "I know I keep saying this, Gwen, but I really don't want to hurt you."

"And I keep telling you I'm a big girl and can look out for myself. Last night was special for me, and I hope for you. But don't read any more into it than it was." She slid out of the bed. "Go back to sleep if you want, but I've got to see to the animals."

She walked into the bathroom and closed the door, needing a few minutes to gather her thoughts. She'd never had a man spend the entire night in her bed, but waking up next to Jarvis had seemed so natural, so right—like he should always be there next to her.

She stared at her reflection in the bathroom mirror. Her hair was a tangled mess, and her lips looked swollen.

She ruthlessly pulled a brush through her hair, trying to tame it, finally pulling it back into a ponytail. A splash of cold water helped wash away the last vestiges of sleep from her face. Even though she didn't get much sleep during the night, it didn't seem to impact her energy level.

She dressed in her usual jeans and T-shirt. After brushing her teeth, she stepped back out into the bedroom.

Jarvis was already dressed. "You wouldn't happen to have an extra toothbrush and razor, would you?"

"Under the sink. I hope you don't mind that the razor is pink." She bit back a smile.

He wrapped his arms around her. "I think my manhood will stand up to a girlie razor, as long as you don't tell Jake. He'd never let me live it down."

"It's a deal." She grinned. "Although I'd be willing to testify just how well your manhood does stand up."

Jarvis laughed. "Thank you. I aim to please."

She blushed. "Yes, well, I think I've bolstered your ego enough for one morning."

He kissed her freckled nose. "I'll be down in a few minutes. I'm not exactly dressed for chores, but I cook a mean omelet. How long will your chores take? I thought maybe we could spend the day together."

"I'd like that. It'll take me about half an hour to get the most important things done."

"Sounds good." He let go of her and headed into the bathroom.

She skipped down the stairs to where the dogs

waited on the porch to be fed. The whole world outside seemed extra bright and beautiful, but Dozer and Larry were too busy eating to notice. But she did. Oh yes, she surely did.

With a neat flick of his wrist, Jarvis flipped the omelet onto Gwen's plate. She made all the appropriate admiring noises as he added perfectly fried bacon and golden brown toast. Then he served himself and sat down.

"This is delicious! Another talent I can testify to." She arched an eyebrow and smiled at him from across the table.

"Keep talking like that and you'll have me blushing." Honesty made him add, "But before you go bragging about my cooking, you might want to know that omelets are the sum total of my repertoire. If it weren't for restaurants and carryout, I'd starve."

It didn't take long for them to finish off everything he'd cooked. He figured it was a tribute more to their bodies' need to replenish after their energetic night than to his cooking skills.

When he took his last sip of coffee, he asked, "Where would you like to go today?"

"Do you have any preferences?"

"Nope, I'm up for anything."

She laughed and said, "I don't doubt that, after last night."

He loved seeing her so relaxed and happy. "Okay, let me rephrase that. I'll be your willing chauffeur. You pick the direction and I'll drive."

"Sounds good. Give me a couple of minutes to change clothes, and I'll be ready." She put her dishes in the sink and headed upstairs.

He quickly cleaned up the kitchen and then went out to his car to get some clean clothes.

Gwen came downstairs just as he finished pulling on his shirt. "Oh good, I was going to offer you another one of Chase's shirts if you wanted something fresh to put on."

"I spend a lot time on the road, so I've learned to carry extras." He picked up his clothes. "So, have you decided where'd you'd like to go?"

"I haven't been to the zoo in St. Louis in years." She gave him a hopeful look.

He'd never been to the zoo at all. "Sure. I'll need to make a quick call and then we can leave."

"Are you on call again? We don't have to go all the way into St. Louis if you really shouldn't go that far." She was putting on a good front, but he could see the disappointment in her eyes.

"Nope, I'm all yours for the day, and tonight, too." His smile was full of promise. "I just need to let Jake know where I'll be." While she locked up the house and gave the dogs extra water, he dialed his friend's number.

Luck was with him; he got Jake's voice mail.

Jake wouldn't have missed the fact that he'd been gone all night, and he was in no mood to answer any questions. He left a terse message, telling Jake that he'd be out of touch for the next twenty-four hours.

He closed the phone and turned it off, feeling like he was back in high school and cutting class—except it was a lot more fun playing hooky with a beautiful woman than by himself. The thought had him smiling as they got in the car and roared up the highway.

Gwen didn't know which was more fun: watching all the exotic animals or watching Jarvis experience the zoo for the first time. He'd laughed at the antics in the monkey house, and had sheepishly admitted that the reptile house gave him the creeps. She'd dragged him into an alcove for a hot kiss to take his mind off the snakes and lizards.

Now they were headed for Big Cat Country, the outdoor enclosures built for the lions and tigers. The day was bright and sunny without being too hot. Walking along together and holding hands just made the day seem that much more perfect. At the top of the incline that gave visitors a view over the enclosure, Jarvis paused to look down at the cats.

He grew quiet as he watched the lions panting in the Missouri heat.

"They sure are beautiful," Gwen said. Then she

saw the odd expression on Jarvis's face. "What's the matter?"

He stepped back from the railing. "I hate to see predators penned up. I know they're endangered, and the zoos help keep up the breeding stock, but they never look right living behind fences."

He watched in silence for a few seconds. "They've done a terrific job with the animals' habitats, but I wish things were different for them."

She looped her arm through his, leaning in close to his shoulder. "I think we all do, but we do our best."

One of the tigers stood up and stretched before padding off to the edge of the shade. Before he lay down, he stared up at the sky, the afternoon sun reflecting off the orange-and-black stripes of his coat. He looked sleepy and sedate, but then he turned those eyes in Gwen's direction. She shivered at the weight of that predatory glance. Abruptly the big animal turned away and flopped down in the grass and closed his eyes.

Jarvis looked down at her. "Something wrong?"

She smiled up at him. "Nothing—just my overactive imagination." She pointed toward the tiger. "He's so beautiful, it would be easy to forget how dangerous he really is. Such a handsome package for a stone-cold killer. Nature should mark those born to kill with some kind of warning sign."

"Those teeth and claws aren't enough of a signal? Besides, I doubt anyone ever asked him if he wanted to kill for a living. He has a job to do, and he does it well."

Jarvis smiled as he said it, but for some reason she sensed the smile was on the surface only. She'd just been making conversation, but her words had obviously struck close to home.

Maybe it was time to move on. "Can we check out the bird house next?"

He gave the tiger one last long look. "Sounds good. And I don't know about you, but I'd love a cold drink."

She pulled out the map they'd picked up near the entrance of the zoo. "Looks like there's a refreshment stand right on the way."

They walked away, leaving the tiger to his own dreams.

Chapter 11

*T*he traffic jam on the highway finally broke up, giving no indication of what had kept everyone moving at a snail's pace for the past ten miles. One minute they were creeping along, and then suddenly the road ahead was clear of congestion. Glad to finally be moving, Jarvis pressed the accelerator.

He'd enjoyed their day in the city, but he looked forward to leaving the crowds behind. They'd stopped at a small Italian place for dinner, laughing over pasta and wine, and holding hands between courses. It was a favorite restaurant of his, located close to his apartment. He'd considered asking Gwen if she'd like to stop by his place after dinner, but in the end he hadn't.

The idea had been tempting, especially the possibility of getting naked with Gwen faster. But he could tell that she was starting to fret about leaving all her animals unattended for so long.

God, he hoped the evening chores didn't take long! He'd spent most of the day half aroused just by being with her. Once they were alone, he wouldn't be able to keep his hands to himself.

"You're looking pretty fierce there, mister. Somebody cut you off for going too slow or something?" Gwen had been dozing for the past few miles, but now was sitting up and looking around. After a glance at the speedometer, she snickered. "Guess not."

He immediately let up a little on the gas. "I'm fine. I figured you were probably in a hurry to get home to check on your four-footed friends."

"I appreciate that." She stared out the passenger window for a few seconds, looking a bit wistful. "I love what I do for a living, but it does make it hard to take time for myself."

"Any regrets about how things have turned out for you and Chase?"

"Not many." She turned her attention back in his direction. "There've been some tough times, but that's true for everyone."

"Think you'll want to do something different, now that your brother's almost grown?"

"I can't imagine what it would be. I like the freedom of working my own hours, and I get my creative fix with my design business. I never was one for city crowds, and that hasn't changed."

He shouldn't ask questions he didn't want answers to, but he couldn't seem to help himself. "Ever think about finding someone to share that farm with?"

Her eyes narrowed as she considered her answer. "Sometimes. More when I was younger, but back then there was never enough time to think about anything but keeping the bills paid and meals on the table. Most of the guys I knew either went off to college or got married and settled down. A couple of guys were possibilities, but nothing serious ever came of it."

Good. Maybe he was selfish for thinking that way, but he couldn't seem to help himself.

"Turnabout is fair play, Jarvis. Any exes I should know about?"

"No. Most women seemed trained to recognize a bad risk."

There had been one or two who might have been willing to go past that second or third date, but he'd always bolted before they got that far. It was better to disappoint them by not calling than to screw their lives up completely by sticking around.

Gwen's expression was hard to decipher. "Sorry, I don't buy that. I can't believe that every woman you've ever met was a fool, Jarvis." Then she changed the subject before he could argue. "How long until you have to go back to wherever it is you go?"

Or maybe it was part of the same discussion. "If I'm lucky, not until sometime tomorrow. I've had my cell turned off, but I'm going to have to turn it on again when we get back to the farm. After that, it's anybody's guess if they'll call me in or not."

When she didn't respond, he added, "That's the way it is for me, Gwen. Always has been and always will be. I can't change it, and wouldn't if I could." Sometimes honesty sucked.

"I know."

"Do you want me to leave after I get you home?" He braced himself for her answer, knowing he wouldn't blame her for trying to protect herself from hurt.

"I probably should, but I don't." She held out her hand for his. "Let's get some carryout on the way to the house and watch movies in bed."

"Are you sure?"

"About watching movies? No. About spending the evening in bed with you? Most definitely."

The Chevelle's engine revved as his foot pushed down on the accelerator, and Gwen laughed.

Jarvis unfastened his seat belt even before the car was completely stopped. Gwen did the same, and they came together in the middle of the front seat with enough heat to put an Ozark summer day to shame. She went straight for the zipper on his jeans, needing to get her hands on the hard evidence that he wanted her as much as she needed him.

Oh, yeah! He leaned back to give her free rein as she worked the button loose and then eased the zipper down as their tongues danced together. Frustrated, she broke off the kiss.

"Give me some room to work here!" she demanded, tugging on the waist of his jeans.

He froze briefly, his eyes widening when he realized what she had in mind. "Are you sure?"

She kissed him softly. "It's all I've been able to think about since we got in the car. Let me do this."

He reached over and yanked on the lever that let the back of the seat drop back, then dragged his jeans down past his hips. She heard his breath catch when she smiled and leaned down to trace the length of his erection with the tip of her tongue.

A gentle squeeze of his sac had him moaning. She liked that and the sense of power it gave her. To show her approval she did it again, this time taking him deep into her mouth, swirling her tongue around the tip of his cock. He tugged the elastic band out off her ponytail, letting her hair cascade over his lap. Then his hands clasped either side of her head, helping her to find the exact rhythm to have him thrumming with pleasure.

All too soon, though, he gasped, "Gwen, honey, we need to stop."

She paused. "You don't like this?"

His laugh was shaky. "I love it, but I don't want to finish without you."

"Too bad. I'll let you make it up to me when we get inside." She stroked him again. "Okay?"

"Oh, yeah," he sighed as she took him in her mouth again.

To prove he was a man of his word, he paid Gwen back for that thrill ride three times over. Once in the kitchen, once up against the wall outside of her bedroom door, and then again in her bed. She'd made her appreciation for his efforts abundantly clear.

But just his luck, the cell phone had rung about thirty seconds after the two of them had made themselves comfortable in the big old claw-foot tub. He'd so wanted to ignore it, but duty called.

Gwen hadn't said a word when he grabbed a towel and stomped out into the other room to answer the phone. But when he came back in, the water was already swirling down the drain and she was dressed in her robe with a resigned look on her face.

Ten minutes later he was peeling out of her driveway in a pissed-off spray of gravel. The sun had finally gone down, leaving him to rip down the road with his headlights cutting through the heavy darkness that fit his mood perfectly.

Jake was waiting when Jarvis pulled through the

security gates and parked. His friend had only been doing his job by calling him in, but that didn't alleviate his need to punch something or somebody.

"Sorry, J-man."

Jarvis cut off the apology. "Don't go there. Just fill me in."

"One of the guys decided to go for a stroll down some of the lesser-used caverns. When he didn't come back, I went looking for him." Jake's expression turned hard. "Someone else had already found him, and they'd really worked him over. Doc thinks he might recover, but it's iffy."

"Son of a bitch! Who was it?"

"Hunter Fitzsimon." Jake opened the door and waited for Jarvis to go in first. "If he survives, he's going to be seriously pissed at Doc."

"Why's that?"

"Hunter's vain about his hair, and they had to shave half of it off to stitch his scalp back together. I'd like to be hiding in a corner the first time he gets that first peek at himself in the mirror."

"Let's hope he gets the chance." Jarvis's stomach bunched up in a tight knot. "Did the barrier go down for long?"

"That's what's so odd: it never went down. So if there were Others in the back tunnels, they didn't come through the main cavern."

"Son of a bitch! Just what we need—another fucking mystery to solve around here."

He punched the elevator buttons three more times, knowing full well that wouldn't bring it up any faster, but standing and waiting was simply beyond him right now. He was on the verge of heading for the stairs when the doors finally slid open.

"Let's go to the lab first and check on Hunter. Then you can show me where you found him."

Jake's face got a little pale. "If it's okay with you, I'll get our weapons while you check in with Doc. I've spent enough time in the lab lately."

"All right." He stared after Jake's fast retreat.

How bad were Hunter's injuries if Jake couldn't bear to see him again? Considering the horror they all lived with year in and year out, it had to be pretty damn bad.

The lab doors were just ahead, and he braced himself. It hadn't been all that long ago that he'd paced this very hallway waiting for Trahern to be put down permanently. Brenna Nichols had pulled off a miracle, talking him back from the wrong side of insanity. Jake was right: they'd all been spending way too much time in the lab.

He pushed the doors open and stepped inside. One look at the patient strapped down to the surgical steel table made him want to go right back out again.

"Dear God Almighty!"

He thought he'd whispered the prayer, but Doc

Crosby looked up from the report he was read-ing. As soon as he saw Jarvis, he set the chart aside and motioned him into the room. Jarvis crossed the short distance with leaden feet, struggling to breathe, much less talk.

Hunter had had several hours of healing time, and if this was an improvement, Jarvis was damned glad to not have seen him before. There didn't seem to be a square inch of skin that wasn't stitched together or didn't have a tube running out of it. The poor bastard looked more like a slab of raw beef than a man. What had they done to him? And more important, why?

He stared at Hunter's chest, hoping that he hadn't only imagined seeing it move, however slightly. No wonder Jake said Hunter's chances for revival were iffy.

Jarvis struggled to put a lid on his rage. Dying again and again until their humanity was used up was the price they all paid in the war against the Kalith. But *no one* deserved to be sliced and diced like that.

Judging by Dr. Crosby's face, he wasn't the only one who felt sickened. Considering the physician's vast experience in treating fatal battle wounds, that said a lot.

Jarvis nodded toward Hunter. "Can I do any-thing, Doc?"

"Kill the bastards who did this to him." He

looked back toward the beeping machinery. "And don't make it fast or easy."

"I hear you." He put a hand on the physician's shoulder. "Bring me up to speed on his chances."

"Not good." Doc rubbed his hand on his whiskery chin. "I had to literally patch pieces of him back together. Though you bastards have an uncanny knack for healing, there are limits. It doesn't help that his blood type is one of the rarer ones. I can transfuse him with O neg or even regular human blood if I have to, but I'd rather give him the right type of Paladin blood."

Dr. Crosby rolled his shoulders to stretch out the kinks. "Of course, that's predicated on his heart beating hard enough to pump the blood."

"What's his blood type?"

"AB neg."

"Then maybe Hunter's luck is changing because so am I. I can afford to run a quart low if it will help him."

"Thanks; it may come to that. I should know in the next few hours." The older man ran his fingers through his hair, looking every one of his fifty-plus years. "Are you going to be around if I need you in a hurry?"

"Jake and I are going to do some exploring, but you can try my cell phone. If that doesn't work, use a landline and tell the guards to hunt me down. I'll come running."

"Thanks, Jarvis."

It was the first time Jarvis had ever seen the man look so lost. "Why don't you get some sleep, Doc? If—*when* Hunter starts reviving, he'll need you fed and rested. Have one of your techs sit with him if you don't want him to be alone, or I can have one of his friends come up. They'd probably appreciate the chance to help out."

"I sent most of my crew to catch some sleep while it's quiet. If you can spare someone, I'd appreciate the break."

"The barrier feels stable, so I'll send a couple of the guys up. It will be easier on them to have someone to play cards with, rather than having nothing to do but stare at Hunter. They can take four-hour shifts and let you sleep."

"I'll be in the next room, close by."

"You're a good man, Doc. We might not tell you often enough, but we appreciate all you do for us."

"Yeah, yeah, yeah. Try to remember that the next time you're the one on that table bitchin' about my bedside manner."

Jarvis managed a small laugh for the doctor's sake. "I'll try."

Then he walked out, relieved to be out where the air didn't reek of medicine and old blood. Sometimes it felt like he was stuck on the merry-go-round from hell, watching friends die over and over, killing one crazy bastard after another, knowing nothing was ever going to change. Not until everything inside that made him human was used up, and then, after a burst of insanity, he would know peace at last. It was a helluva thing to be looking forward to.

He made his way farther down in the caverns where Jake was waiting for him. With his cell phone turned off he'd been able to pretend that this reality didn't exist, and found some real peace with Gwen. She'd made him forget that he was as much a killer as that tiger in the zoo.

Gwen was so easy to be with, funny and warm, and so damned sexy. But the best part was that he could be with her without having to pretend. She had no idea what a balm to his soul that was. She knew he had secrets that he couldn't share, yet she liked him anyway.

Of course, once she found out what those secrets were and how they'd affect her brother, she'd hate him. It would be harder for her now that they were lovers, but he wanted these few days or weeks of normalcy. He deserved to rot in hell for his selfishness, but that day was coming.

For now, he needed to find out what had happened to Hunter.

Jake saw him coming and shut down the computer game he'd been playing. When Trahern's Brenna had been there, she'd admired the computer game Jake had designed. He'd sent her a prototype to play, asking for her feedback.

"Did you hear back from Brenna on your killer dragon?"

Jake grinned. "She likes the game so much, Trahern's starting to complain about how much time she spends playing it. She got a kick out of one of the dragons being named after her."

Jarvis shook his head. "Damn it, Jake, are you trying to get yourself killed? I've already warned you about messing with Trahern's woman. If you want to be gutted with a rusty sword, just keep on doing what you're doing."

Jake turned guileless eyes in Jarvis's direction. "They're two thousand miles away. Besides, he should cut me some slack. Getting shot with someone is bound to bring people closer together."

"Trahern got shot then, too. That doesn't mean he wants to cozy up with you."

Jake looked back toward the lab. "I wish Hunter had a woman to fuss over him like Trahern did when he had trouble coming back. Maybe it would help."

"Yeah." Once again, his thoughts turned toward Gwen. Doc Crosby always did his best for them, but it would be a damn sight better to wake up from the dead with someone like Gwen standing over him, with her woman's scent and soft hands.

Now was not the time for those thoughts, though. Not with killers haunting the tunnels. He took the sword Jake was holding out to him.

"Take me to where you found Hunter, and we'll go from there."

"Sounds good." Then Jake took a couple of quick sniffs near Jarvis's shoulder.

"Get away. What are you doing?"

"Did you know you smell like roses?" Jake's mouth spread in a wide grin. "What were you and Gwen doing when I called? Something hot and kinky, I hope."

"None of your damn business." The last thing he needed was for Jake to know they'd been taking a bubble bath. He'd never hear the end of it.

"Okay, but you'd be better off telling me. Otherwise my imagination is going to run wild—and you know how I like to run off at the mouth."

"Imagine whatever you want to." He punched his friend on the arm, hard enough to hurt. "But keep your ideas to yourself, or I'll tell Trahern you're having wet dreams about Brenna."

Jake mimed zipping his lips and crossing his heart. Maybe he had more sense than Jarvis gave him credit for.

They'd left the main cavern far behind and were following a winding path through the maze of smaller passages that nature had started and the Paladins had expanded over the years. He didn't have to ask when they were getting close; the scent of dried blood made it unnecessary.

Dear God, how could anyone have bled that

much? The passage here was ten feet across, most of it covered in splashes of blood. Even the walls were decorated in macabre patterns from arterial spray.

His gut rose up and then plummeted as if he'd just crested the top peak on a roller coaster. He automatically reached out to touch the cave wall to steady himself but then jerked back from the bloodstains.

"You okay?"

Jarvis nodded, surprised that Jake's voice sounded so calm. Then he noticed his friend had his eyes pinned directly on Jarvis's face.

"Let's move on and see if we can see where the bastards came from."

The passage narrowed down again, and most of the time they had to walk single file. They continued on for a considerable distance in silence. If there were Others somewhere ahead, they didn't want to alert them that death was on its way.

They'd been traveling for about an hour when Jarvis stopped. The most commonly used caverns and tunnels were lit with motion-activated lights. He and Jake had reached the point where they'd need flashlights and other equipment to keep going.

They'd have to turn back—without the fight he so badly needed. He needed a safe target for the rage that had been building inside him since the minute the phone had rung.

Closing his eyes, he bashed the flat side of his sword against a stone outcropping and imagined the sweet feel of the blade slicing through Other flesh. The impact vibrated painfully through his bones and teeth, giving him something to focus on, something he could control. He swung the sword again and again and again. He might have been screaming, but he didn't know. Right now, the clang of metal against the cold, hard rock wall was all there was.

"Uh, Jarvis, buddy." Jake's voice sounded as if it were coming from a long distance away. "Shouldn't we head back now? Maybe come back later with more men and lights? If we bring some GPS equipment with us, we can get a fix on this place."

At first the sound of his voice was no more than background static on a radio station that wasn't quite tuned in. As Jake repeated himself over and over, individual words began to seep through, then stringing together as whole phrases, and finally sentences.

His rage had burned too bright and too hot to last long. Inside Jarvis's chest, it felt as if an on-off switch was abruptly flipped. One second he was out of control, in mindless pain; the next, his chest was heaving with the need for oxygen, but his mind was rational and clear.

Jake ventured closer. "So, got that out of your system?"

"Mostly." He rested the sword tip on the ground. "But I still have a few good swings left in me, if you insist on being such a pain in the ass."

"I go with my strengths," Jake said nonchalantly.

Jarvis cracked up, unsure which of them he surprised more, himself or Jake. "There's nothing more to be done here. Depending on the status of the barrier tomorrow, we'll return prepared to trace this back far enough to figure out where they gained access. Maybe there's a narrow strip of barrier in an open cavern that we don't know about."

The trip back passed uneventfully. As soon as they reached the main cavern, one of the on-duty guards flagged Jarvis down.

"Sir, Dr. Crosby asked me to have you report to him as soon as you can. He said it wasn't an emergency, but sooner was better than later."

"Did he say what he needed?"

"No sir, just that you were to see him ASAP."

"Thank you."

Jarvis handed his sword to a passing Paladin and headed quickly toward the lab, Jake hard on his heels.

Inside the lab, the doctor stood over Hunter with an enormous smile. "I think Hunter turned the corner about half an hour ago. He has a long way to go, but there's a definite improvement. He's breathing regularly and his pulse is up enough that I want to give him a transfusion. That's why I sent for you."

Jarvis stuck his arm out. "Take as much as he needs."

"We'll start with two pints. I don't want to over-tax your body or his ability to assimilate the blood."

He pointed toward a gurney pushed up against the far wall. "Jake, bring that over here, then head for the cafeteria. Jarvis is going to be here awhile, so I want you to bring him some dinner and several bottles of water."

"Sure thing, Doc." Jake rolled the gurney across the room and then disappeared.

Jarvis stretched out on the gurney while the doctor gathered his supplies. "Thanks for giving Jake something to do, Doc. Knowing him, he's carrying a fair load of guilt over Hunter getting hurt."

"Why? He's not the one who did this to him."

"I know that and you know that, and even Jake knows that. But he's probably thinking that if he'd noticed Hunter was missing sooner, maybe he could have gotten there in time to save him from some of this."

"That's bullshit." Doc swabbed Jarvis's arm with alcohol. "He might have walked in on something that was too big for the two of them to handle, and then I'd have *two* critical patients."

"How much has he improved?" Hunter still looked like a train had hit him head-on.

"Enough. After all these years, I'm still amazed at the recuperative powers your kind have."

"Our kind?" That hurt, but he kept his reply light. "We're human, like everyone else. We just got the deluxe package."

"I know, Jarvis." Doc looked at him over the top of his glasses. "And I can't imagine a finer group of men to serve with. I just wish we could tell more people about the sacrifices you guys make for the rest of us, over and over again."

"Quit it, Doc. You're going to embarrass me."

The doctor just smiled and started palpating Jarvis's arm for the best vein. "Just relax. This won't hurt."

"That's what you always say." Jarvis looked away until the needle was imbedded in his vein and taped in place. Then he watched the steady line of blood winding through the clear tubing to fill the blood pack at the other end. He wasn't overly fond of needles, but he'd drain himself dry if it would help bring Hunter back faster.

Dr. Crosby waited by his side to make sure that everything was working correctly. "It won't take long for the first bag to fill. This will jump-start his healing process."

Jake walked back in, laden with a tray heaped high with food and water bottles.

"Please take it in the other room, Jake. After Jarvis is done here, I'm going to have him sleep here tonight." Turning back toward Jarvis, he frowned and sniffed the air.

"Something wrong, Doc?"

"I keep thinking I smell roses."

Jake's eyes sparkled with mischief. "That *is* odd, Doc. I was just telling him the very same thing."

Jarvis closed his eyes and ignored Jake's laugh. He'd exact his revenge when he was back up to full strength.

"See ya, Jordan!"

Chase waved as his friend pulled out of the driveway, then headed for the back door. He could hardly walk with the dogs bouncing up and down, demanding his attention. He finally dropped his duffel and sleeping bag on the grass and knelt down to let the two fur balls get their scratches and rubs.

"I was only gone for a couple of days. From the way you're acting, you'd think that I'd died or something."

Gwen stepped out the back door. "Did you have fun?"

"Yeah, we did." He hefted his bags and walked toward her. "We spent most of the time rafting and swimming. It was a long hike back down to the car, so I'm tired, but good tired."

"And hungry?"

He gave her a one-armed hug. "Always, but I need to shower first. After I eat, I'm going to crash for the night."

"And your chores?" She crossed her arms and gave him one of *those* looks.

"Oh, yeah." He started to drop his bags. "I'll do them now."

She smiled. "I've already done most of them. You can double up tomorrow to make up for it."

"That's a deal."

When he came back downstairs, Gwen had dinner ready to go on the table. "You didn't have to wait for me."

"I didn't mind." She passed him the meat loaf. "I hate to bring up a touchy subject, but do you have everything you need for school?"

He grimaced. "Rats! I'd successfully blocked it from my mind. I probably need a couple of pairs of jeans and three or four shirts. I've got enough saved up to cover it."

But he wouldn't have much money to live on until football season was over, when he could look for part-time work. Then he noticed the smug look Gwen was giving him.

"What?"

"Wait here." She disappeared into the spare bedroom, came back with three large shopping bags, and set them down by his side of the table.

"What's this?"

"Happy senior year, big guy! You're going to start school in style."

She ruffled his hair, just as she used to when

he was a kid. He normally would've ducked out of reach, but under the circumstances he'd put up with a little fussing. He opened the bag and pulled out the jeans and shirts.

"Thanks, Sis! This is perfect. But you didn't have to buy all this; I've been saving up."

"I know, but I wanted to do it." She nudged his size-thirteen foot with her much smaller one. "Besides, you'll need new shoes, too. Those can be your contribution to the Send Chase to School Fund."

He stuck his foot out and studied it. "I didn't want to tell you that these are already feeling a bit tight."

"Good grief, I'm going to have to quit feeding you so much! If you don't watch it, you'll be as big as Jarvis. I think he wears a fourteen."

That tidbit got his attention. "And how would you know that?"

"Just guessing."

She picked up an armload of dishes from the table and carried them over to the sink. He might have taken her statement at face value if she hadn't blushed.

He took his empty plate over to the counter and set it down. "So how much time did he spend here while I was gone?"

"He stopped by night before last, so we ate left-overs and watched a movie."

There was more she wasn't telling him. "And what else?"

She frowned at him. "Yesterday he took me into St. Louis to the zoo, which was a lot of fun. But not long after we got back, he got a call from Jake and had to leave."

That left the time after the movie and before the zoo unaccounted for. From the way Gwen was acting, he suspected Jarvis never went home in between.

He'd decide how he felt about that later; but right now he was too tired. He'd better go to bed before he opened a can of worms neither of them wanted to deal with.

"If you don't need me for anything, I'm going upstairs."

"No, go ahead. I won't be far behind you."

"I'm glad you weren't alone the whole time I was gone." That was true.

"I had a good time." She smiled. "Can you believe that Jarvis had never been to the zoo?"

Somehow, that didn't surprise him. "So, you two are dating now? I mean, it sounds that way."

Gwen wiped her hands on the dish towel and set it aside. "We are. For a little while, anyway."

"It's nice that you have someone your age to hang out with."

She laughed. "Well, I don't know about the age part. He's actually about seventeen years older than I am. Can you believe he's forty-five?"

"No way!"

She laughed. "Yes, way. That's what he told me."

"Why do you think he looks so young? Is it part of this whole healing thing we both have?"

She looked thoughtful. "Sounds logical. Ask him the next time you see him."

"Maybe I will. See you in the morning."

As Chase's head hit the pillow, his last thought was he ought to be make a list of questions for Jarvis—including what his intentions were toward Gwen.

"How are you feeling this morning?"

Jarvis rolled over and glared at Dr. Crosby. "I was doing great until you turned the lights on." He sat up and rubbed his eyes. "What time is it?"

"Close to noon. You've been asleep for about fourteen hours. I wouldn't wake you now, but Jake called and asked if you wanted him to take your lesson today."

"Do you think you'll need my vein again? If so, I'll stick close and let Jake go in my place. Otherwise, we may both go." He swung his legs over the side of the bed.

"No, I've been giving Hunter IVs and that seems to be helping."

Jarvis looked toward the lab. "How's he doing?"

The older man looked grim. "His numbers are improving a little at a time, but there's been no sign of him coming around. That's hardly surprising, though. He'll need more time than usual to recover completely. It could be weeks before we know if any of the nerve damage is permanent or not."

Son of a bitch.

"Keep me posted."

"Will do."

Jarvis pulled on his clothes and headed out, stopping to check on Hunter first. The man looked like death warmed over, but if you looked hard enough, you could see a few spots that had healed. Great—the poor bastard had a few square inches that didn't hurt every time he breathed.

Leaning down close to Hunter's ear, he whispered, "Hey, buddy, glad to see you're on the mend. Don't worry, we'll get the bastards that did this to you."

One of the machines hiccupped and beeped loudly a couple of times as Jarvis straightened up. He'd like to think that meant Hunter had responded on some level.

On the way out of the lab, he put in a call to Jake.

"I'm going to my quarters for a shower and shave. Give me thirty minutes and then meet me at the car."

The thought of spending the afternoon with the Moselys was a definite mood booster. Maybe Jake could keep Chase busy while Jarvis and Gwen finished that bubble bath? He sighed. A man could dream.

Chapter 12

Jake lifted his water bottle and chugged down half of it. Wiping his mouth with the back of his hand, he nodded in Chase's direction. "What's up with him?"

Jarvis kept his eyes on Jake, trying to make it less obvious that they were talking about the boy. "I suspect he found out that I spent a lot of time with his sister while he was gone. He'd warned me once about not messing with her, so I'd guess he's working himself up to another lecture."

"She told him that you were doing the horizontal tango?"

Jake sounded incredulous, right up until Jarvis's fist connected with his stomach. Then he sounded like a whole lot of pain. He hit the floor hard, holding his gut with a moan.

Chase's eyes were the size of plates when he worked up his courage to approach. Noting the boy stayed on the far side of Jake, Jarvis gave him points for good sense. A smart man avoided getting in the middle of a fight until he found out which side he was on.

Staring down at Jake, Chase asked, "Is he okay?"

"I'm fuckin' fine." Jake pushed himself up to his feet, glaring at Jarvis. "I didn't think—"

Jarvis cut him off. "That's exactly right: you *didn't* think. Now shut your damn mouth before I give you a second lesson in manners."

Chase backed away a step. "Do you two have these lessons often?"

"Too damn often," Jake complained. "Don't worry, kid—he only uses his fists when he thinks somebody hasn't been listening close enough."

"O-kay." Chase put his hands behind his ears as if trying to hear better. "What do you want me to do next, Mr. Donahue, sir? I'm all ears."

Jarvis laughed. The kid had gumption. "I want you to go open that red gear bag by the door and bring back what's in it. Carefully."

He and Jake waited to see Chase's reaction to the three swords. Hopefully Gwen wouldn't poke her pretty nose in anytime soon. Even if Jarvis could convince her that swords were a normal part of martial arts practice, he wanted to put the discussion off as long as possible.

"Cool!" Chase sounded reverent as he lifted the first sword out of the bag.

"Take a few practice swings with it and then do the same with the others. When you're done, I want to know which you like best and why."

Jake moved up beside him, a silent apology, which only made Jarvis feel more like a shit.

"It's different this time." There'd never been another time that even came close.

His friend managed a small smile. "Tell me something I don't know." After a few seconds, he said, "Hey, Chase has some good moves already. I think he's a natural. He'll take to the job like a duck to water."

Normally that would have pleased Jarvis because God knows they needed any additional manpower they could get. But prying Chase out of his sister's fingers was going to be tough. If they could tell her the truth about the very real threat the constant invasions from Kalithia posed, not only to this country but also in other spots scattered around the world, she might understand.

"Might" being the operative word. It was easy to flag-wave when it wasn't your ass on the line or that of someone you loved. But no matter how Gwen felt about it, Chase would man up to do the job, just as Jarvis and Jake had when they were his age. It was hardwired into his genetic makeup.

Which reminded him—Chase had never said a word about his father, not since Jarvis had given Gwen the picture to pass along to her brother.

Apparently, she hadn't done so. He'd respect her decision for now, but would ask her about it later. Eventually they'd have to tell Chase more about Harvey, to help the boy understand who and what he was. And sooner would be better, because Jarvis was already planning a field trip for Chase.

The time to introduce him to others of his own kind was coming. Chase would probably get a kick out of working out with some of the younger Paladins. It was just another step in the process of bringing him into the fold.

Chase was on the last sword now. He hefted it and then waved it around a couple of times before doing a couple of quick lunges. It wasn't hard to tell that he'd found his favorite. His bright blue eyes gleamed as he carefully put the other two back.

Jarvis crossed his arms over his chest and gave Chase his best drill sergeant stare. "Why that one?"

"I don't know, except that it feels better. Right, somehow."

"How so?"

Chase brought the sword up into fighting position and held it there as he tried to formulate an answer. Finally, he brought the sword straight up in front of his face. "The other two felt heavier and sort of awkward. This one feels like an extension of my arm, as if the pommel was made for my hand."

Jake clapped him on the back. "See, I told you, Jarvis. The boy's a natural, with fine taste in swords." He stage-whispered to Chase, "That's the one I picked out for you."

True enough. "Okay, smart-ass, you put him through his paces. I'm going to see what Gwen is up to. If we're taking up Chase's time, she might need help with the chores."

Chase's excitement visibly dimmed. Time to nip this in the bud. "You got a problem with me helping your sister, Chase?"

The boy rested the sword on the ground, his hands crossed on top of the pommel. "And if I do?"

"Spit it out."

"I've already warned you once." He handed the sword off to Jake and squared up his shoulders. "Right now she seems happy about the way things are between you. If that changes, we'll have a discussion like the one you had with Jake—only I'll be the one doing the talking."

Chase had to know he wouldn't stand a chance against Jarvis in a fair fight, if there even was such a thing. He couldn't fault the boy's instincts and respected the loyalty that drove them.

"Fine. We'll talk." Before he could go two steps, Jake caught him by the arm. "What do you want?"

His friend's eyes were flint hard. "She's a nice lady. If Chase needs help explaining things to you, I might help him clarify a few points."

Jarvis shrugged off Jake's hand and walked away. When he stepped out of the barn, he turned toward the woods rather than the house; his mood was too volatile to be around anyone. A quick hike might help.

Then he saw Gwen standing at the corral fence. There was no way to avoid being seen, and if he ignored her, it would only cause more problems.

He joined her at the fence. She was watching the alpacas so intently, he wasn't sure she noticed him.

"Something wrong?" He put his foot on the lowest railing and rested his arms on the top one.

Gwen shook her head as if to clear it. "What? Oh, no. Everything is fine. I was just seeing sweaters."

He couldn't resist the urge to tease her. "I would have thought their coats would keep them warm enough this winter. Knit hats and booties might help, though."

She laughed and poked him in the ribs with her elbow. "Very funny."

"Seriously, though, what do you see when you look at them?"

"Colors, mostly. I prefer to work with the natural colors of their fiber. One of the other breeders in the state is selling some of his breeding females, and I'm trying to decide if there are any colors I'd like to add to my bunch."

"Are they expensive?"

"Oh, yeah. If I want to buy one or two, I'd have

to sell a couple of mine to swing the payment." She lapsed into silence again, her eyebrows drawn together in a frown.

"If it's a matter of money, I've got some I'm not using."

Paladins were well paid for the duration of their fighting years. Of course, there were no retirement benefits, since they all left the job in the same way: at the wrong end of a lethal injection.

"You're sweet to offer, but no thanks. I don't really need another animal; I just want one."

"The offer stands if you change your mind."

She raised up on her tiptoes and kissed his cheek.

The sound of a muffled shout, followed by raucous laughter, drifted from the barn. Gwen turned in that direction, a pleased smile on her face. "So how is the training going?"

"He's good, and will be really good before long. He and Jake are practicing some new moves." Ones that would help Chase become a proficient killer.

"It's so nice of you and Jake to give up your free time to help him. Other than various sports coaches, he's never had a man to show him the ropes. It means a lot to both of us."

Maybe now was the time to ask about the picture. "Chase has never mentioned the photo I gave you of his father. Did you decide not to tell him about Harvey?"

"Not exactly. I told him his father's name, but he didn't seem very excited about learning even that. I could have pushed it more, but . . ."

"But what, Gwen?"

"This might sound silly, but it's just been the two of us for so long. It's hard to know whether telling Chase about his father will help him or hurt him. It's not like he'll ever have a chance to meet the man."

Jarvis turned to stare out toward the woods. "I wouldn't presume to interfere, but maybe even a small connection, especially knowing his father was a good guy, might help Chase learn his place in the world. It's not easy for teenage boys at the best of times, and anything that sets them apart just makes it that much harder. Your brother has a lot in common with Harvey. Maybe it would help for him to know that."

Gwen turned to stare at her herd. After a bit, she said, "You're right, of course. I guess I have a hard time sharing, which is stupid. It's not like the man is going to swoop in and steal Chase away from me."

No, Jarvis was going to do that. "Look, I'm going to take a walk in the woods for a few minutes. When I get back, it will be time for Jake and me to head out."

"Mind if I come with you?"

Yes. No. Maybe. Hell, he didn't know. Chase

wouldn't like it, but maybe that was too damn bad. "Sure thing. I've been shut in too much. A walk along the river just sounded good."

She whistled for the dogs, who came charging around the corner. "Come on, boys, let's see if there are any varmints in the woods for you to chase."

As they followed the excited dogs toward the path into the woods, Gwen slipped her hand into Jarvis's. At first she wasn't sure he was going to respond, but after a second's hesitation he gave her hand a soft squeeze before letting go. Something was obviously bothering him, but she didn't feel comfortable prying. Maybe he'd tell her if she was patient.

After a bit, he draped his arm around her shoulder. She snuggled closer and cupped the side of his face with the palm of her hand. Seeing the sadness in his eyes, she raised herself up high enough to kiss him. His arms immediately tightened around her, holding her close and with such care. The brief embrace had a far different feel than any they'd shared before. This time, she offered him comfort and sweetness instead of heat and passion. She hoped it helped. The air in the woods was heavy with humidity, but a small breeze kept it from being unbearable. Other than the occasional rustling in the bushes or the call of a bird flitting around in the trees, the woods were quiet and peaceful. It always seemed as if she shed her worldly problems there.

She wished she could say the same for Jarvis. Maybe she could get him to talk about whatever was weighing him down. "I know you can't tell me what was wrong the other night, but I hope whatever Jake needed you for wasn't too serious."

"Serious enough, but the, uh, situation is improving bit by bit."

"That's good." So much for that topic of conversation.

She tried again. "Chase's first game is this coming weekend. He'd love it if you could come—if you're free."

"Sounds like fun. Tell me when and where, and I'll try to be there. Things at work are a bit dicey right now, but if I can get free, I'll meet you there."

She understood he had obligations, but they'd be easier to accept if she had a better idea of what they were. "That'll work. I really hope you can come."

They'd reached the edge of the river. She sat on a boulder and tugged her shoes off to dangle her feet in the cool, clear water. Patting the space next to her, she said, "Come join me. The water is perfect."

He immediately pulled off his boots and rolled up his jeans. As soon as he stuck his feet in the water, he yelped and yanked them back out. "That's not perfect! That's damn cold!"

She giggled and splashed the water with her feet. "Wuss. It feels great."

"If you say so." Even as he groused, he eased his feet back into the water. Then he tugged on her braid. "You caused me a big problem the other night."

"Really? What did I do that was so terrible?"

He leaned down to scoop up a handful of rocks to toss in the river. "Jake and another coworker kept sniffing the air around me and saying they could smell roses. I thought I was going to have to threaten one of them to make them stop."

"Would they think less of you for taking a bubble bath?"

"Actually, I think they'd be green with envy. Any guy in his right mind would fight for the chance to take a bath, bubble or otherwise, with such a beautiful woman." His fingers tangled with hers, and his voice grew rough with heat. "I get hard just thinking about wrapping myself around all your sweet-smelling skin. If I thought we could lock Jake and Chase in the barn, I'd suggest we pick up where we left off."

Then he pulled her close for a long kiss, the kind that had her curling her toes and actually considering nailing the barn door shut for a while. She ran her hand up under Jarvis's shirt, loving the feel of all that warm skin and smooth muscle.

He broke off the kiss, resting his forehead against

hers. "If I could bottle the taste of your kisses, I'd put all the candy companies out of business."

"Your kisses ought to come with a warning label, because they melt my bones." She brushed her lips across his. "Not that I'm complaining."

He immediately took control of the kiss, his tongue plunging in and out of her mouth, reminding her of how it had felt when he'd used the same rhythm to bring her to a shattering climax the other night. She just couldn't get enough of this man.

He laid her down on the boulder, then unbuttoned her shirt far enough to reveal the top of her breasts. He whispered hot words of approval as he teased her with his lips and tongue, tasting her skin and leaving heat in their wake.

She pushed him away just long enough to release the front catch of her bra, and his eyes turned the color of melted chocolate as he tongued her nipples into hard peaks. His callused hand palmed one side as he suckled hard on the other. If he kept that up, she was going to come right there. She was half naked right where anyone walking through the woods could see them, but she wouldn't miss it for the world.

Then he found the damp heat between her legs. No other man had ever stoked her fires to such an inferno before.

He reached for the snap of her cutoffs, when all of a sudden the dogs came bounding back, barking their fool heads off. She snarled at them to shut up, but stopped when she realized that their attention was focused on the ridge above them, the fur on their necks standing up. Their low growls doused the rest of her passion completely.

"Jarvis?"

He shushed her with his fingers over her lips. "Straighten your clothing and go back to the barn and stay there. Tell Jake to come running with my gear bag. He'll know which one. Hurry."

Her sweet-smiling lover was gone. In his place stood a warrior, his face harsh and fierce, his entire body rigid with tension. Without taking his eyes off the ridge, he gave her a hand up off the boulder and picked up her shoes.

"Go *now*, Gwen, and *don't* come back with Jake. We'll be fine, but I can't afford to have any distractions."

She put on her shoes but didn't wait to tie them. The faster she got to Jake, the faster Jarvis wouldn't be alone in the woods with whatever had both him and the dogs so spooked. And he seemed to know exactly what the threat was.

As she ran back toward her farm she struggled to button her blouse, hoping Jake and Chase would assume her bedraggled appearance was because she'd been running.

"Jake!"

She hollered his name again when she came

even with the pasture gate, and then repeated it until she turned the corner toward the front of the barn. He was already charging out of the door with Chase right behind him.

"Gwen! What's wrong?"

"Jarvis wants you to bring his equipment bag and come running. He's waiting a short distance down the path. Hurry, because something's got him and the dogs really spooked."

"Son of a bitch!"

Jake disappeared back into the barn and reappeared immediately with a bright red duffle that clinked like metal inside. He took off at a dead run and Chase started after him, but Gwen blocked his way.

"He said only Jake, Chase. He didn't want any distractions."

Her brother tried to step around her, but she managed to keep herself planted in front of him.

He grabbed her waist and set her out of his way. "Damn it, Gwen, those are my friends and my dogs out there. I'm not going to stay here like some helpless child."

She didn't bother trying to catch him, knowing that he'd easily outdistance her. All she could do was wait and pray for all three of them, and hope that whatever was out there didn't hurt any of her menfolk.

• • •

Jarvis was clearly not happy to see him, but too bad. He wasn't some child to be left out of the action.

"What's up?"

The two men ignored him as they unzipped the red bag and pulled out a pair of swords and a couple of handguns. They checked the two automatics over with deadly-looking efficiency.

Did they know what was out there? No one in their right mind went hunting with swords, for God's sake. At least no one he'd ever heard of.

Jake held out a smaller version of the gun he'd just stuck in the back of his waist. "Do you know how to use one of these?"

"I'm more familiar with a twenty-two rifle, but I've shot something similar to this a few times at a firing range with my friend and his dad."

Jarvis nodded. "Good. Keep the safety on. I don't plan on you needing it at all, but I don't want you unarmed, either. It would be better if you went back to your sister, but I figure that's not going to happen."

"No way." These were his woods. If they were no longer safe for him and his sister, he wanted to know why.

Then Jarvis picked up his sword. "Chase, you hang back, no matter what happens. Got that?"

Jarvis's voice of authority made him want to salute. "Yes sir."

"Okay, let's get this show on the road." Glancing

at the dogs, Jarvis said, "Come on, boys. Show me where they are."

For once, Larry showed good sense and let the more experienced Dozer lead the way at a slow lope, splashing across the river and then up-hill. When they neared the top Dozer stopped and waited until his people caught up with him. Smart dog. When Larry started to pass him, Dozer shoul-dered him aside.

Jarvis reached the dogs first because he'd gone straight for them while Jake had angled off to the right. Following his lead, Chase moved to the left, but stuck closer to Jarvis, figuring caution was the name of the game. Especially when his hands were shaking and the lump of what felt like fear almost choked his throat closed.

When they were all the same distance from the crest of the ridge, Jarvis made a forward motion with his hand. Chase did as he'd been ordered and waited a count of three before following his com-panions over the top.

Memories of playing soldiers with his friends in these same woods flashed through his mind, but this was no game. He'd never seen anyone look as deadly as Jarvis and Jake. In an odd sort of way, fol-lowing the two of them into the face of danger felt right.

They continued down the other side about twenty feet before Jarvis stopped. The dogs ranged out ahead, nose to the ground and sniffing like crazy. Jarvis knelt down to study the ground while Jake did the same thing farther on. Chase did the same thing, even though he didn't know what he was looking for.

A broken twig on a nearby bush caught his attention. He duck-walked closer, studying the ground. Anything could have accounted for the damage: a raccoon, a coyote, a deer. He moved the branch out of the way to study the ground, hoping for some kind of paw print.

What he saw made his pulse race again. It was a footprint. Judging from the condition of the leaves on the twig, someone had passed through here recently. If it had been hours before, the leaves would have wilted; days before and they would be dry and crumbly.

He gave a soft whistle, catching Jarvis's attention. He in turn signaled Jake, who moved closer to stand watch while Jarvis joined Chase on the ground.

"Tell me what you see."

Pointing at the broken twig, he pushed it aside to show Jarvis the clear print. "Someone passed through here recently enough that the break in the stem is still wet and the leaves aren't wilted."

Jarvis nodded. "Go on."

"The heel print ends here, the toe there. I wear a thirteen, and this is smaller, maybe an eleven. Still plenty big enough for an adult man."

"Male. We call them males." Jarvis unfolded to his full height. "What you see here, what we tell you here, stays between us. You can't tell your sister or your friends. If you can't handle that, go home and stay there. Argue the point, and Jake will personally haul you back. You might be close to our size, but don't doubt his ability to take you out."

Curiosity won out over temper. "I won't tell."

Jarvis stared into his eyes for an eternity before nodding. "See if you can tell which way he went, and if there's more than one male."

Chase moved off, keeping his eyes to the ground, trusting Jarvis and Jake to stand guard. "Here's another print."

He measured the print against his own foot. "Probably the same male who made the first one."

Following the same direction, he went on for a few yards before turning back to the last print. Using it as a focal point, he walked ever-widening arcs, looking for another trace that someone—or something—had passed that way. His mind whirled with questions. Why males and not men? Why swords? Although both Jake and Jarvis had guns, it was clear that the blades were their primary weapons.

"I'm not finding anything. The ground gets rockier from here on out."

Jarvis muttered a string of obscenities. When Chase looked up, the dogs were sitting at the base of a limestone cliff and staring up toward the top. He walked over beside them and studied the rocky surface. The tops of a few stones were damp, as if they'd recently been disturbed. Again, an animal might have knocked them loose, but he didn't think so.

"If he went up there, he did it without any climbing equipment or the rocks would show fresh cuts." He felt Jake come up beside him. "Unless this male could fly?"

"No, he can't fly."

Jake scanned the cliff that towered thirty to forty feet above them. "Someone who knows what he's doing might be able to scale that without a bunch of equipment, but I think he probably had help."

Jarvis had been studying the ground past where they stood. "He either went up or he flew."

Chase snickered at the disgust in Jarvis's voice. "Jake just told me he couldn't fly."

"Yeah, we're done here."

Chase nodded and whistled the dogs back.

"Let's head for the farm. Gwen's bound to be frantic by now." Jarvis turned back to face him. "Chase, when we get there, we're going to need to get our story straight. It has to be something that makes sense but won't keep your sister up nights worrying."

"Okay." He gave it some thought. "How about a sick coyote? They're normally skittish around humans, but one that's sick or hurt might threaten the dogs."

"What would you do if you saw one?"

"Go after him with the dogs and our twenty-two."

"You wouldn't call in the authorities?"

"Not unless we thought it was rabid. If it's just been injured, we'd put it down. Doesn't happen often, but it wouldn't be the first time."

"Jake? Any thoughts?"

Jake shrugged. "I'm a city boy. Chase knows the area. Sounds reasonable to me. What would you do with the carcass?"

Chase didn't hesitate. "After we check in with Gwen, I'll come back with a shovel to bury it. I'll have to cover the spot with rocks to keep other animals from digging it up."

Jarvis patted him on the shoulder. "Good plan. Do you want the privilege of shooting our coyote? That knothole in that second tree to the left looks pretty vicious to me."

Just that quickly, the mood turned from deadly intent to black humor. Chase clicked off the safety and took aim with the compact automatic that Jarvis had given him. With a firm squeeze of the trigger, he hit the knot dead-on.

"Nice shot, but it might be playing possum. Maybe another shot to make sure." Jake held out his bigger gun.

Chase traded with him, making sure to engage the safety on his first. Holding Jake's gun in two hands, he finished the tree off, hitting it only about two inches from his first shot.

Afterward he put his hand over his heart. "A moment of silence, please, for the deceased."

Jake tried to cuff him as Chase danced back out of reach. Then he held his hand out for the gun. "Come on, brat, fork it over. We need to get back."

Chase reluctantly handed it over. It was a sweet little weapon.

On the way, Jarvis asked, "You sure Gwen won't want to see the body?"

"No, she has a soft heart for furry things. She'd pull the trigger herself if an animal is suffering, but she'll be relieved we took care of it."

Jarvis checked his watch. "Shit! Jake, we need to haul ass. We're going to be late."

The three of them picked up the pace, the dogs having already headed for home.

"I know you've got questions, Chase, but now isn't the time. How much longer until your birthday?

"About three weeks."

"After that, I have some people I'd like you to meet. Until then, we continue as we have. Fair enough?"

"It will have to be."

He tried not be disappointed, but it was hard. He'd really liked feeling like part of the team.

As if reading his mind, Jarvis gave him a commiserating look. "Give it time, Chase. It will be worth the wait."

He mulled that over as they walked back to the house. His gut told him that Jarvis was being honest with him. They clearly had answers for Chase. He just wondered what the questions were.

Chapter 13

$\mathcal{A}$s in most small towns, high school football was a community event, so the bleachers were crowded with friends and family. The team was gathered around the coach, getting last-minute instructions. Even without being able to see Chase's number, she could pick him out of the crowd of red-and-gold jerseys. Only one or two other boys even came close to his size.

It was hard to think of him as on the verge of manhood, but he was. Soon he'd be eighteen, legally an adult and able to make his own decisions. She'd been only two years older when she'd taken on the responsibility of raising him. They'd both come a long way.

The game was but minutes away, and still no sign of Jarvis. Reminding herself that she was here to support Chase, she forced herself to stop watching the parking lot for his car. He'd said he come if he could. She shivered, hoping he and his buddy Jake were safe.

The team captains walked out to the center of the field with the refs for the coin toss. The visitors' side cheered when their side got first choice. The home team defense put on their helmets and ran out onto the field as everyone held their breath for the kickoff. The teams lined up and as the ball flew through the air, the game was on.

On the second play, Chase knocked down the pass and one of his teammates snagged it for an interception. She and everyone else around her leapt to their feet, cheering at the top of their lungs.

When she sat back down, a familiar voice said, "Glad I didn't miss that."

Her heart skipped a beat as she beamed at Jarvis. "Me, too."

"Sorry I'm late. Things took longer than I expected." He had his eyes on the field, but his arm snaked around her shoulders to pull her close.

She had to ask. "Is Jake okay, too?"

"He's fine."

When the play ended, Jarvis turned to face her, his dark eyes serious. "It's sweet of you to worry, but I wish you wouldn't. You know better than most how resilient the two of us are."

"Yes, but that doesn't mean you don't hurt."

He turned away, a strange expression on his

face, making her wonder what he was thinking as
he watched the game. The offense was moving
steadily down the field. Chase was walking up and
down the sideline, his helmet in his hand. When he
looked up toward the stands, Jarvis waved.

Her brother's immediate response was to grin
and wave back, but then he frowned. Clearly he
was not happy about something, but then his team
scored, and he got caught up in the celebration on
the sidelines.

When the crowd quieted down, she said, "I
wonder what's up with him."

"I suspect he's happy I came to the game, but
he's not sure he likes me being with you." He gave
her a small squeeze.

So Chase hadn't liked seeing Jarvis's arm around
her. Well, that was too bad. She liked keeping Jarvis
as close to her as possible.

"He needs to get over that."

"He might have a problem with anyone you
bring home, at least until he decides the guy's not
going to hurt you. Considering what happened to
his father, Chase probably figures I'm a bad risk."
He softened the comment with a smile, but it didn't
reach his eyes.

The regret she heard in his words hurt. She
didn't know which one she wanted to throttle more:
her brother for trying to interfere, or the good man
sitting next to her who thought so little of himself.

She caught his chin with her hand, forcing him to look at her. "He's wrong. And so are you, Jarvis Donahue. You've been up-front with me about what you can offer me and what you can't. A lesser man would have lied just so he could get in my . . ." Then she remembered where they were. "Good graces. Get in my good graces."

The devilish twinkle was back in Jarvis's eyes. "I can't remember when I enjoyed being in someone's good graces quite so much."

"Behave!" she hissed.

The trouble with being a fair-skinned redhead was that she blushed so easily. It didn't help that he took one look at her face and laughed before planting a quick kiss on her mouth.

"Watch the game!"

"Yes, ma'am. Anything to stay in your, uh, good graces."

His eyes made a quick trip up and down her body, telling her exactly which graces he had in mind.

Turning her attention to the football field, she watched her brother's team fight the good fight and walk away with the victory.

As Gwen waited to congratulate her brother, Jarvis tried to think of the last time he'd had so much fun. He still chuckled every time he thought about Gwen and her good graces. They'd have only the few minutes' drive back to the farm alone, which was disappointing, but he needed to tread carefully around Chase.

If the boy had problems with Jarvis's arm being around Gwen, he'd take it very badly to find Jarvis at the breakfast table tomorrow morning. Nothing was ever simple.

"After you talk to Chase, want to go somewhere for a while? Maybe get a bite to eat?" Anything to keep her to himself for as long as possible.

"I've got sandwich makings at home, if that's okay."

"That would be good, too." If that was the only way he could extend their time together, he'd settle for sharing her with Chase.

Several of the football players came filing out of the locker room, and Gwen waved to get her brother's attention. He made his way through the throng with a trash bag in his hand.

Jarvis moved up beside them. "Great game, Chase. That was a heck of a play when you batted that pass down to your teammate. I bet your coach was happy."

Chase ducked his head, looking embarrassed at all the attention. "Yeah, he may have mentioned it a time or two."

Gwen gave her brother a quick hug. "Well, we're proud of you, too."

Jordan yelled from across the hall, "Hey, Chase? The dance is starting."

"Yeah, I'll be right there." He handed the bag to Gwen. "Here's my uniform. Thanks for taking it home for me."

"You're welcome. The dance ends at midnight, so you'll be home by one?"

"I told Jordan I'd give him a ride, so that sounds about right. I'll call if it's going to be later."

"Okay. Have fun and we'll see you when you get home."

Chase's good mood dimmed. He looked over Gwen's head to stare down Jarvis. "You'll still be there?"

"That depends on your sister, and whether or not I get called in." In other words, Chase had no say in the matter.

Gwen put her hand on Chase's chest, forcing him to pay attention to her. "We'll probably watch a movie and make popcorn. I've got one of my mushy chick flicks already picked out. You go have fun with your friends."

Chase snickered and met Jarvis's gaze. "Enjoy your movie. But keep a box of tissues handy; she likes real tearjerkers." Then he was gone.

As they walked out of the school, Jarvis asked, "You were kidding about the movie, weren't you?"

Gwen grinned. "We might get around to it—but I thought you might enjoy getting into my good graces first."

Watching her laugh as she skipped ahead of

him, Jarvis was pretty sure his tongue was hanging out. He tried not to trip over it as he followed her to the car.

With Chase's eighteenth birthday almost upon them, their time together was running out, making Jarvis a desperate man. He and Gwen had seen each other a handful of times over the past two weeks, but never alone. As in getting naked, hot and sweaty, mind-blowing sex alone. The situation was killing him. The stolen kisses and full-body-press hugs were great, but all they did was throw gas on the fire.

But today he had a plan. He pasted an innocent look on his face as he pulled into the driveway in the middle of the afternoon, not wanting to scare Gwen with the intensity of his need. Nor did he want to set off all those protective urges Chase was prone to.

He'd decided that a picnic along a private stretch of a river was just the ticket. A blanket, a bottle of wine, and skinny-dipping all added up to a perfect afternoon. He hoped Gwen would think so, too.

Gwen stepped out on the porch, looking pleased but surprised to see him. Good. She came straight into his arms.

"I wasn't expecting you. What's up?"

He decided not to point out the obvious if she hadn't noticed it for herself. "Grab your swimsuit. I got the afternoon off and don't want to waste a minute of it."

Bless her, she didn't hesitate or stop to ask questions. "I'll leave Chase a note."

Score!

So far, so good.

The screen door slammed open, and Gwen came out carrying a beach bag and wearing a smile. Another quick kiss, and they were off and running.

Twenty minutes later, he turned off the state highway. The road ahead was unmarked and not on any maps. "My friend owns this place and said we could use it this afternoon. I wanted you to myself, and this is as private as he can make it."

Actually, the Regents used it for training new recruits, both Paladins and guards, but there weren't any classes going on today. After another half mile, the road came to an abrupt halt right at the edge of the water. From there, a narrow foot bridge would take them to the trail on the other side.

"We're here. I'll grab the picnic basket out of the back."

She took his hand as they crossed the river into the woods. "This is lovely, Jarvis."

After a short walk they reached their destination, a wide spot where the river pooled deep enough for swimming. He spread the blanket out on the grassy bank and set the basket down.

Gwen looked around. "Where do I change into my suit?"

He grinned. "I'm only going to strip it off you as fast as you put it on."

Her answering smile was all he could have wished for. "Better move that blanket into the shade, then. No use in getting sunburned in awkward places."

The woman knew how to get a picnic off to a perfect start. And he planned on making the most of each minute they had left to them, hoping to build enough memories to last a lifetime.

Jake shifted in the Chevelle's front seat. "Chase has been looking forward to this day for weeks. I guess now that he's eighteen, he gets to register for the nonexistent draft and to vote."

"That's why Gwen invited us to the celebration. He's officially a man." It was also the beginning of the end for him and Gwen.

"You know, I don't think I've ever been to a birthday party." Jake seemed oblivious to Jarvis's mood as he reached for the radio.

"Touch that button and I'll break your fingers."

His friend sank back in the seat. "This may

come as a surprise to you, but music didn't die in the seventies. There are whole decades of music you've never heard."

"I've heard it. I just don't like it."

"You're showing your age, old man."

Hmm. Considering Gwen was closer to Jake's age, maybe he should try listening to something more current. He pushed a button and country western filled the car.

Jake covered his ears and moaned dramatically. "I surrender: Put the oldies station back on; I won't complain."

Jarvis laughed and turned the radio off. "We're almost there anyway."

"Thanks. But back to the party. What did you get him? My dad gave me a new sword for my eighteenth birthday, but you couldn't very well do that. Not around Gwen, anyway."

"No, although I thought about it." He flexed his hands on the steering wheel to ease his tension. "Gwen and I went together on his present. She thought it was time he had his own truck, so I helped her pick one out. My part is to help him tune the engine, along with a gift certificate to the auto parts store. I thought he'd get a kick out of doing the work himself."

Jake fiddled with the envelope in his hands. "Great idea. I know he's a big Rams fan, so I bought him tickets to one of the games."

"He'll love that. Should make for some happy memories for his birthday."

Jake turned serious. "Now that he's eighteen, are you going to bring him to the Center for training?"

"Yeah. Tomorrow is the big day, unless he changes his mind."

"You actually think he'd turn down the chance to finally see what we do for a living? He's been champing at the bit to find out ever since we started training him."

No, he wouldn't back out, and Jarvis knew his duty was to introduce Chase to his future. There was satisfaction in knowing that they helped make the world safer for everyone, even if no one outside the organization had any idea the battles the Paladins fought.

But he had this awful premonition that the minute he took Chase to see the barrier, the death knell would start ringing for him and Gwen.

"Hey, buddy, don't go all glum on me. We're going to a party, not a funeral."

"She'll hate me when she finds out what's in store for her brother."

"I hate to point out the obvious, but that woman has some powerfully strong feelings for you, old man. Even Chase has made peace with the idea of you and his sister being involved long-term."

Jarvis's temper exploded. "And how fucking well do you think *that's* going to work out, Jake? Are you looking forward to being the one to break the news to her that I'm dead?"

His friend flinched. "Hell, no. Are you crazy?"

"No, but I will be, and then I'll be dead. Have fun with Gwen at my funeral."

He could have cut the silence with a sword. He fought to control the anger boiling through his blood. "Look, I'm sorry, Jake. I didn't mean to take your head off."

After a bit, Jake looked at him. "It doesn't have to be that way, Jarvis. Look at your buddy Trahern and Brenna, and Devlin Bane and his Handler. Maybe things are changing for us. No point in digging a grave when you might not need it for a long time to come."

That idea tasted a little too much like hope. But the jury was still out on how long those relationships would last. And neither one had a complication like Chase to deal with.

He slowed to turn into the driveway. As he pulled in, Jake had the last say.

"Let it go, Jarvis. No one can foresee the future. You've got something pretty special going. Don't throw it away on the chance that something might go wrong."

Jarvis had arrived at the house looking more grim than usual, which worried her. With the help of Chase and Jake, he'd soon shaken off the gloom-

and-doom attitude. Her brother was so buzzed about his birthday, it would have taken a lot more than Jarvis to dampen his enthusiasm. He kept giving her a hopeful look, asking without words if it was time for presents.

She smiled. When it came to unwrapping presents, he still had a lot of little kid in him. Hopefully he'd manage to hold onto that excitement for years to come.

"Okay, birthday boy, do you want pie or presents first?"

There was no hesitation. "Presents!"

"Lead the way into the living room. You can start in there."

Chase started to charge out of the kitchen, but then he stopped and waited for his two guests to go first. Jarvis shot her a bemused look before following Jake down the hallway, and the four of them settled around the room. She perched on the arm of the couch next to Jarvis and watched her brother try to hide his disappointment at the small pile on the coffee table. She supposed that at eighteen, two envelopes and a small box didn't look like much.

Jake snagged one of the envelopes and tossed it at Chase. "Happy Birthday, brat!"

"Thanks, Jake."

Chase pulled out a pocketknife to slit open the envelope. He quickly scanned the card and then opened the smaller envelope inside. Two tickets fell into his hand. He stared at them in shocked silence, then his face lit up as he turned toward her and held them up.

"All *right*! Rams tickets!" Then he studied them again. "Jake! Who did you have to kill to get these?"

"Chase! I taught you better manners than that."

"They're in the first row on the fifty-yard line, Sis."

She could understand her brother's reaction. She turned a suspicious eye in Jake's direction. "Okay, like he said. Who did you have to kill?"

He gave them both a pirate's grin. "That'll be my secret. I wouldn't want you to have to testify against me if the case ever comes to trial."

Chase carefully put the precious tickets in his wallet before reaching for the next card. She and Jarvis had debated over what order they should have Chase open their two gifts. He was bound to think a gift certificate to an auto parts store was a pretty boring, practical gift until he found out it was so that he could work on his own truck. But if they gave him the keys first, he'd hardly notice Jarvis's gift. They'd settled on letting Chase make his own random decision. It didn't take long for him to fish the gift card out of the envelope.

The enthusiasm he'd shown for Jake's tickets was missing when he politely said, "Thanks, Jarvis. The truck could use some new shocks."

Jarvis gave him a solemn nod. "You're welcome."

Then Chase reached for the small package and the card from her. Despite the simple wrapping and stick-on bow, Chase took a great deal of time peeling away the paper. When he held the small box up to his ear and shook it, he frowned at the rattle it made.

Jake's patience broke. "Come on, Chase, open it! At the rate you're going, we'll still be sitting here when you turn nineteen. Besides, I want pie."

Chase lifted off the lid, then tipped the contents into his hand. His eyes locked on to the pair of keys, his expression someplace between hope and confusion. He slowly raised his gaze to meet Gwen's. When she nodded, his eyes went wide in shock.

"Where? What?"

The two men laughed and Jarvis clapped him on the shoulder. "I thought that gift card might help you with your sister's present. Why don't you head for Mr. James's farm with Jake to see what that key fits?"

"Man oh man!" Chase stood immediately, jingling the keys.

Jarvis tossed the keys to the Chevelle to his friend.

"Thanks, Sis! You, too, Jarvis!"

As Chase charged out to the car, Jake looked back and rolled his eyes.

Jarvis waited until the car was out of sight before pulling her into his arms—right where she wanted to be.

"You certainly made your brother's day." He nuzzled her neck. "Think we could send him and Jake on a long drive?"

"I wish. But as soon as they get back here with his truck, you know all three of you are going to spend the rest of the evening with your heads under the hood, making plans to get all greasy together."

"True enough. But you know I'd rather spend the time with you."

Then he kissed her, curling her toes and making her want to drag him over to the kitchen table. She used her hands and her tongue to tell him exactly what she wanted, until they heard the crunch of gravel as his car and Chase's truck made the turn into the driveway.

They broke apart when Chase came bounding across the yard to sweep her up in his arms and swing her around. He was hollering loud enough to raise the dead, and the dogs joined in the celebration by barking and jumping up and down.

Chase set her back down. "It's perfect, Gwen! I couldn't have done better myself. Hey, Jarvis, thanks for helping her. Can we go look at the engine now?"

Just as she predicted, the three males immediately disappeared under the hood to admire the arcane mysteries of the combustion engine. It was good for Chase to have two such men to hang with and learn from. Despite the secrets that surrounded them, they were good influences on Chase.

His volatile temper had dropped to a more manageable level, and just knowing that he wasn't the only one with his amazing ability to heal had gone a long way toward helping him to feel like less of a freak.

Tomorrow, the two men were taking Chase to visit the place where they normally trained. Her brother had jumped at the chance. Between that and his birthday, it was a big weekend for him.

She took one last look at Jarvis's backside before heading into the house, heartily approving of the way he looked in well-worn denim. She liked him a whole lot better naked, but there wasn't any chance of that happening with Jake and Chase around. Maybe they could fit in an evening walk in the woods before he and Jake had to head home.

Meanwhile, there was pile of dirty dishes waiting for her. As she waited for the sink to fill with water, she puzzled over Jarvis's odd mood when he'd arrived. Something had been bothering him, but there hadn't been any chance to ask him about it. He seemed to be better, but more than once she'd caught him looking at her with a strange, almost sad look in his eyes. The last time had sent a shiver through her while at the same time making her want to hold him close.

It probably had to do with his job, so all she could do was make sure he could relax and enjoy himself while he was with her. Satisfied with her plan, she set out dessert dishes and clean forks. If she wasn't mistaken, the guys had just slammed the hood down on Chase's truck. Time to cut the pie.

What was going on? When they'd invited him to go visit their gym, neither Jarvis nor Jake had made mention of blindfolds. How long had they been riding around? It seemed like forever.

"Jarvis, is this some kind of joke? Are you driving in circles to make me think we're really going somewhere, but we're really only a mile from the farm?"

He cocked his head to the side, trying to detect some familiar sound over the blare of the radio. Jarvis had picked him up right after breakfast, telling Gwen that they'd be back after dinner. A short distance down the road, he'd pulled over on the shoulder of the road and ordered Chase into the backseat and handed him a black scarf. After telling him to tie it over his eyes, Jarvis had peeled out and proceeded to drive without a single word of explanation.

"No joke, Chase. I apologize about the blindfold, but it's necessary." The car made a slow left turn. "We're almost there."

"Almost where? I thought we were going to some gym where you and Jake train." Though he normally trusted Jarvis, right now he felt as if he were being kidnapped.

"We are. You're safe with us, Chase, but I can't let you know exactly where we're headed. For now, it's against the rules."

"*Whose* rules? You make it sound like we're headed for some top secret government installation." But what kind of government agency armed its agents with swords?

"You're not far off the mark, except we're in the private sector. I promise to explain everything in a few minutes. Right now it would only confuse you more."

Damn straight he was confused. Could things get any more bizarre? The car slowed abruptly, slinging him forward against the seat belt, and he grabbed the armrest. Wait till he told Gwen about all this weirdness.

The car lurched to the side as the road surface changed to gravel, which explained the sudden reduction in speed.

He tried to count off seconds to judge how far they were traveling along the mysterious road. They hadn't passed another car in a long time, so the main highway was pretty far back. Whoever ran this mysterious facility sure didn't want close neighbors. Why? What did they have to hide?

The car slowed to a stop. "You can take the blindfold off now, Chase. And I'm sorry that I had to do that to you."

Chase yanked the scarf off his face and blinked against the bright morning sun. They'd stopped just shy of a high chain-link fence with a double coil of barbed wire running along the top. A uniformed guard stepped out of the small building next to a closed gate. Evidently he recognized Jarvis's car since he left his automatic rifle slung casually over his shoulder.

Jarvis twisted around to face him. "The security is necessary, but don't let it weird you out. Jake's expecting us, so you'll be with friends the whole time you're here. But I can take you back home now if you're not ready for this."

Chase gave it less than a second's thought. There was something pulling at him, and whatever it was felt important, making him want to find out what the big mystery was. They were the only two men he'd ever met that had the same physical abilities he did. Maybe there were more like them behind that fence.

"I'm ready. Let's go."

"One more thing, Chase. I must have your promise that you tell no one what you're going to learn here today. Not your friends, not your teachers, and especially not your sister. You'll understand the need for all the secrecy before you leave here today, but you need to promise before we can go through that gate."

The only other time he'd seen Jarvis look that grim was the day they'd tracked the mysterious footprints through the woods. Both he and Jake had looked like those highly trained military guys as soon as they'd picked up their weapons. He wanted some of that action for himself.

Jarvis was asking him for his word man-to-man, and he liked the feel of that. "You have my word, Jarvis. Everything I see here today will be kept secret."

"Good."

Jarvis rolled down his window and waved at the guard, who immediately pushed the button to open the gate. They drove through and headed for an unmarked building across the parking lot. Jake must have been watching for them, because he stepped out the door and waited for them to park.

"Hey, kid, welcome to our little corner of the world!"

He held the door open for them and then followed them into the mysterious building. Jarvis keyed a series of numbers into a security pad by an elevator door. After they stepped inside, the three of them rode down in silence. A flock of butterflies fluttered in Chase's stomach, making him feel queasy, but he tried to look as calm as his companions.

He had the strangest feeling that this would be life-altering. For good or for bad, he wouldn't be the same kid when he took this elevator back up to the top.

Chapter 14

*J*arvis kept his eyes straight ahead, allowing Chase some privacy. The boy was doing a damn fine job of hiding his nerves, even though Jarvis could hear the pounding of his heart racing and the shallow rasp of his breathing.

The cave could wait. Before he exposed Chase to the beautiful bitch that would rule the rest of his life, he wanted to explain things and introduce him to some of the other Paladins. The kid had enough to absorb without showing him the door to another world first.

"My office is down this hall."

Chase kept pace with him, his eyes open wide as he took in the strange surroundings. "How far underground are we?"

Good question. Jarvis had wondered if he'd realized how long the elevator ride had taken.

"About four floors. There's another one below this."

Chase reached out to drag his fingertips along the limestone wall. "Cool."

Inside the office, Jarvis sat behind his desk and motioned Chase toward one of the two chairs that faced it. The boy perched on the edge, too wound-up to relax.

"Jake, why don't you snag us something to drink and a few sandwiches? I don't know about Chase here, but breakfast was hours ago and lunch is still a ways away."

"Sure thing." He patted Chase on the shoulder. "I'll be back in a couple."

Jarvis propped his feet up on his desk, trying to project a relaxed image, as if he wasn't about to turn Chase's idea of reality inside out. "Okay, I guess this is where we get down to the nitty-gritty. A lot of what I'm going to say will sound crazy, especially at first, but I promise I'm not yanking your chain. I'll answer any questions you might have, but let me give you the basics first. Does that sound reasonable?"

"Yeah, I guess." Chase leaned forward, his elbows on his knees. "I feel like I should take notes in case there's a test."

Jarvis chuckled. "I promise no pop quizzes. So, here it is in a nutshell. You probably know that Missouri is chock-full of caves, and this installation is parked right on top of one of the biggest. It's not on any maps, and we work hard to keep it that way. What makes it special is that there's an energy barrier that runs through it that separates our world from another one."

Chase's jaw dropped and then his eyes narrowed, clearly not buying what he heard. It was a typical reaction by those who hadn't been raised around their Paladin fathers.

"I know it sounds crazy, but I'm not asking you to accept everything on faith. I'll go over the basics, we'll eat something, and then we'll take a tour. Once you see the barrier and talk to some of the rest of the guys around here, you'll find this all easier to accept."

Jake arrived with a tray piled high with food. As he set it down on Jarvis's desk, he grinned at Chase.

"Judging by the look on your face, he told you about the barrier and the world on the other side of it. Do you feel like you wandered onto the set of *The X-Files*?"

"Kind of."

Jake tossed him a can of pop. "And the Paladins' world only gets weirder." He took the other chair and grabbed a sandwich.

Chase opened a bag of chips. "What's a Paladin?"

"They're some of the toughest sons of bitches on this planet. Paladins are natural-born warriors, and damn near impossible to kill." Jarvis bit into his apple, giving Chase a chance to absorb that much. After swallowing, he added, "And just like me and Jake, that's what you are."

His pronouncement startled Chase into choking. Jake slapped him on the back and handed him the pop he'd set down.

"You following me so far?"

Chase took another drink and nodded. His voice sounded rough when he spoke. "Let's see. There's a cave below us that backs up on another world, and we're natural-born warriors and the toughest sons of bitches around."

Jake beamed with approval. "Nice summary, kid."

Jarvis dropped his boots back to the ground as he unwrapped his sandwich. "The barrier isn't always stable, and waiting right on the other side is a bunch of crazed killers we call the Others, although they call themselves the Kalith. Every time there's an earthquake, the barrier gets weaker and weaker until it fails completely. Then the crazies come charging over. Our job is to shove 'em back across to their world, or kill the ones who insist on staying on our side."

Chase drained his pop and set it aside. "And how long has this been going on?"

The kid was holding up better than Jarvis had expected.

"Good question. Wish I had an answer for you. The Regents, who are like a board of directors over our organization, have records going back for several centuries. Chances are, there were Others leaking over into our world for a helluva long time before that."

"And where did the Paladins come from?"

"As far as we can tell, Kalith have occasionally managed to come across and jump into the human gene pool. We're the result. I forgot to mention that the Others are a humanoid species, capable of mating with *Homo sapiens* and producing viable young. They've left a mark on the Paladin genetic makeup, passing along a few of their traits, although some of our abilities seem to be unique to us."

"Why do they want to come here?"

"We've learned more about that in the past few months. Seems their sun is dying, so their world is getting darker. The ones who can't tolerate that go nuts and try to fight their way into our world for the light."

Jarvis thought of Barak q'Young, the first Other to become a part of the Paladin organization. He still thought Devlin Bane was nuts for letting the bastard live, but the rumor was that he was no longer the only one of his kind attached to the Seattle Paladins.

Chase brought him back to the moment. "So besides healing fast, what other superpowers do we have? I hope it doesn't involve tights and a cape."

"Nope, no spandex or big red *P* on your chest." He admired the boy's ability to roll with the punches. "But all of your senses are better than the average human's. When you fill out to fit that frame of yours, you'll be stronger, too. And when I said Paladins were hard to kill, what I really meant is that even if someone does manage to kill one of us, we don't usually stay that way."

Right up to that point, Chase had been liking what he was hearing. "Bullshit! What happens then? Do we turn into zombies?"

Jake said, "He's telling the truth, Chase. Remember the night your sister found Jarvis out in your woods? He'd been tracking down an escaped Other by himself. Normally we hunt in pairs, but the fighting had been brutal. I couldn't back him up because I was dead. I had two broken legs and a fatal stab wound."

He pulled up his shirt to show Chase the faint trace of a scar that ran from the center of his stomach around to his left side. "It's not the first time I've died, and it won't be the last. We don't exactly keep score, but Jarvis rates as a legend around here."

Damn, Jarvis wished Jake wouldn't say things like that. Even if the younger Paladins felt that way about him, that didn't mean he liked being reminded of it. When a Paladin had been around long enough to become a legend, he was probably running out of the ability to come back from the abyss intact. Jarvis's chances for surviving death anymore were running from slim to none—but now wasn't the time to share that with Chase. He had enough to assimilate without knowing the nightmare his life would become one of these days.

"And my father, he was a Paladin, too?"

"Yes, he was. Harvey Fletcher lived and fought in this area. From what I've been able to find out, he must have died shortly after your mother got pregnant. My guess is that no one in the organization knew about her, so she was never notified of his death. I'm truly sorry about that." He reached in his drawer and pulled out copies of the pictures he'd given to Gwen.

He held them out to Chase. "You look a lot like him."

The boy's hands were unsteady as he studied his father's face for the first time. "Does my sister know about this?"

Jarvis nodded and tried to choose his words carefully. "She wasn't sure whether or not to show you."

Chase's knuckles went white as he held the papers in a death grip. "She should have given them to me as soon as she had them. Why didn't one of *you* two show them to me, especially when it became clear she wasn't going to?"

"Because until yesterday, she was your legal

guardian. Now that you're eighteen, you can make more of your own decisions." And because Jarvis didn't want to lose her one minute before he had to, but that was his problem and not Chase's.

"Later you can look at the file that Jake assembled for you. Right now, I'd like to introduce you to some people before heading down to the barrier." He wadded up the wrappers from the sandwiches and tossed them in the trash, while Chase and Jake did the same.

"Why don't we start in the gym and go from there?"

Chase followed his two friends, trying his best to act like he fit in. But holy crap, it was hard to know what to think about everything Jarvis had told him. At first he'd been convinced the man was jerking his chain, but something in Jarvis's expression said he was down-to-the-bone serious about aliens and other worlds and dying but not dying. And Jake had confirmed every word Jarvis had said.

They were currently walking down a hallway carved out of limestone in an underground chamber located beneath an unmarked building. Memories of the armed guards and the coils of bright, shiny barbed wire were all too clear. If they were pulling a fast one on him, they'd sure gone through a lot of trouble for a joke.

They hadn't crossed paths with anyone else

since they'd entered the building. They were sup-
posedly on their way to meet with some other Paladins, but if there were any around, they were sure
making themselves scarce. What the heck *was* a
Paladin, anyway? The word had something to do
with knights. Was that why Jarvis and Jake carried
swords?

The silence was getting on his nerves, so he decided to ask, "Do you use swords because the word
'Paladin' means some kind of knight?"

It was Jake who answered. "I've always suspected that we're called Paladins because the origi-
nal ones were knights of some kind. But the reason
we use swords more than guns is because bullets
can damage the barrier. We can control blades better than bullets that miss their targets. Besides, we
often fight in close formation. We'd end up shooting each other as often as the enemy."

How could they be so matter-of-fact about killing and fighting? And if they were right about him
being one of them, is that how he would sound in
a few years? The shiver that went through him had
nothing to do with the chill of the underground
cave.

Then the muffled sound of voices and the clang
of metal on metal echoed down the hallway. Finally,
he was going to see some action.

"Here we are." Jarvis pushed open the double
swinging doors. "Come on in."

Chase had been picturing the gym at the high school, with a basketball court surrounded by wooden bleachers. This place looked more like the health club that opened in the next town over. There were all kinds of muscle-building machines lining the walls, gym mats here and there on the floor, and a long rack of swords hanging at the far end. And were those really axes those two guys were swinging? Hot damn, they were!

The clanging noise came from men who'd paired up for sword practice. Having a little experience now, he could only imagine how long these guys had been practicing to get that good.

Jarvis stuck his fingers in his mouth and let out a shrill whistle that brought everything to an abrupt halt. Everybody immediately lowered their weapons or stepped off the equipment, turning their attention toward the three of them. Chase fought the urge to slide behind Jarvis and Jake to hide.

Jarvis's big hand clamped down on his shoulder, either in a show of his support or to keep him from bolting out the door. The touch gave Chase enough courage to stand up to the open curiosity coming at him in waves.

"Gentlemen," Jarvis announced, pitching his voice to carry to the far corners, "I'd like to introduce you all to my friend Chase Mosely. For those of you old enough to remember, his father was Harvey Fletcher."

That pronouncement brought several men to full attention. A couple of them immediately handed off their swords to their companions and started toward Chase with big smiles on their faces.

The first one to reach him held out his hand and said, "Welcome to the clan, Chase. Your old man and I were good friends. It's damn nice to meet you. My name is Court."

His companion followed suit. "I'm Terry. Harvey was a helluva Paladin, one of the best. He taught me how to fight when I first got here. You're sure the spitting image of him."

"Thank you, sir." A lump formed in his throat to hear these men's obvious affection for his late father. He'd only just found out about Harvey, but their comments helped make the man in the faded pictures more real.

Terry glanced at Jarvis and then back to Chase. "So are you here to stay, or only visiting?"

"Visiting." At least he assumed so. Jarvis hadn't said anything about keeping him here.

"Chase turned eighteen yesterday. Jake and I have been working with him at the farm he shares with his sister, but we thought it was time to give him a peek at our world."

"Great." Terry yelled back over his shoulder. "Someone get this guy a sword. Let's see what bad habits he's picked up from these two. Knowing

Jake's lack of technique, we probably have our work cut out for us."

Jake snorted. "Go to hell, Terry. I'll let Chase see how old men fight, then I'll take over."

While the good-natured insults continued, Chase turned to Jarvis for guidance. "Should I?"

"Go ahead, Chase. You'll dazzle them." He walked away, stripping off his shirt as Jake did the same. The two of them picked swords from the rack and started hacking away at each other.

Even more than before, he felt like he'd been cut adrift from the normal world. He tossed his shirt over with the others and accepted the blade Terry held out to him.

They saluted each other, and then the fight was on.

The house felt empty. Gwen spent a lot of time alone, but it normally didn't bother her. Today felt different, though she couldn't put her finger on why. Maybe because Chase was normally home on Sundays during the school year. Other than the necessary chores, they always took it easier on Sundays, spending the day watching television while she knitted and he caught up on homework.

But he'd gone charging out the door this morning as soon as Jarvis had pulled into the driveway, and the two of them had waved good-bye from the car. If she was honest, she'd admit that it had hurt her feelings a little that Jarvis hadn't even taken the time to come in for a cup of coffee or a quick kiss. Instead, he'd looked more distracted than happy to see her standing on the porch to watch them leave.

What was going on with him? Granted, it had been a while since they'd had more than a few minutes alone. She'd been planning to ask if he wanted to take an overnight trip together, but she'd never gotten him by himself long enough to ask. It was almost as if he didn't want to be alone with her.

Which *really* hurt. Worse yet, she'd found herself resenting the time he was spending with Chase. It was an awful thing to be jealous of her own brother, but she was. Did that make her a rotten sister? She suspected it did.

Dozer whined in his sleep, his feet twitching as he chased varmints in his dreams. She smiled as she stepped over him, and he lifted his head long enough to blink before going back to sleep. Even Larry was content to lie in the shade of a bush. The day wasn't all that hot, but there wasn't even a breath of a breeze.

She sought out the sanctuary of her workshop. After flipping on the light switch and the overhead fan to stir the air, she propped the door open in case the dogs wanted to join her. Pulling out her desk chair, she sat down to boot up her computer. Her in-box had a satisfying number of new orders for yarn and patterns. If her small Internet business continued to expand, she'd soon have enough money for a down payment on a new truck.

It wasn't much of a cushion, but it felt good to have that much without having to sell off any of her herd. Of course, she might need the money for Chase's schooling next fall. So far she hadn't been able to talk him into registering for the local community college; he told her he wanted to get a job and work for a while before he decided what he wanted to do with his life.

It didn't seem like all that long ago that she'd been his age, with a world of possibilities open to her. Then her mother had died and all those choices had narrowed down to one. Although she'd never regretted her decision, she wanted more for him.

Dozer stuck his nose in the door and whined as he waited for a formal invitation. She pulled a doggy treat out of the bag she kept in the desk drawer and held it out. He crossed the floor to take it from her fingers then settled under the ceiling fan before crunching down on his prize.

She counted off the seconds, figuring Larry would need about twenty from the sound of the first crunch to come charging in to get his fair share. He made it in nineteen. Thank goodness for their undemanding company.

Now that they were settled in, she started printing out the orders and the shipping labels. Paperwork was her least favorite part of the business, so she always got it out of the way before rewarding herself with spinning wool or designing new patterns.

Anything to keep her hands and mind occupied and off Jarvis and her brother, but it was hard. Instead of heeding Jarvis's warnings about how he wasn't a forever kind of guy, she'd let herself get used to him being a part of her life. There was something about him being around that felt so right.

Maybe that had more to do with the lack of eligible men in her social circle, but she didn't think so. From that first night when she'd dragged him home half dead and bloody, she'd felt a special connection to him. Even if it was because she'd helped save his life, he'd taken up residence in her heart. That he was such a positive influence over her brother just earned him bonus points.

Drat, there she went again. Mooning over the man and not getting anything done. Maybe music would help. She put in a couple of CDs and hummed along with the songs as she started filling the orders so she could ship them first thing in the morning.

As long as she kept busy, maybe she wouldn't feel like she was rattling around in an empty cage. Darn Jarvis for making her feel lonely, instead of just alone.

• • •

Chase collapsed on a stack of mats and leaned his elbows on his knees, hoping his heart wouldn't give out before his lungs caught up on oxygen. He thought he'd done well enough with his sword work not to be a complete embarrassment to Jarvis and Jake. But judging by the bruises on his arms and back, he still had a long way to go before he caught up to Paladin standards.

He watched Jarvis take on two Paladins at once, his moves so smooth and fast that it was hard to follow them. Every so often he'd call a halt to the proceedings to repeat a maneuver for the other two, going in slow motion so that they could duplicate it. Then he'd show them how to counter it as well. Chase tried to memorize the instructions so he could try out a few of the moves next time he got a chance.

Jake joined him on the mat and watched the match for a few seconds before speaking. "No matter how hard I try, I can't duplicate his moves. The only one I've seen come close is his buddy Trahern, one of the Seattle Paladins who was here awhile back. Everybody always stopped what they were doing to watch the two of them go at it. Then the bastards challenged all of us at the same time, and they still came out on top."

"I'd like to have seen that."

"It was amazing—though I try not to bolster Jarvis's ego any more than I have to."

Jake grinned, but then his smile disappeared. "Oh shit."

Chase tore his gaze away from the match. A man in a wheelchair had entered the gym, his movements awkward as he tried to maneuver the chair through the heavy door. Even from this distance, it was easy to tell he'd been badly hurt. Chase watched as he slowly rolled across the floor, skirting the other Paladins. The closer he got to where they were sitting, the worse he looked.

"What happened to him?" Chase thought he'd whispered the question, but the man's head immediately jerked in their direction and he pinned Chase with an angry gaze. Obviously Jarvis had been serious about Paladin senses being better than the average human's.

Jake didn't bother to keep his voice down. "Others caught up with Hunter in one of the outlying caverns. They played with him for a long time before leaving him for dead. He looks a damn sight better than he did when we first found him."

The man parked his chair a few feet away from them. From the sweat pouring off his face, the effort had taken a lot out of him. Every square inch of skin that showed was that sickly green of old bruises. If he looked good now, Chase was glad he hadn't seen him before.

"Hey, Hunter, I'm going to get Chase and myself a bottle of water. Can I bring you one, too?"

"No."

"Pop?"

"No."

"Anything else?"

"No." Hunter's fists clenched and unclenched. "Just leave me alone."

"Fine. Chase, I'll be back in a minute." Jake loped off toward a cooler in the corner.

Hunter turned in Chase's direction. His voice was a rough whisper. "Have you looked your fill, kid, or would you like me to pirouette in case you missed anything?"

Chase's face burned hot and then cold. "I'm sorry, sir. I didn't meant to stare."

"Yeah, right. Just like all those cars that slow down as they pass a bad accident aren't hoping to see something gruesome to tell all their friends."

He'd already apologized; what else could he say? Chase was relieved to see both Jake and Jarvis on their way toward them. Jarvis made it first.

"Hunter, it's good to see you up and about. I assume Doc Crosby okayed your being down here." He wiped his face with a towel and accepted his shirt back from Chase.

"I don't need or want his approval. There's nothing more he can do for me up in the lab." He glared up at Jarvis from his chair.

Bitterness and pain dripped from every word, making Chase want to put some serious distance between himself and the angry Paladin. He must have made some move in that direction, because Jarvis caught his eye and shook his head.

"I don't blame you for wanting a break from the lab, Hunter, but we both know the rules. No one leaves the lab without Doc's permission. Overdoing it won't help you heal any faster."

"Like I'm going to heal at all. From what Doc says, I'll be lucky to get even eighty percent of my mobility back." Hunter's voice cracked. Abruptly, he spun the chair around and started back toward the door. Several of the other Paladins approached him, but he waved them off.

Jarvis's gaze followed his progress before turning back to Chase. "Son of a bitch, I wish you hadn't had to meet Hunter right now. Normally he's one of the best, but he's not taking his convalescence very well."

Jake was still watching Hunter. "Do you blame him? Eighty percent? Doc might as well have—"

Jarvis threw his sweaty towel at Jake's face. "Will you shut the fuck up? Nothing is set in stone. Doc's been wrong before. Look at Trahern!"

A loud crash had all three of them staring across the gym. Hunter had stopped by the free weights, and they watched in silence as he picked up another dumbbell and heaved it against the wall.

"Jake, take Chase to lunch and I'll join you there." Jarvis headed for the wounded Paladin, who was reaching for another weight.

Chase stood to pull on his shirt. "Is Hunter a friend of his?"

"We're few enough in number that we all get to be pretty close, but it's worse for Jarvis. Every installation has one Paladin who is more or less in charge. Jarvis has filled that role here for a very long time. He always takes it personally when he loses one of us; and Hunter came that close"—he held his forefinger and thumb a fraction of an inch apart—"to dying permanently. If Doc's right about his chances for recovery, it might have been better if he had."

Then he clapped Jake on the shoulder. "But Hunter should fine eventually. None of us make good patients, and the longer it takes to heal, the worse we are. Now, how about some lunch?"

"Sounds good," Chase lied, trying to ignore the sick feeling that had settled in his stomach.

As they left the gym, he looked back at where Jarvis was squatting down beside Hunter, obviously arguing with his friend. It was hard to tell from this distance which one came out ahead, but Jarvis stood up and pushed Hunter out the door and out of sight.

As the two of them disappeared, Chase's skin rippled with goose bumps.

Chapter 15

"**D**amn it, Jarvis, leave me alone. I don't need a nursemaid!"

"No, Hunter, what you need is your ass kicked. Right now your coloring is the same crappy gray as that limestone wall. It's bad enough you snuck out of the lab, but did you have to roll yourself all the way down here?"

Jarvis kept the chair moving fast enough that Hunter couldn't grab on to the wheels and wrest control away from him. Right now, he was mad enough that his hands itched to smack the wounded Paladin. When they reached the elevator, he let Hunter do the number punching.

As they waited, Hunter looked up at Jarvis. "So who's the kid?"

"His father was Harvey Fletcher, who probably died before your time. I met the kid by accident when I was left cut up and half dead in the woods near Chase's family farm."

"And I'm guessing today was his first visit here."

"Yeah."

There was real regret in Hunter's expression. "If I had known, I wouldn't have . . ."

"Don't sweat it, Hunter. The kid will be okay. It's you I'm worried about." He leaned against the wall.

"Yeah, but the last thing a new recruit needs to see is a chewed-up mess like me." He pounded his fist on his leg.

"You're not going to get any better if you insist on ignoring the doctor's orders, Hunter. These things take time. It's not like all you needed were a couple of stitches and a Band-Aid this time."

Jarvis wished there was more he could do to make things easier, but there wasn't. They were born with the instincts of a warrior, with a burning need to serve. A crippled Paladin was only half a man, and they both knew it.

"Trahern says he has a friend in Seattle with some of the same problems as you have. Let's see how much Doc can do for you before we go jumping off the deep end. But if you'd like, I'll get you the guy's e-mail address."

Hunter sneered as the elevator door finally opened and he rolled himself in. "Oooh goody, my very own support group. Maybe we can meet on the second Tuesday of the month over tea and cookies."

"All right, so don't contact him. I'm just saying I haven't been where you are right now, but this Penn Sebastian has. Maybe talking to him would help."

"Yeah, and maybe I can get the Regents to install some artillery on my wheelchair, so I can be the first member of the Paladin artillery division."

The doors slid shut, cutting off the conversation as Hunter went back up to the lab. Jarvis closed his eyes and prayed for patience. The last thing he wanted right now was lunch, but he couldn't abandon Chase for long. He had to work some kind of damage control, to make sure the boy understood that what had happened to Hunter was almost unheard of. But damn, it hurt to see the lines that bitterness and pain had carved in Hunter's face in such a short time. It couldn't be easy to hear that the life you'd planned had just taken a major turn for the worse.

Which reminded him. He needed to find out where they were on backtracking the tunnel where Hunter was attacked. If there was a hole, they needed to get it plugged up. But right now he had more immediate concerns.

He thought about calling Doc Crosby to warn him about Hunter's mood, but decided against it. The Paladin was feeling crowded enough without having Jarvis ride herd on him. Maybe later he'd get Jake to take Chase home, while he kept Hunter company in the lab.

He pushed off the wall and started for the cafeteria. He'd never been a coward, and he wasn't going to start now. He'd take Chase home himself because it was the right thing to do. The boy would have a ton of questions he wanted to ask, and might feel more comfortable doing so in the car, when none of the others could hear him.

Besides, Jarvis needed to see Gwen. He'd spent so much time and energy warning her that she should keep him at arm's length, but he hadn't listened to his own advice. It had almost ripped his heart out to merely wave at her that morning, as if seeing her standing there hadn't had his pulse racing and his body wanting the sweet touch of hers.

Cursing himself for a fool, he headed into the cafeteria, hoping his dark mood didn't spoil the rest of the day for Gwen's brother.

Chase had an odd look on his face, and Jake was too busy jawing at one of the other Paladins at the table to notice.

Jarvis set his tray down across from the boy and sat down. "What's up? Something wrong with your pizza?"

"No, the food's great." Chase leaned closer. "I keep feeling like something is humming in the back of my head, only it's more than that. It's like something is pulling on me, or watching me, or something."

"The barrier's doing that to you because you're a Paladin. We all sense it, and the feeling gets stronger the more you're around it. When we serve near a particular stretch of the barrier for a long time, we can sense its moods even from a distance—especially when it's weakening or about to go down."

Chase took another bite of his pizza as he mulled that over. Jarvis waited for him to swallow, knowing he'd have more questions.

"So, different parts of the barrier feel different? How many places like this are there?"

"Yes, to the first question. If we were to visit the Pacific Northwest, the barrier would resonate on a slightly different frequency. Up there, the barrier is affected not only by earthquakes but also by the volcanoes stretching from California all the way up into Alaska. The more unstable the volcano, the more unstable the barrier. You can imagine what Mount St. Helens does to it on a routine basis."

He popped the top on his cold drink and took a long swallow. "We have installations all over the world, but there are more in regions where the tectonic plates are more unstable, or where there are more active volcanoes. Once you're trained, you can request a transfer to pretty much anywhere you'd want to go."

"Cool! Do guys move around a lot?"

"A few do, but most tend settle in one area after a while. I've served here for over twenty-five years. My friend Trahern trained under me here, and then moved to Seattle for personal reasons—which you can translate as woman trouble." He smiled. "Sometimes those reasons jump up and bite you on the ass. He came back awhile ago because the woman was in danger. When he returned to Seattle, she went with him."

Chase looked around the room full of men. "So there are no women Paladins?"

"No, it's one of those chromosome things. Doc Crosby knows more about it, so ask him sometime if you want to learn more. My understanding is that women can carry the gene, but they don't become Paladins themselves."

"Do all these guys live here?"

"Some do. Some, like me, keep a place up in the St. Louis area or one of the nearby towns. We try to rotate duty so that everyone gets some time off from the barrier, especially when we get a quiet stretch. It's nice to get away from all of this when we can." Even if it felt like pulling a giant rubber band that wanted to snap them right back where they belonged.

"So if some guys live here, is it like the military, where there are separate quarters for men with families?"

So that's what was driving this conversation. "Come on. Let's take a walk."

They cleared their trays and left the listening ears behind. When they reached the staircase, Jarvis opened the door. Once they were inside and safe from being overheard, he tried his best to answer Chase's questions—even the ones the boy hadn't asked yet and Jarvis had no real answer for.

"Paladins don't often have families, Chase. We age slower than most humans, and we aren't exactly easy to live with. The job demands too much of our time and energy to leave much for the demands of family life. We're on call twenty-four/seven for life. There's no retirement, no time off for good behavior. Even though I occasionally take breaks at my apartment in St. Louis, I get edgy and irritable if I'm away from the barrier for too long."

Their steps echoed in the stairwell.

"I'd like to tell you differently, but you're in this for the long haul. Sure, you can put off joining us long enough to go to college. A lot of the guys pursue other interests even after they start serving here—computer science, medic training, geology. Some even do a stint in the military. If there's something you're interested in, go for it. But eventually you won't be able to stay away."

"It's Gwen who really wants me to go to college. She's been saving money for my tuition and stuff."

That wasn't a surprise. "I guess the real question, Chase, is what do *you* want?"

"I'm hanging in long enough to graduate high school, but it's not easy to be cooped up all day." His shoulders slumped. "I was planning on getting a job for a while and then try school again. Doesn't sound like there's much point, if this is where I'm going to end up anyway."

"No, Chase. You don't have to take the weight of the world on your shoulders yet. You're still only eighteen. No one, least of all me, is pushing you to pick up a sword and join in the fight today. You've got plenty of time to make your own choices."

"So why have you been teaching me how to fight if you don't expect me to need those skills?"

"That was only part of it. Mainly, you needed to learn the control that martial arts and weapons training could give you. We come prepackaged with a whole shitload of aggression. If we don't learn how to channel it, there's no telling what could trigger an explosion. Hell, I don't have to tell you that. And it's been helping, hasn't it?"

Chase nodded. "Yeah. My coach and teachers have all noticed. It makes school bearable, now that kids aren't cringing every time I walk by them. I hated getting in fights all the time, but it was like something was driving me to lash out at the least little thing. I don't know how many trash cans Gwen had to pay for because I kicked them to death. Better that than . . ." His voice trailed off, but his meaning was clear.

God, they'd barely found Chase in the nick of time. Another few months of feeling crowded and out of control could have ended up in total disaster. And it would have killed Gwen to have her brother end up in prison for killing somebody in a fit of uncontrolled rage.

How many of their kind were out there with no one to bring them into the fold? The Regents kept an eye on the medical records of the military, watching for any hint that someone had healed faster than expected or had survived what should have been fatal wounds. More than one Paladin had been discovered among the ranks of the armed forces, especially special ops. A few more had channeled their abilities into serving in law enforcement and fire departments.

But none of them had had an easy time of it out in the world. At least they'd found kindred spirits and a home among their own kind with their fellow Paladins. They lived together, fought together, and died together, saving the world in their own secret war.

They'd reached the bottom of the stairs. "Okay, kid. Hold your breath and be prepared to be dazzled."

● ● ●

"Was I right?" Jarvis stood beside him, letting him absorb the glorious colors of the barrier.

"Heck, yeah. It's amazing."

He had no names for the colors that swirled and billowed in the wall of energy that ran from the ceiling to the floor throughout the length of the enormous cavern. The cave itself was enough to leave him speechless, but it was nothing compared to the barrier.

"How far does it go?"

Jarvis shrugged. "It winds all throughout this area. Like I told you earlier, there are bits and pieces of it scattered over the world where the tectonic plates come together or the volcanoes are active. The good news is that there are only a few places where the Kalith cross regularly. This seems to be one of their favorites, although Seattle is right up there with us."

"How often does it go down?" Chase peeled his gaze away from the barrier long enough to briefly look at Jarvis.

"Too damned often. We get long quiet spells followed by total chaos. It has to do with the type of earthquakes in this area. Although there's occasionally a big lurch, we usually get swarms of shallow quakes that can go on for weeks. Individually, the shallow ones are too weak for humans to detect, but they play hell with the barrier's stability."

The colors were changing again, this time

shades of deep blue and purple fading into reds and oranges. Chase had to clench his hands into fists to keep from reaching out to make sure the barrier was real. Jarvis had already warned him that one touch carried enough voltage to melt the fillings in his teeth. Not to mention that it would fry his brain and burn out his nerve endings at the same time. Evidently there were a few injuries that even Paladins couldn't come back from.

Which brought the Paladin in the wheelchair back to mind. "What's going to happen to that guy Hunter? I mean, from what you've told me, nothing makes the need to be near the barrier go away completely."

Jarvis stared at the barrier for several seconds before answering. "I don't know. Our bodies can heal almost anything over time, so I'm hoping that Doc's wrong about Hunter's chances. There's another Paladin with similar problems out in Seattle, so I've been in touch with my friend Trahern to see how that guy's doing."

He crossed his arms over his chest. "I don't want you to worry about Hunter, though. He'll be fine. We take care of our own."

Who was Jarvis trying so hard to convince of that? It didn't matter. Despite all the outlandish things he'd learned today, Chase felt pretty good about all of it. He fit in here. For the first time in his life he didn't stand out because of his size or his temper or his weird ability to heal. Even his inborn aggression would be considered an asset instead of a danger.

Gwen wasn't going to like his decision, but he couldn't wait until he became a full-fledged Paladin. Even if he had to keep it secret, it would be enough to know that he had a purpose in life.

"Fuck, no!" Jarvis took off at a run to hit what looked like a fire alarm on a nearby wall. As soon as he did, a loud horn started blasting away.

"What's wrong?" Chase shouted over the racket.

"The barrier!" Jarvis hollered back as Paladins came pouring into the cavern from all directions.

Chase turned back to the barrier and saw that the bright colors were gone, replaced by greens the color of pus, with pulsing streaks of black.

Jake came charging across the cavern carrying three swords. He tossed one to Jarvis and shoved the second into Chase's hands. Chase clutched the pommel like a lifeline. As the Paladins formed up in ragged lines and faced the barrier, the klaxon shut off, leaving his ears ringing.

Jarvis snagged Chase's arm and dragged him toward a narrow tunnel at one side of the cavern. "Chase, get back out of sight and stay there. The stairs and elevators are in lockdown to keep the bastards from escaping, so you're trapped down here with us for the duration. There's a small chance the barrier will stabilize, but no matter what, I don't want you getting mixed up in this. Use that if one of the bastards gets past us, but don't try to be a hero."

Then he was off, running right up to the front of the formation. Chase fought the urge to follow him. What had he been training for, if not to fight? He inched farther forward until he could see into the main cavern. In a flash of light, the barrier blinked out. He blinked to clear his vision. Shadows were moving in the darkness that slowly took shape and form.

It looked like a scene straight out of hell. The shadows surged forward, becoming solid nightmares. The Others were built like humans, although their coloring was off. They shrieked and screamed as they swung their swords with reckless abandon, facing the equally determined Paladins. Blade on blade they fought. After a few seconds there were already bodies writhing on the floor, as blood-splattered swords arced through the air.

The noise was horrific as some men screamed in challenge and others in agony. One of the Paladins went down close to where Chase stood. The injured man barely got his sword up to block an attack from a second Other. Between one heartbeat and the next, Chase threw himself between the downed warrior and the bastard trying to kill them both.

The sword felt different from the one he was used to, awkward and slow to respond. Even so, he managed to hold the cold-eyed killer at bay long enough for the Paladin behind him to get up off the floor. Between the two of them, they forced the Other to back off.

"Thanks, kid, I'll take it from here." The Paladin shouldered him aside and charged his enemy, bellowing curses at the top of his lungs.

Chase retreated, knowing he'd be more of a hindrance than a help if he tried to do more. But it was hard to sit this out, seeing the men he'd just met bleeding and hurt.

His eyes automatically sought out the two men he knew best. Jarvis and Jake fought side by side, slowly forcing their opponents to give ground, gradually pushing them back to where the barrier had once stood.

If the situation hadn't been so grim, he would have thought their grace and speed beautiful to watch. How could anyone move that fast with the heavy weight of steel in his hand? He'd never again complain about the endless repetitions of the training drills. Now that he knew that lives depended on his ability to fight, he would take whatever Jarvis dished out.

The barrier flickered in and out. A shout warned the Paladins, and they made one last concerted effort to push the Others back into the shadows of their own world. When the barrier finally snapped back into full strength, only a handful of the enemy was still standing on the wrong side. They were quickly eliminated, along with their wounded, while the Paladins started helping their own wounded up off the floor.

The violence ended as abruptly as it had started. Now that it was over, Chase threw up, his stomach wrenching in painful spasms. When his gut had emptied itself, he leaned against the tunnel wall for support. When he was sure he could stand again, he picked up his sword from where he'd dropped it, hoping that Jarvis wouldn't kick his ass for treating a good weapon so carelessly.

He was about to rejoin the others to see if he could do anything to help, when he heard soft footsteps on the stone floor behind him. He looked around, and too late, he realized that it wasn't one of the Paladins coming to check on him.

Cold steel cut through his T-shirt like butter. He staggered back as a gush of hot blood poured out of his gut. The pain didn't start until he'd stumbled several steps out into the cavern; then it came in unrelenting waves with the screams that clawed their way out of his throat.

As Chase hit the floor, he heard Jarvis's battle cry and his sword cut straight through the enemy they'd all missed. Chase was dimly aware of Jarvis stepping over the bloody body; then the Paladin knelt beside Chase and took his hand in his.

"Hang in there, buddy. You'll be fine. The first time's always the worst."

Chase used the thick sound of Jarvis's voice to seek out his friend's worried face. The last thing he saw, as darkness reached up and grabbed him, was the streaks of tears running down Jarvis's face.

"Jarvis, why don't you get your depressing ass out of here?"

"Keep pushing, Hunter, and we'll both find out if Doc notices the extra bruises you'll have." Jarvis was too tired to put much energy into the threat, but right now he was in no mood to take shit off anyone.

"We both know the boy's going to live, so why don't you go get some rest? I'll call you myself when he comes around." Hunter's voice was softer, tinged with what sounded an awful lot like sympathy. Or worse, pity.

Jarvis forced himself to respond civilly. "I appreciate the offer, but I need to be here when he wakes up."

Even if guilt wasn't riding him hard, he cared enough for Chase to make sure his first transition from death back to living went smoothly. Shit, could this nightmare get any worse? He wondered what excuse Jake had given Gwen for Chase not coming home tonight. Tomorrow was Monday, and she wouldn't like the fact that their little field trip made him miss school.

Telling her the truth was impossible.

"Hey, Gwen. Sorry, but your brother was accidently killed today when aliens invaded. I knew there was a chance they'd do that, but I figured it was worth the risk. I'll be glad to help him with any homework he misses over the next couple of days while he recuperates."

"No problem, Jarvis. Just drop him off at the farm when he's up and around. Oh, and don't bother ever speaking to either one of us again. You set one foot on my property, and you'll find out just how good I am with my rifle."

"I understand. Take care and have a good life, Gwen. I'd like to hope that you find someone else to get in your good graces soon, but I'm not that generous."

"Go to hell, Jarvis."

"I'm already there."

The door to the lab swung open and Jake poked his head in. "How's it going?"

Hunter eased himself off his bed and into his wheelchair. "Has this place turned into Party Central? I'm out of here. If Doc starts looking for me, tell him I'll be back when I feel like letting him use me for a pincushion again."

He rolled past Jake, glaring at him for holding the door open for him. "I can do things for myself."

"I know. But I can't stop helping you, since you're always so damned grateful."

Hunter shot him another nasty look before disappearing down the hallway.

Jake approached Jarvis, who was slumped in an uncomfortable molded plastic chair. "How's he doing?"

"As well as can be expected. The machines have already started picking up a heartbeat or two every few minutes. Once he starts breathing again, he should come back pretty fast. Doc wants to be here for that, but he needed a break after stitching everybody up. I offered to keep an eye on Chase so he could catch some z's." He nodded toward the still form chained down on the stainless steel table. "Luckily, he was the only fatality. Most of the other wounds were pretty minor."

The memory of seeing that Other swinging his sword and Chase's blood spraying the floor made his own gut hurt. It had all happened so quickly, but Chase sinking to the floor had seemed to flow in slow motion as Jarvis had fought his way through the crowd to catch him. Would he ever get over the look of betrayal in the boy's eyes as the light in them had faded and then disappeared altogether?

Jake held out a cup of coffee. "It wasn't your fault, Jarvis. Him dying like that, I mean."

"Try telling that to Gwen. She'll never forgive me . . . or any of us for putting her brother in danger. I should have known better than to let him get that close."

Damn, his eyes felt like sandpaper. He pinched the bridge of his nose, trying without success to relieve the headache he'd been fighting for hours.

"That's bullshit and you know it. Introducing Chase to the barrier is not just your job, it's your duty. If you hadn't taken him down there, I would have. No one has control of the barrier. If you want to blame someone, blame the bastard who swung the sword!"

"I would, but he's dead." Which reminded him. "I've been meaning to ask: did you happen to see where that Other came from? We'd already finished the mop-up of the few who didn't cross back over. How did we miss him?"

"I don't know, but I'll ask around to see if anyone else saw what happened."

"As soon as the mop-up is done, I want a team to explore that tunnel where Hunter was caught again and see if that's where those crazy bastards are coming from. If we have to blow up the whole fucking tunnel to stop them, I'll light the fuse myself."

Jake snagged another chair and straddled it, resting his arms on the back. "It's a shame we can't tell Gwen that her brother's a hero. He stayed right where you told him to, but when one of our guys went down, Chase jumped in long enough to give Toby a chance to get his wounded ass up off the floor. As soon as he did, Chase retreated to the tunnel. Smart kid. When Chase wakes up, Toby said to tell him he owes him big time."

He doubted that would comfort Gwen in the least. "Speaking of Gwen, how did that go?"

"About as well as you'd expect. She's glad everyone is okay, what with the car going into a ditch. I told her you'd call and let her know when she could expect Chase to get home. I bought you some time—but the longer you put off talking to her, the worse it's going to be."

Yeah, he should have called her himself, but he'd chickened out. As soon as Chase was definitely on the mend, though, he was going to drive out and bring her here, the Regents' need for secrecy be damned. He wouldn't be the first one to bring a civilian in when the circumstances warranted it. Only a few months ago, Trahern had introduced Brenna Nichols to the hidden world of the Paladins when her life was in danger. So far, there hadn't been any major repercussions from the powers that be.

Of course, Brenna's father had been a Regent himself, although she hadn't known about that part of his life. That, plus the fact that she was head over heels in love with Trahern, had ensured her silence.

Gwen's circumstances were nowhere near the same. First of all, she wouldn't want her brother to be a Paladin, and she was going to want Jarvis's guts for garters for lying to her for weeks.

The only thing he hadn't lied about was how he felt about her—not that he'd ever told her in words. Now he never would.

An hour later, Hunter rolled back into the lab.

"Don't you guys have your own rooms?"

Hadn't they just gone through this a little while ago? "If you don't want company, find someplace else to hang out."

Before Hunter could respond, the machines surrounding Chase blipped again, this time for several more beats than the last time. Jarvis leaned forward, trying to read the numbers on the display. Was Chase breathing?

Jake sat up straighter. "What's up?"

Jarvis fought to keep his excitement tamped down. "I think I saw Chase breathe."

He crossed to the table with Jake hot on his heels. Hunter rolled closer and leveraged himself up high enough to see. The three of them hovered over Chase, their eyes straining against the dim light to see if the boy's chest had just expanded.

"There! He did it again."

They all watched as Chase's lungs took a series of shallow breaths. When they continued to do so, the three men backed away to celebrate. Even Hunter was smiling. He twirled his chair in a tight circle and then headed for the phone.

"I'll call Doc. He'll want to know."

Jarvis let him make the call; it was good to see Hunter excited about something. He and Jake continued to hover near Chase, as if their presence would ensure the boy continued on his journey back to the living.

A few minutes later, Doc charged through the doors. He was still buttoning his shirt and he had a bad case of bed head, testimony to his own excitement. He grabbed his stethoscope and plugged it into his ears before gently applying it to Chase's chest with his eyes closed.

Apparently satisfied with what he heard, he pressed his fingers to Chase's wrist and whispered numbers under his breath as he stared at the clock on the far wall. Even though the machines were probably busy monitoring the same data, Jarvis didn't blame Doc for wanting to judge the boy's recovery with his own senses.

"He's back. It may come in fits and starts, but his pulse is getting stronger, and his lungs sound clear." He grinned at Jarvis, his tired eyes sparkling over the top of his reading glasses. "I'd give him another few hours at most before his eyes open."

Damn good news!

"Doc, I know you didn't like it when we brought Trahern's woman in here to fuss over him, but I'm going to be doing the same thing. Chase's sister will need to see for herself that he's all right. If you've

got a problem with that, speak your piece now—
but it won't stop me."

Doc set his stethoscope aside and came around
to Jarvis's side of the table. "No, I certainly did not
appreciate Brenna Nichols being in my way, or the
peremptory way Dr. Young took over my lab. But
their interference undoubtedly saved Blake Trahern's life. There are nights I can't sleep, thinking
about how close I came to killing that man unnec-
essarily."

He looked back down at Chase. "If this boy
needs his sister, you won't get any complaints from
me."

"Do you want me to go get her?" Jake offered.

He'd played coward long enough. "I appreciate
the offer, but I need to face her sometime." Jarvis
rested his hand on Chase's bare shoulder, needing to feel the boy's body warming up as his blood
started pulsing through his veins and arteries.

"She's going to be upset, Jarvis, but she'll get
over it."

"I got her brother *killed,* Jake. That's too much
to get over."

Hunter poked his nose into the discussion. "If
she's anything like that Brenna Nichols or Dr.
Young, maybe you're selling her short. Those two
could face down a mob of crazed Others all by
themselves. Hell, they managed to tame two of the
toughest Paladins in creation."

"Shut up, Hunter." He had to get out of there before he broke down completely. It was hard enough to take that first step toward Gwen and total disaster.

But Jake joined right in. "Damn it, Jarvis, you know Gwen. She'll—"

He held up his hand. "If anything changes, call me. Otherwise I'll be back in a couple of hours."

After all—once Gwen banished him from her life, where else could he go?

Chapter 16

$\mathcal{T}$he crunch of gravel in the driveway snapped Gwen out of her exhausted stupor. She charged out of the house, not sure if she was going to hug the two males who were hours and hours overdue or knock their heads together for scaring her so badly. Why hadn't they called again if they were going to take this long? Jake had tried to make the accident sound like nothing major, but there'd been something in his voice that had convinced her that blood or even broken bones had been involved.

She skidded to a halt when she saw the Chevelle. The sky was just starting to brighten, but the barn lights made it clear that there wasn't a mark on the car. The grim look on Jarvis's face as he climbed out of the car worried her deeply. He looked as if he hadn't slept in days, his face shadowed with exhaustion. But what sent the blood plummeting from her head was the lack of expression in his dark eyes. They looked dead.

Whatever had happened to her brother had been bad. Very bad. Jarvis caught her before she hit the ground, but just barely. He swung her up in his arms with ease and carried her onto the porch, setting her down in the rocker.

"Put your head down until the dizziness is gone. I didn't mean to scare you."

She fought him. "Tell me *now*."

"Breathe, damn it. I'll tell you everything when you're no longer the color of pea soup."

His big hand relentlessly pushed her head forward until it touched her knees. It didn't take long for her to feel back in fighting form. She batted at his hand until he released her.

"Go slow, Gwen, or you'll be right back down there."

She managed to raise up without her head spinning out of control again. Then she mustered up the courage to open her eyes to face the bad news she knew would be reflected in Jarvis's.

"Jake lied. Your car wasn't damaged, and Chase wasn't hurt when the car went into a ditch." Anger burned through the accusation.

"No, it wasn't a car accident. Jake lied because I ordered him to. Be mad at me, not him." Jarvis rocked back on his heels, giving her a little room to breathe.

"How badly is Chase hurt? What hospital is he in? They should have called me, even if you didn't! I should be with him, not waiting here at the farm!"

"Chase is doing fine now. If you'll gather what you need for a couple of days, I'll take you to him." He slowly rose to his full height. "And I'll explain everything on the way."

She couldn't think. She couldn't plan. "I can't leave for days. The animals can't take care of themselves."

"I'll take you to Chase. On the way, you can write down what needs to be done, and I'll come back to take care of the farm. I might not have your touch with the alpacas, but I can shovel shit with the best of them."

She was in no mood for humor. "That doesn't surprise me, because you can also dish it out with the best of them. Now tell me what's wrong with my brother! And I want details, Jarvis. I'm running on pure worry and no sleep, but don't you dare try to wrap it up in a pretty package for me. You have no right to decide what I can handle and what I can't."

He jerked back as if she'd physically struck out at him. She was too furious about being kept in the dark so long about Chase's injuries to worry about hurt feelings.

"I'm waiting, Jarvis."

His eyes slid past her toward the east, where the

rising sun was setting the hills afire. "He was gutted with a sword because of a lapse in my judgment. Is that blunt enough for you, Gwen? Or do you want to know how much blood he lost before the doctor got him stitched back together?"

She gasped. A sword?

He winced and ran his fingers through his hair. "I'm sorry, but I haven't slept either. I made a bad decision, and it cost Chase a lot of pain. Saying I'm sorry won't change that, but I promise that he's going to be fine. You, of all people, know how well he heals. It'll only be a matter of days before all he has left is a scar, and eventually even that will fade."

"But the memories won't, will they?" She brushed past him to pack. "He'll carry those for a long, long time."

"Yeah, he will. We all will."

For a moment, she thought he was going to follow her upstairs, but he went only as far as the kitchen table. He sank down in his usual chair and reached across to pick up the cold cup of coffee she'd left sitting out. He swigged it down without even a grimace at its cold, bitter taste. She considered telling him to make a fresh pot if he wanted to, but right them she didn't have it in her to be nice.

She made it all the way to the top step before she stopped. Damn the man, anyway! She marched back down the stairs. "Are you hungry?"

"You don't have to play hostess for me, Gwen."
He sounded weary beyond bearing.

"I know that, but you look like death warmed
over. I don't want to get in a car with you running on empty. Food and caffeine will help." She
grabbed a skillet and banged it down on the stove.
"You make the coffee."

He didn't argue, just headed for the cabinet
where she kept the coffee and filters. It hurt to be
reminded how at home he was here in her kitchen.
How could he know her house so well, and her
so little? She could forgive almost anything but
dishonesty. If he'd told her the truth about Chase,
she would have hated waiting until Jarvis got
there to pick her up, but she wouldn't have spent
the night pacing the floor and imagining horror
upon horror. Somehow she'd known deep inside
that Jake hadn't been completely forthcoming
about what had happened. Then the truth had
been so much worse than anything she could have
thought of.

She set the eggs down before her shaking hands
lost control and dropped them. Or threw them at
him. "Did you really say someone used a *sword* on
Chase?"

"Yes, I did."

There was far more to the story; she'd bet her
last dime on it. "Since when were weapons part of
his training? Did you think I would allow him to get

involved in whatever you and Jake do for a living? Especially considering how we met?"

Then realization hit her like a physical blow. She wheeled around to face him. "I can't believe I was so naïve. That was your plan all along, wasn't it? From that first morning: to drag him into your secret little world."

He didn't have to answer. The truth was there in the straight slash of his mouth. For a moment she couldn't think. Couldn't process. What had she been doing? Oh yes, breakfast. She broke egg after egg until Jarvis stopped her by moving the carton out of her reach.

"I think eight eggs will be plenty for the two of us, Gwen."

That did it. The dam broke, and the tears she'd been fighting gushed down her face. Jarvis gently pulled her into his arms, probably figuring he was the last person she'd want comfort from right then. He was wrong about that, but that only made matters worse.

His right hand moved in soothing circles on her back, and the left gently cradled her head against his shoulder as she soaked his shirt with tears.

"He's going to be fine, Gwen. I wouldn't lie about that." His voice was thick and rough.

"But you've lied about other things—like what you were really doing with Chase, and why."

"Yes. Or at least, I didn't tell you the full truth."

"Same thing."

"I know."

He went back to making coffee. She took the overheated skillet off the stove to give it and her temper time to cool down; then she whisked the eggs and poured them in. Some bread in the toaster, and breakfast was under control. She wished it was as easy to do that with her life.

They ate in silence. She choked the food down, figuring she'd need all the strength she could get to deal with Chase's injuries. While she went upstairs to pack her overnight bag, she could hear Jarvis cleaning up the kitchen. Maybe they'd get past this, but it would be hard. Even if she were willing to forgive him for this mess, something about his attitude made her think that he'd have a harder time forgiving himself.

She was chilled-to-the-bone scared for her brother. Yes, she knew firsthand about Chase's ability to heal, and that Jarvis had the same talent. She should have known that he'd think Chase would be a perfect candidate for the same kind of work. How many times had she looked at Chase with Jarvis and Jake, and thought how well he fit in with them? But she'd turned a blind eye to the situation because she'd hoped they'd help him gain some control.

Her conscience pricked at her. Maybe she hadn't wanted to see it, because having Jarvis around had been such a wonderful change in her life, too.

She tossed in more clothes than she'd probably need, but there was no telling how long she'd be gone. After grabbing a spiral notebook, she went back down the stairs.

"I'm ready."

Jarvis took her bag from her. On the way out, he turned off the kitchen lights and locked the door behind them. The dogs were waiting outside on the porch, and she noticed their bowls were full of kibble and their water had been topped off. Dozer whined softly, clearly picking up on her emotional state.

"I'll be back with Chase, boys. Be good."

The Chevelle roared to life, and then they were flying down the highway, driving right into the morning sun.

Gwen was doing her best to ignore him, keeping her eyes focused out the passenger side window, but she wasn't going to wait much longer for him to make good on his promise. And delaying the inevitable wouldn't change the outcome.

"What I'm about to tell you is not for public broadcast, Gwen. I'll be up to my ass in alligators for telling you—but that's not why I'm asking you to promise you'll honor that secrecy."

He waited until she looked at him before continuing. "There are a lot of good men and women who work hard to keep this world safe. More than just their lives would be at risk if word of their mission were to get out."

She didn't exactly sneer, but it was a close thing. "And this super secret mission involves my brother?"

"Yes, it does. And I need your word on this, Gwen, or I'm going to turn this car around and take you right back to the farm." He would do no such thing, but hoped she wasn't completely sure about that.

"You have my word, for what it's worth."

"I mean it, Gwen. Lives depend on it."

"I said you have my word, Jarvis," she snapped, holding her hand up as if swearing an oath in court.

She looked insulted that he'd been so insistent, but too bad. If she went to the media with stories of aliens and warriors who could survive even death, all hell would break loose.

"Okay. I'm going to tell you the same thing I told Chase. And just as with him, I want you to hear me out before you start asking questions or telling me I'm crazy." He glanced in her direction. "Let me start by saying I'm sorry you had to run up against the world I live in."

"But not Chase. You aren't sorry about Chase getting involved, are you?" Those green eyes saw too much.

"If he had any choice in the matter, I would have disappeared from your life after that first morning,

Gwen. But as much as you're going to hate it, the bottom line is that he doesn't."

Her temper exploded in the small confines of the car. "Do not—I repeat, *do not*—try to tell me that my brother is condemned to live like you! I won't have it, Jarvis. You have no right to screw up his life like that. No right at all."

God, could there be a worse time to be having this discussion? They were both tired and worried and totally sick about Chase. But she had to know what she was walking into; he owed her that much. Rather than get into a shouting match over Chase's future, he settled for explaining the present.

"You've known all along that Chase and I share the same ability to heal, as well as the inborn aggression that makes us good fighters. Some of the best in the world."

"Maybe that's true for you but—"

"Damn it, Gwen, stop it! You want the truth? I'm giving it to you. I never promised you'd like it, but you're damn well going to hear me out because I won't take you to Chase until you do."

She crossed her arms over her chest and glared at him some more.

Then he let the truth pour out—the Paladins, the Others, the Regents, the ongoing war, everything. And right at the end, he let slip the one thing he'd meant to keep to himself. He foolishly told her he loved her.

Her silence spoke far more than any words could have.

Gwen felt the stares and heard the whispers from the men they passed by, but she ignored everything except the soft pressure of Jarvis's arm around her shoulders. She would've shrugged off the protective gesture, but right now she needed his support. And maybe he needed hers.

The guard at the gate had clearly not been happy to see Jarvis drive through with her in the car. They'd had the elevator to themselves, but after that they'd passed a number of men who'd looked startled by her presence. When Jake had stepped out of a doorway to join the two of them, she'd almost wept at the relief of seeing a familiar face. At least he had the presence of mind to run the others off.

"Come on, guys, let's give her a break. She's here to see her brother." He made shooing motions with his hands until the men broke ranks and disappeared back to wherever they'd come from.

Satisfied they'd be left alone, he took her hand in both of his. "Sorry about that. Can you tell we don't get many women through here?"

"So it appears." She didn't bother smiling. She was too tired, too wired, and just as mad at Jake as she was at Jarvis.

She pulled her hand free and stepped clear of Jarvis's embrace. "How's Chase?"

Jake met Jarvis's gaze over her head before he answered. She poked him in the arm to force his attention back to her. "Take me to my brother. Then you two can swap secrets to your hearts' content."

The younger man's eyes reflected his regret. "Chase is doing much better. Dr. Crosby is waiting to talk to you. He will answer any questions you might have."

"Go with her, Jake, and get her anything she needs. I'll have my cell if you need me."

Jarvis did an abrupt about-face and walked away, leaving the two of them staring at his back.

Jake frowned as his friend disappeared back down the hallway. "I take it things didn't go well between the two of you."

"About as well as you could expect, considering he's been lying to me from the start."

She wrapped her arms across her waist, wishing she could rewind her life and start over from the night she'd found Jarvis in the river. How could she have been so blind? And now, when everything had gone to hell and back, he dared tell her that he loved her? Was that just another in a long line of lies? How could she tell? And what did it matter?

Two days ago she would have given anything to hear those words from him, but not now. His deceit had almost cost Chase's life. Of course, Jarvis had told her some fairy tale about how these Paladins' talents went far beyond the ability to heal severe injuries. Yeah, right.

Jake sighed. "Gwen, I know you're having a rough time right now, and have every right to be seriously pissed at both Jarvis and me. But even if you can't believe anything else, he's the most honorable man I've had the privilege to know. Having to keep secrets from you has been eating him alive."

He walked away, leaving her to follow. Beyond the next turn in the hallway, he stopped in front of a pair of swinging doors that said "Lab" on them. He put a finger across his lips, telling her to enter quietly.

Inside, the air was heavy with the usual hospital smells of antiseptics and remembered pain. There were several stainless steel beds in the room, but only one of them was occupied.

Despite the faint light, she recognized her brother's profile and hurried to his side. Her frantic eyes soaked in the sight of his steady breathing and slightly worried expression, as if he hurt enough to be uncomfortable, but not enough to keep him awake.

"Chase, honey, I'm here."

At the sound of her voice, an older man poked his head out of an adjoining room. As soon as he saw Gwen, he ducked back out of sight for a few seconds. When he came back, he was shrugging on a lab coat.

"Dr. Crosby? I'm Gwen Mosely, Chase's sister."

He held out his hand. "I'm sorry we couldn't have met under better circumstances, Miss Mosely, but at least I can tell you that your brother has been making steady improvement. He'll be up and around before you know it."

"What are you doing for him?"

He tugged back the thin blanket to show her the bandaged wound. "Paladins are a tough lot. Once we get the bleeding under control, we pretty much let their bodies take over. Jarvis said you raised Chase, so I would guess that you already know quite a bit about Chase's ability to heal, as well as the need for restraints."

Tears stung her eyes as she touched the chains. "I've used rope in the past."

"As soon as he wakes up, we'll get them off. I'm sure you'll want to take him home as soon as I can release him to your care."

The sympathy in his eyes was almost her undoing. The need to cry and scream knocked around in her chest, forcing her to waste precious energy on holding herself together. And wishing Jarvis was there beside her only made it worse.

"As soon as possible." She brushed her brother's cheek with the back of her fingers, then settled her hand gently on his shoulder.

"I know this hasn't been easy for you, Miss Mosely, and telling you how bad everyone around here feels isn't going to help much."

"No, it won't."

"Can I get you anything?"

"No." Then she changed her mind. He was only trying to help. "Actually, I would love a cup of tea and maybe a sandwich."

The small request pleased the doctor. "Jake, can you take care of that? Bring enough for all of us, plus Hunter. He's due back for treatment."

"Are you sure that's wise?"

Gwen had forgotten all about Jake. If she hadn't turned around at that second, she would have missed the odd look that had accompanied Jake's question. Before she could decipher what was going on, the doors behind him banged open as a man in a wheelchair pushed himself into the room.

Jake looked resigned. "Never mind. I'll be back in a jiff."

Gwen watched as the door swung shut. What was wrong with him? Meanwhile, the man in the wheelchair rolled himself over to where the doctor was waiting for him. If he found Gwen's presence odd, he gave no indication of it as he peeled his shirt off over his head. She stared in horror at the raw scars that crisscrossed his back. She must have made some noise, because his head whipped around to glare at her.

"I'm sorry . . . I didn't mean to . . ."

He snarled, "Can't we have any privacy around here, Doc?"

"Of course, Hunter. Sorry, I wasn't thinking. Let's go in the other room."

They filed out, leaving Gwen alone with the buzz and whir of the various machines. What had happened to that man? Who could have done such a thing to another living being? Once again she drew what comfort she could from touching Chase's shoulder, relieved to feel the warmth of his skin.

Jake reappeared, breathing hard as if he'd run the whole way. "Hope turkey and cheese is okay."

"Anything will be fine, Jake."

She pulled a chair over next to Chase and sat down. After setting the tray of food on a small rolling cart between them, Jake followed suit.

Between bites, he asked, "Where'd Doc and Hunter go?"

"In the next room. I couldn't control my shock when Hunter took off his shirt." She dropped her voice. "I know you can't or won't tell me what happened to him, but please say that he's going to be okay."

"We're keeping our fingers crossed."

Considering how quickly Jarvis and Chase both recovered from injuries, either Hunter's ability wasn't as strong or he'd been hurt far worse than Jarvis had been. But it wasn't any of her business.

Nor would it be Chase's, after she got him back home where he belonged and away from all of this. She concentrated on choking down her sandwich.

After a time, her lack of sleep caught up with her and she drifted off to sleep.

"Hey, Sis."

The words were barely more than a whisper, but they jerked Gwen out of a sound sleep. She lurched upright, her neck protesting the sudden movement. The small pain was nothing in comparison to the relief to see her brother awake and looking around sleepily.

"How long have I been out?"

She glanced at the clock on the wall. "About thirty-six hours. I've been here about twenty-four of that."

Jake's chair was empty, so they had the room to themselves for now.

She brushed the hair back off his forehead. "How are you feeling? Are you in pain?"

"Not bad, considering." He arched his head to look around. "Where's Jarvis? I want to thank him for saving my life. He killed the guy who did this to me."

Shock jarred through her. "*What*? He said you'd been hurt with a sword. I assumed it was an accident." Despite Jarvis's promise to tell her the truth, he'd still managed to skirt revealing all of the facts.

"Don't be mad at him, Sis. He made sure I was someplace safe during the battle." He blanched. "Damn it, I'm probably not supposed to tell you any of this."

Then he conveniently closed his eyes and fell back to sleep.

Gwen wanted to punch something—or better yet, somebody. Her brother had been dangerously close to a battle? What had Jarvis been thinking? Accident be damned, he'd had no right to drag Chase into his ugly world. If half of what he'd told her about the Others and their world was true, it was the stuff of nightmares.

Well, that was all over with. Once Chase was up and around, the two of them would go back to the farm and forget all about this disaster. If Chase needed martial arts, she'd find a regular place for him to study.

It was time to get the doctor. The sooner he released her brother, the sooner they could get down to rebuilding their lives without Jarvis and company. As the man had said over and over again, he wasn't a forever kind of guy.

Even if he *had* said he loved her. It had taken all her strength not to admit her own powerful feelings for him when he'd whispered those words, especially when his voice had cracked in pain. But what kind of love was built on lies and almost got her brother killed?

No, she was going to put all of this behind her. She was strong. She could do it. One step at a time, one day at a time, she'd go forward and ignore the fact that her heart was bleeding pain with each beat it took.

"Doctor, can you come now? Chase was awake and talking."

When the physician came out, she stood out of the way and prayed for the strength to get through the days ahead.

Earlier, Jake had driven Gwen's truck to headquarters so that she could bring Chase back to the farm when Doc Crosby released him. A short time ago, Jake had called to give Jarvis a heads-up that they were on their way home. It was good to hear that Chase had checked out with flying colors. Although he'd have to be careful in the locker room at school to avoid awkward questions until the scar faded, he'd been given a clean bill of health.

That was damn good. He shook his head at something else Jake had told him. Gwen had evidently hovered near her brother the whole time to keep him from being left alone with anyone who might continue to indoctrinate him about becoming one of them. Did she think they were some kind of cult, out to recruit new members?

Given the genetic makeup of Paladins, they

were better off within the Regents' organization than they were out on their own. Especially when they were approaching the end of their humanity. But if Gwen hadn't wanted to hear about the good parts of being a Paladin, she sure wouldn't have wanted to hear how her brother's life was preordained to end.

Jarvis moved farther back into the woods when headlights flashed at the top of the driveway. Gwen had made it clear that he was persona non grata in her life, but he reserved the right to watch over her.

Once the Moselys settled for the night, and if all was quiet, he'd head back to headquarters to check the progress on his special project. He'd had several of the Paladins tracking the GPS location of the far end of the tunnel where Hunter had been tortured. The Kalith who'd attacked Chase had definitely come from that same direction. So far they found at least two openings to the outside that would need to be closed off.

So for now, he was operating under the assumption that no one was safe until they knew where all the Kalith were gaining access to the surrounding countryside. Jarvis was reluctant to leave Gwen and Chase alone and unprotected, especially at night, until the Paladins plugged that hole in their defenses.

Gwen's truck pulled up in front of the barn and stopped. The bright security lamps illuminated her face, sparking off her fiery red hair. He could almost feel its warmth, and his forefinger and thumb rubbed against each other as he remembered its silky feel. He was too far away to see her freckles clearly, but he knew they were there. That he'd never finished counting them was another regret he'd have to live with.

Chase winced a little as he got out of the truck, but he straightened right up and walked toward the house, shaking off his sister's attempt to fuss over him. Jarvis grinned, figuring the boy had endured enough of that in the lab. Then Chase paused on the porch step and looked straight out at the exact spot where Jarvis stood in the shadows of the trees. When Gwen noticed what he was doing, she frowned and looked around herself, then urged her brother to get inside.

Had the boy somehow sensed his presence?

It didn't matter. They were home and safe for now. He eased back into the darkness and prepared to walk away from the one bright spot he'd ever known.

Chapter 17

*G*wen was staring out the kitchen window and considering her options when Chase crossed the room to stand beside her. "It's been two days, Sis. Don't you think it's time we talked?"

She wasn't ready, but evidently he was. "We don't need to rush anything."

"Come on, Gwen. You're the one who's always told me to face up to problems before they controlled your life."

Chase's big hands settled gently on her shoulders. She closed her eyes and enjoyed the small connection. He'd stayed home from school for the past two days, giving credence to the excuse that he'd had emergency surgery while visiting friends out of town. She *hated* the lies upon lies, but they'd needed a plausible story to cover his absence and the new scar.

They'd yet to figure out what kind of fictional surgery would have left a massive scar across his abdomen that would have healed up completely within such a short time, so Dr. Crosby had given Chase a note to excuse him from P.E. and football for several more days.

Her brother was right. They needed to talk about so many things. She patted his hand on her shoulder before stepping away from the window.

"Have a seat while I fix us a snack. I do better on a full stomach." Which was another lie. She'd been off her feed since Jake's phone call telling her that Chase had been hurt.

She stuck a package of popcorn in the micro-wave and punched in the cooking time. While she waited for it to pop, she poured each of them a tall glass of iced tea. The four minutes of popping time whizzed by much too quickly.

She was going to have to face the shambles her life had become and decide what she could sal-vage . . . and what she couldn't. As the final seconds ticked down on the microwave, she fought the need to rub her chest to soothe the pain that had taken up residence there.

"You want extra salt or butter on the popcorn?"

Chase took the bowl from her. "I don't want the damned popcorn at all, Gwen. What I want is to talk about what happened and what happens next."

He pulled a chair out and gave her a gentle push

to make her sit down. Then he pushed his own seat close enough so that they were knee to knee.

Feeling cornered, she clenched her hands into fists and snapped, "So talk."

Chase leaned forward, resting his elbows on his knees and looking far older than his eighteen years. "Gwen, it wasn't Jarvis's fault. It wasn't anybody's fault."

Somebody had to be responsible for Chase's . . . death. God, just the thought of it sent a shudder right through her soul.

She dug her nails into her legs. "You *died*, Chase. You actually died. How can that be no one's fault?"

"But I didn't stay that way. Is my being a Paladin more than you can handle? I know the healing thing was hard enough for you to deal with."

"You're my brother and I love you, no matter what special abilities you have. And you're not a Paladin. Not yet." Not ever if she could stop it.

"You're lying to yourself, Sis. You and I both know I don't function very well out in the normal world." His voice cracked and he abruptly sat back and took a long drink out of his glass. "You have no idea how *good* it felt to be in that gym with all those guys who were just like me. I didn't have to worry about being so big that I'd hurt someone when we worked out." He paused for a few seconds.

"Not only that, my natural ability to fight was

something to be admired, not feared. At school, no one even wants to line up opposite me on team scrimmages. I would've quit football, but the physical contact helped me maintain some control."

The level of pain in his voice scared her. How much had he been hiding from her all this time? She wanted to wrap her arms around him and hold the rest of the world at bay, as she had when he was younger. But he was too grown-up now to accept that from her.

"Chase, I don't know what to say. There must be something else we can do to make it easier for you."

He squared his shoulders, a warning that she wasn't going to like what was coming next. "There is something, Gwen. I'm going to become a Paladin, with all that means. I've talked to Jake and set up a training schedule around school and my chores. When I can't get to the Center, I'll practice here, but that's only temporary. Once I graduate, I'll be moving into the barracks with the other guys."

She'd thought her heart was already shattered. But as the tears started to burn down her face, she wondered if she'd ever feel whole again.

"It's not the kind of future I wanted for you, Chase."

His eyes softened as he snagged a paper towel and gave it to her. "I know. But the good news is that Jarvis said the Regents will pay for any schooling I want to pursue."

She scrubbed her face dry, the need to cry re-placed by a flare of temper. "I didn't think you were interested in college, Chase. I've been trying with-out success to talk you into it for the past two years. Now, just because Jarvis is the one to suggest it, you'll do whatever he wants?"

"You can't blame all of this on Jarvis and Jake, Gwen. I've said all along that I'd consider school when I knew better what I wanted to do with my life, where I fit in. Well, now I know. I'm a Pala-din."

When she didn't immediately respond, he went on. "Yes, that means I'll be serving along the barrier to keep our world safe. That's a good thing to be doing. If you'd seen those crazies, you'd be glad to know there are guys like Jarvis and Jake who know how to stop them. I want to be part of that so badly I can taste it. Did you know that I can feel the bar-rier from here? It calls to me, especially when it's about to go down."

No, she hadn't known that—but she had to try one more time. "But you're going to spend your life with a sword in your hand, either being killed or else killing."

Anger flashed in his eyes. "When it's necessary, yes. But at least I'm well suited for the job because of my DNA. The rest of the time, I can do other things. For example, Jake knows computers inside and out and designs computer games to sell. The

Regents need geologists, doctors, medics, all kinds of professions, and I get to choose.

"And be honest: if I wanted to sign up for special training in the regular military, you wouldn't be fighting it, would you? And they fight for a living, especially these days."

"Maybe you're right." As much as she hated to admit it, he was. Men from their family had fought in every war. "You've grown up, Chase. I guess I have to get used to that, and to you making your own decisions."

Then she pointed at him to let him know she was serious. "But if your grades slip, we'll revisit the issue. Is that clear?"

"Yes, ma'am. Clear as glass." His relieved grin reminded her how young he still was, regardless of his new veneer of maturity.

"Okay. Well, I guess we've settled that."

When she started to stand up, Chase blocked her way. "We may have settled my future, but we still need to talk about yours."

"Oh no you don't. This is something I'm not ready to talk about."

He didn't budge. "Turnabout is fair play, Sis. You've had your say about my decision. I want equal time."

She was *so* not in the mood for this, but she recognized the stubborn tilt to his chin. It was one feature they had in common.

"Speak, then—but I won't promise to listen."

"You're letting your pride get in the way with Jarvis. I don't want you to end up here alone, and that's what's going to happen if you don't get your head on straight."

She shoved free and stood up. "Jarvis lied to me, and those lies got you killed, Chase! How do you expect me to forget that?"

"I don't. I expect you to be smart enough to understand it, though. He's eating himself alive with guilt, and that's not fair. It's his duty to recruit new Paladins and train them. There aren't nearly enough of us to go around, and you can't fault him for doing his job. And he risked everything to bring you to me. Jake says they're still waiting to see what the Regents are going to do to him for that breach in security."

Chase backed away, giving her a little room to breathe. "Jarvis is an honorable man. We both know that about him. And he tried not to lie to you any more than he absolutely had to. It's so obvious that he has strong feelings for you. Did you know he's spent the last three nights out there in the woods just to keep you safe? And that's after spending all day trying to figure out how the Others are getting loose."

She reached for the paper towel again. "Yeah, I knew."

That admission took some of the wind out of his sails. "You did?"

"Do you think I haven't noticed you sneaking off after you're supposed to be in bed? Not to mention that my dogs are spending more time in the woods than they do on the porch?"

It was time to walk out on the ice and hope it didn't crack beneath her feet. "But I said some awful things to him, Chase. The kind of things a man would have a hard time forgiving."

"How do you know that?"

"Because I haven't been able to forgive myself for saying them. Looking back, all the signs were there about what he was up to. I just didn't want to admit it because I didn't want him to lure you away from me, but also because I couldn't stand the thought of him never coming back."

"Why is that, Gwen? And no one was trying to steal me from you. We're family and always will be, but you need to give Jarvis a chance. He made you happy. You know he did."

She shook her head. "Anything else I have to say on the subject, I need to say to Jarvis directly. Do you know if he's coming tonight, or can you find out?"

"Yeah, Jake said Jarvis is insisting on coming every night while they plug the holes where the Others have been getting out. They finished exploring the tunnel where Hunter was caught and determined its GPS location. Now they're using dynamite to close it off. Jake wanted me to tell you not to worry. They'll make sure they've covered all the possible escape routes."

He frowned. "They're beginning to think my father was killed in these same woods, but that the tunnel closed when the ground shifted in an earthquake. It probably opened up the same way."

"It seriously creeps me out to know that." She carried the popcorn bowl over to the counter. "Looks like I'll be camping in the woods tonight, so you stick close to the house."

"Afraid the Others will get me?"

She grinned. "No, I've got plans for Jarvis that might traumatize your innocent young eyes."

Chase cleared his throat. "Uh, I'd wish you good luck with that, but I suspect you won't need it." He quickly disappeared upstairs.

Yeah, he was all grown-up all right—except when it came to his sister wanting to seduce the one man she'd ever loved.

Checking the time, she figured she had about three hours' time to prepare for her mission. She'd use all the ammunition she had at hand—a bubble bath, sexy underwear, and a home-cooked meal in a picnic basket. Once she'd marshaled all her forces, she'd head out to the woods and set her trap.

She was going to stage an all-out attack on Jarvis Donahue. With any luck, the man wouldn't know what hit him until it was too late.

It felt good to smile for the first time in days.

• • •

The sun burned bright red as it sank behind the hills. Jarvis stopped to enjoy the view for a few seconds before continuing down the trail. He wanted to set up his makeshift camp before darkness blanketed the woods. The straps of his backpack were biting into his shoulders, but he could put up with the discomfort long enough to reach the clearing where he'd been spending his nights.

Tonight would be the last one he needed to stand guard over Gwen's farm. Yesterday, a crew of Paladins had finally finished surveying the system of tunnels where Hunter had been tortured. Today they'd swarmed over the woods to locate any openings big enough for an Other to slither through. He lit his own share of fuses, taking satisfaction in blowing their tunnels all to hell. Gwen was safe now, but he'd been unable to stay away. Tonight would be his good-bye.

As he reached the last bend in the trail, he caught a faint whiff of wood smoke. His gun was in his hand before he was even fully aware of reaching for it. No one used these woods for camping. He left the path and cut through the woods to avoid making an obvious target of himself.

Someone had set up a tent right by the boulder where he and Gwen had dangled their feet in the river. Well, they wouldn't be there for long. The last thing the Moselys needed was some squatter this close to the house. He braced himself to confront the intruder.

Then he saw a flash of red hair and his heart stopped. What was Gwen doing out here? Frozen in midstep, he drank in the sight of her.

She held a cup of something hot in her hand as she gazed at the setting sun. He wished he had a camera; the sight of her beautiful red hair against the sunset was art in its most basic form, natural and compelling.

"Are you going to stand there staring all night or come join me by the fire?" She waited a few seconds before slowly turning to face him. "I won't bite."

He forced his feet to move, unsure of his welcome, but needing to get close to her this one last time. "I hope I didn't scare you."

"There's a lot about you that scares me, Jarvis Donahue, but not in the way you mean." She sat on the boulder, leaving room for him.

He dropped his backpack next to the tent and sat on the rock, leaving a small distance between them.

He swallowed hard. "What's up, Gwen?"

"As my brother so reminded me, it's always been my belief that facing a problem head-on is the best course of action." She stared into her cup as if all the answers of the universe were contained in its depths. "And you, Jarvis Donahue, are one major problem for me."

"I didn't mean to be."

"I know—and I was wrong to put the entire blame on you." She tossed the dregs of her coffee out and dropped the tin cup on the ground. "A lot of it was me.

"You've been good for Chase, even though I'm still trying to come to terms with him becoming a Paladin. It's not the life I would have chosen for him. But I do understand that life takes unexpected turns, and you can either do the best with what you've got or waste your energy fighting an uphill battle."

Her smile was a little sad. "I'm proud of him, though. He's gone from being an angry kid to a young man with a future, one that he's proud of and excited about. That's more than most kids his age have going for them."

"I won't tell you that it'll be an easy life for him, Gwen. But he'll serve with the best group of men I've had the honor to know. And we won't be rushing him to the front lines anytime soon—not until he's fully trained and has finished whatever schooling he wants to go after." He'd see to that personally.

"I appreciate that. So I guess we've got Chase all taken care of." She shifted so that she was facing him directly, cross-legged. "That leaves us."

"Us?" He didn't know there even was an "us" left to discuss.

"I owe you an apology, Jarvis. I'm still not happy about your sneaking off with Chase like you did, but I figure I didn't give you any choice." Her fingers fiddled with the hem of her jeans.

"Gwen, I . . ."

She put her fingers across his lips. "Let me finish. I've done a lot of soul-searching since bringing Chase back home, and I haven't liked some of what I've learned about myself. I allowed you to split yourself down the middle just so that I could spend time with the easy half.

"Maybe if I'd met you under different circumstances, that would have been all right. But because of that first night, I knew about the other half—the part of you who suffers so that people like me can be safe in our beds at night."

"Gwen, don't make me out to be some kind of hero." A pedestal was an uncomfortable and lonely place to be.

"You and all of those other Paladins *are* heroes. But I'm not here to argue about that."

Which brought them back to the real question. "So, why are you here?"

Her green eyes looked straight into his only briefly before focusing beyond his left shoulder. "I'm here to say that I don't want to be friends with only half of you. I want the whole man. No more secrets, no more half-truths from either of us. No more pretending to be a normal guy and then going off to be someone else I don't know."

Friends. The word dropped like a rock in his stomach. If she wanted honesty, he'd give it to her.

"I can't be friends with you, Gwen. It's not enough."

Her sweet mouth curved up in a siren's smile. "Then I guess I'll have to offer you more than that."

She slipped her jacket off and let it fall to the ground. Then she reached for the top button on her blouse, then the next one. All he could do was watch and hope that he didn't explode as each new inch of skin was revealed.

His honorable side finally kicked in. "Gwen, you don't have to . . . we don't . . . we're not . . . Oh hell."

She cupped the side of his face with her hand. "Jarvis, did you mean it when you said you loved me?"

That was a no-brainer. "My timing could have been better, but I was feeling pretty desperate."

"Maybe. But the point is, I never responded. I was too upset about Chase. I'd like to respond now, if it's not too late." She opened another button.

His heart kicked up a ruckus and his voice cracked. "No, no, it's not too late."

"Before all this stuff with Chase blew up, I

knew I'd fallen hard for you. But I naïvely thought you could continue to compartmentalize yourself, keeping me separate from the dangerous part of your life."

There went another button. How did she expect him to concentrate on what she was saying?

"I didn't want that violence to touch your life, Gwen. When I was with you, I could pretend to be a normal guy—one a woman like you might fall in love with."

"And I love the guy who pets my dogs and makes me feel beautiful, but you're so much more than that."

Her blouse joined her jacket on the ground. "And I love *all* of you."

She held out her hand and tugged him down off the boulder. He immediately wrapped her up tight in his arms. "You're going to freeze out here dressed like that—or *un*dressed like that."

"That's why I brought the tent and sleeping bags. It won't be as comfortable as my bed, but it's more private." She pressed her lips against his. "Love me, Jarvis. Please love me."

"Always, Gwen. Always." Then he kissed her, hardly believing she was back in his arms where she belonged.

"It won't be easy," he warned. "I'll be a Paladin until the day I die for the last time. I won't always be able to come home at night." He nuzzled her neck.

"As long as you come when you can, I'll be waiting here with open arms."

He kissed her tenderly. "Then if you'll have me, I want the whole package: wedding bells and all."

"It's a deal. And the sooner, the better." She shivered. "Let's go inside the tent and get each other warm."

But before they climbed inside, she handed him a flashlight. "Here, I brought this for you."

"Uh, thanks?"

She smiled seductively. "You'll need it, unless you can count freckles by touch alone."

Jarvis laughed. "How about I try it both ways and see which works best?"

Somewhere along the way he lost count, but that was okay. They had the rest of their lives for him to get it right.

Turn the page
for a sneak peek at
Alexis Morgan's next exciting
Talion novel

Dark Warrior Unbroken

Coming September 2008
from Pocket Star Books

Sandor slipped inside a small neighborhood bar and positioned himself at the side of the front window, where he could watch for Lena without her being able to easily spot him.

"Hey, mister, we're not a bus stop. Order something or take a hike." Ham-fisted and built like a linebacker, the bartender had a face that had survived more than a few bar brawls.

Sandor figured he could take the guy, but now wasn't the time.

"I'll take a scotch on the rocks." He pulled out two five dollar bills and tossed them on the bar. "Hold the scotch and the rocks. Keep the change."

The bartender and the couple of patrons at the bar looked at him like he was crazy. Finally, the bartender grinned.

"Turns out we're having a special on that tonight." He pushed a five back across the counter.

Sandor chuckled and accepted the bill. "Thanks."

Back to business. Lena was walking by the window, searching for him, unsure where he could have disappeared to so quickly. It was time to make his move before his prey made her escape.

Grinning, he slipped out the door and pounced.

The door she'd passed a few seconds ago opened and closed with a soft whoosh. It was all the warning Lena had that Sandor Kearn had turned the tables on her. Before she could react, he had his forearm across her mouth, dragging her into the alley. She should've fought him off, but her only coherent thought was wondering how a man his size could move so fast and so silently.

He half-dragged her down the narrow passageway until they'd passed a Dumpster big enough to hide them from the street. If any other man had treated her this way, she would have either kneed him or screamed for help. All she could do was glare up into his dark eyes with a mixture of fury and embarrassment over being so easily captured.

"Let go of me."

Sandor moved in close, crowding her. Was it temper or something else causing his dark eyes to glitter in the fading light? Maybe a mix of things.

"I'm not touching you." He held up his hands to prove his point.

"Then you won't mind if I leave." She stepped to the side, planning on doing just that.

"Actually I do mind." He kept her cornered between himself, the Dumpster, and the wall behind her. "Why have you been following me the past couple of days?"

How did he know it was her? She was sure he hadn't seen her before tonight. "I wasn't—"

He stopped the lie by placing his gloved finger across her lip. Shaking his head sadly, he sighed as if sorely disappointed in her.

"Let me go now and we can both pretend none of this happened," she suggested. Although she figured it would be a long time before she could forget the rich smell of his aftershave combined with the scent of his leather coat. A powerful urge to bury her face against his chest and simply breathe him in washed over her.

He smiled slowly and, she realized, he knew it, the big jerk. She stiffened both her shoulders and resolve. *Lord, get me out of here before I do something foolish.*

"So why were you hunting me, Lena?" he whispered from close by her ear.

Like she'd tell him that! "Hunting? What makes you think I was?"

"You're not ready to hear what I think, little girl." His smile continued to taunt her.

"I'm not a little girl." Especially the way he was making her feel at the moment. She *really* needed to put some distance between the two of them.

But his gaze was fixed on her mouth, and he slowly leaned in so close that his warm breath teased her skin. What was he doing? Was he going to kiss her?

Her world rocked on its axis the second his lips settled over hers. As her ability to think short-circuited, she grabbed onto the first thing she could find to anchor herself: Sandor. Her fingers clutched his arms, the buttery soft leather of his duster doing nothing to disguise his muscular strength.

This had to stop! Perhaps her protest would have been more effective if it hadn't come out sounding more like a moan. She took some pride in that she managed to keep her lips closed, preventing the kiss from becoming too intimate. That worked right up until he nipped her lower lip with his teeth hard enough to sting. When she opened her mouth to protest, he slipped his tongue inside. He was careful of her, but still he tasted of temptation and male anger. She tingled from head to toe, as if he was bathing her with warmth stolen from the sun.

Sandor murmured to her between kisses, but her mind was too far gone to understand him at first. Finally his words began to make sense as he asked the same question over and over again.

"Why are you after me, Lena?"

He was temptation itself, but she managed to hold back the information he was trying so hard to coax out of her.

She pulled back enough to smile up into those dark chocolate eyes of his as she slowly slid her hands down his arms and then dropped them to back down to her sides, ending the connection between them. "It's simple, if somewhat embarrassing. I like the way you look walking around town in that duster."

It was the truth, just not the one he was looking for. It was hard to tell in the dim light in the alley, but his cheeks looked flushed. Was he actually *blushing*? She was smart enough not to give voice to that particular question.

"Now, if you'll excuse me, I—"

Once again he stopped her by putting his hand over her mouth. Who the hell did he think he was? She kicked him in the shin, taking satisfaction in his curse as he jumped back.

"Now if you'll get out of my way."

But he wasn't listening to her. His attention was focused on the far end of the alley. She strained to hear what had put such fierce expression on his face.

There. She heard it. A soft moan, one laced with desperation and pain. Someone nearby—a woman or girl by the sound of it—was hurting.

"Stay here."

In one second, Sandor changed from sexy to lethal as he stalked away, a gun appearing in his hand as if conjured out of thin air. His terse command made it clear that he would brook no arguments on the subject. Yeah, well, maybe that worked on the other women in his life, but not with her.

She waited until he'd gone several feet before pulling her own weapon and fanning out to his left. At the sound of her steps, he shot her a hard look. When he spied her automatic, he frowned but gave her a quick nod. Maybe he was smarter than she thought.

Together they slowly moved down the alley, stopping every few steps to listen again. Finally, he motioned for Lena to stop while he eased around another cluster of trashcans to kneel by a pile of broken up cardboard boxes.

Lena eased closer, trying to see what had caught Sandor's attention. A shoe was laying in a puddle that looked too dark to be water. Then the shoe moved. Holy shit, there was a foot in the shoe, one that belonged to the nylon-clad leg jutting out from under the pile of boxes.

Sandor holstered his gun and used both hands to begin lifting away the pile of cardboard layer by layer until he revealed an injured woman. When it was obvious that she was too out of it to present a threat to either of them, Lena put away her gun and joined Sandor on the ground. She watched as he peeled off his driving gloves before reaching out to push the woman's hair back out of her face. She had a good-sized lump on her forehead. As he trailed his fingers down the side of her face, checking for other injuries, the woman moaned and stirred restlessly before lapsing into a worrisome silence.

"How badly is she hurt?"

"Bad enough." He gave Lena an enigmatic look. "While I check her over, take a look around in case the bastard that did this is still lurking nearby."

His suggestion made sense, so why did it feel as if he were trying to get rid of her?

"All right, but I'll be right back."

"I never expected otherwise."

There was a hint of a smile in his voice. She glanced back at him, but he was running his hands down the woman's arms, looking for the source of what Lena now recognized as a pool of blood. Pulling her gun again, she slowly made her way down the alley, wishing she could see better. The sun had finally ceded the city to the night. Other than the occasional pool of light from a window, the alley was bathed in shadows.

The empty passage gradually narrowed down and came to a dead end. She rose up on her toes to look in a couple of large trash bins then started back to where Sandor hovered over the woman, checking out other possible locations where the woman's attacker could have hidden another body.

As she jumped down off the side of another industrial-sized recycling bin, she caught a flash of light out the corner of her eye. Whipping around, she brought up her gun. Odd. There was nothing moving, only Sandor slowly rising to his feet.

"Did you see a flash of light?"

"Maybe you saw my cell phone. I was getting ready to call 9–1–1 when I heard you coming back."

Again, his explanation made sense but didn't feel right. "How soon will they be here?"

He held up his phone. "My reception sucks so I'm going to the street and call them. Can you stay with her?"

"Will do."

Before he'd gone more than a few steps, she added, "And when you come back, don't sneak up on me. I don't want to shoot you by accident."

"If you promise to kiss where it hurts, I might just let you."

He was still laughing as he disappeared down the alley. The man was certifiably crazy, but that didn't seem to dampen her body's powerful reaction to him. If she wasn't convinced that he and his friends were covering up what they knew about Coop's death, she'd be sorely tempted to drag him back to her hotel room to see if he looked as good out of his clothes as he did in them.

The injured woman stirred, her eyes slowly opening. She met Lena's gaze with a confused look.

"What happened to me?" she whispered.

The fear in her voice hurt to hear. "It's okay;

you're safe now. My friend is calling the police and the EMTs."

When the woman didn't seem to understand her, Lena dropped her guard, hoping her heightened senses would help her find a way to soothe the woman's increasing agitation. She grasped her hands with her own; maybe touch would get through where her words of comfort hadn't.

As soon as they touched, Lena was yanked out of the present and thrown back in time. With a tearing pain in her head, she was no longer kneeling in the alley, no longer herself. She'd become the injured woman—Mary Dubois, reliving her experiences through her memories.

Trapped in Mary's mind, Lena found herself walking along the street, hurrying to get home to her family after a tough day at work. She had been focused on the bus stop up ahead, hoping to catch the early bus. The people gathered there began lining up, warning her the bus had pulled into sight.

Running in heels was never easy. She was making good time when out of nowhere an arm snaked around her neck and jerked her backward. As her assailant dragged her into the mouth of the alley, he increased the pressure on her throat until she could barely breathe, much less scream for help.

Oh, God! Oh, God! Oh, God! She was going to die! Her mind filled with the images of her children—a boy and a girl. Then there was a man, her husband, the one she'd been mad at that morning. How could she die, knowing the last words she'd said to him had been so angry?

Her attacker was taller than she was. He wasn't alone, as another set of footsteps scuffled through the filthy alley. Then a hand covered her eyes and her oxygen-starved body panicked. Flailing her arms, she tried to get her hands on the arm that was slowly killing her. But her mind was growing hazy and strangely calm.

All sensation faded as the strength in her muscles drained away. Her last memory was pain as her head hit something hard and then for a short time there was nothing.

"Damn it, Lena, let go of her!"

Strong fingers worked to break her hold on the injured woman's hands. When they succeeded, Lena's own consciousness came flooding back, identifying the hands pulling her away as Sandor's.

"What the hell were you doing?"

She still couldn't open her eyes. He was angry, but it was because he was worried about her. It was there in the gentle way he helped her to her feet.

"Come on, Lena. Open your eyes and tell me you're all right."

There was a new note in his voice, intense and hot. She was trying to do as he asked, wanting to allay his worries. Before she could manage it, though, he cupped her face with both of his hands. Normally, she would have basked in the warmth of his touch, but she hadn't yet raised her guard to shut out all the sensations that were bombarding her. For a brief second, she flashbacked to the dance club fire and the shadow man who'd killed Coop.

Her stomach lurched at the wave of sick glee that washed through her. More bewildered than ever, her eyes finally popped open. Where had that image come from?

"What the hell?" Sandor dropped his hands away from her face.

As soon as he stepped back out of reach, her mind cleared. She was right back in the alley, staring at Sandor in horror. For a brief second, the man she had kissed only minutes before tasted just like the bastard who had killed Coop.

Then Sandor caught her face in his hands and stared down into her eyes—and suddenly, all the fear faded away.

The approaching sirens made it impossible for Sandor to do more than a down-and-dirty invasion of Lena's mind. It took far more power than he expected to break through her shields and adjust her memories of the past few minutes. As strong as she was, he'd be lucky if his tinkering held long enough for him to get her somewhere safe so he could try again.

The police were cautious in their approach, weapons drawn. Sandor eased his arm around Lena, hoping that they looked like a couple out for an evening stroll. She stiffened briefly, but then relaxed against him. Good girl.

The closest officer gave Sandor and Lena a quick once-over before speaking. "Where's the victim?"

"There." Sandor pointed toward the woman who sat blinking up at them.

The cop knelt by her side while his partner kept an eye on Sandor and Lena. "Was she conscious when you found her?"

"Not really. She was buried under that pile of cardboard. We never would've known she was there if she hadn't made a sound."

"Do you know her?"

Lena answered. "No, but her name is Mary Dubois. I stayed here while my friend went for help. While he was gone, she woke up enough to tell me her name, but that was all."

Damn it, when had Lena planned on telling him that she'd spoken to the woman? When he'd sent Lena down the alley, he'd read a bit of the woman's memory, but her thoughts were too chaotic for him to get much. Her attackers had definitely been Kyth renegades, but she'd given him nothing more to go on. The flash of energy Lena had seen had been his failed attempt to use some of his own store of energy to help stabilize the injured woman.

As worried as he was about Mary Dubois, he was even more concerned about Lena. What had been going on between the two women when he'd returned to find Lena frozen in position, her hands locked onto Mary's with such desperate strength? It had been all he could do to break the connection between them. For now, he'd blocked Lena's memories of the event, but he needed to get her to Kerry and Ranulf. Between the two of them, they should be able to get past the barriers Lena had built up around her thoughts.

He studied her out of the corner of his eye, liking what he saw. There was such strength in this woman. She was athletic, but he was also drawn to her intelligence and the obvious power of her mind. Until he'd met Lena, Kerry Thorsen and the late Dame Judith were the only two women he'd met with such power.

If she was Kyth, it was such a faint trace that he couldn't read it. Maybe Kerry would be able to tell for sure. But there was definitely something different about Lena, something that the average human being lacked. What's more, he suspected that mysterious ability was at the root of her determination to find Coop's killer.

He jerked his attention back to the matter at hand when Lena pulled him out of the way of the EMTs. The cops left the Dubois woman in their care and motioned for Sandor and Lena to follow them out of the alley.

"We need to take your statements." The senior partner got out a form and pen, ready to write. "Can I see your drivers' licenses, please?"

The two of them stood quietly while the officer copied down the information.

"Are you in town for long?" he asked as he handed Lena her license back.

"A couple of weeks. I used to live here and came to visit some friends who work for the fire department."

That caught his attention. "Anyone I know?"

"Maybe. I had coffee with McCabe earlier today." She smiled. "Other than a few more pounds and less hair, he hadn't changed a bit. I've really missed that laugh of his. We had a great visit."

Just that quickly the interview turned from cautious to friendly. "Did he make you pay? He always does me."

Lena grinned. "No, I think he decided to take it easy on me since I was visiting."

"So what were you two doing in that alley?" the cop asked.

"Well, we were looking for . . . a little privacy. We'd made plans to meet over at the Center. We . . . uh, haven't seen each other in a while."

She ducked her head, injecting exactly the right amount of embarrassment to make her statement ring true.

Not that she was exactly lying. Sandor *had* dragged her into the alley to confront her, away from prying eyes. If she'd told the truth, Sandor could very well be on his way to jail—especially if the cops decided that if he'd also been responsible for the attack on Mary Dubois.

He owed Lena one. And knowing her, she'd be sure to collect.

Discover the darker side of desire.

Pick up a bestselling paranormal romance from Pocket Books!

Kresley Cole
Dark Deeds at Night's Edge
The Immortals After Dark Series

A vampire shunned by his own kind is driven to the edge of madness....where he discovers the ultimate desire.

Jen Holling
My Immortal Protector

Deep in the Scottish Highlands, a reluctant witch is willing to do anything to give up her powers—until she meets the one man who may give her a reason to use them.

Marta Acosta
Happy Hour at Casa Dracula

Come for a drink....Stay for a bite.

Gwyn Cready
Tumbling Through Time

She was a total control freak—until a magical pair of killer heels sends her back in time—and into the arms of the wrong man!

Discover the darker side of passion with these bestselling paranormal romances from Pocket Books!

Kresley Cole
Wicked Deed on a Winter's Night
Immortal enemies...forbidden temptation.

Alexis Morgan
Redeemed in Darkness
She vowed to protect her world from the enemy—
until her enemy turned her world upside down.

Katie MacAlister
Ain't Myth-Behaving
He's a God. A legend. A man of mythic proportions...
And he'll make you long to myth-behave.

Melissa Mayhue
Highland Guardian
For mortals caught in Faeire schemes,
passion can be dangerous...